DOLLYBIRD

ANNE LAZURKO

COTEAU BOOKS

Edited by Sandra Birdsell
Designed by Tania Craan
Typeset by Susan Buck
Printed and bound in Canada at Houghton Boston

Library and Archives Canada Cataloguing in Publication

Lazurko, Anne, 1964-, author
   Dollybird / Anne Lazurko.

Issued in print and electronic formats.
ISBN 978-1-55050-563-4 (pbk.).-- ISBN 978-1-55050-564-1 (pdf).--
ISBN 978-1-55050-748-5 (epub).--ISBN 978-1-55050-749-2 (mobi)

   I. Title.

PS8623.A98D65 2013   C813'.6   C2013-903647-4
                                          C2013-903648-2

COTEAU
BOOKS

2517 Victoria Avenue
Regina, Saskatchewan
Canada   S4P 0T2
www.coteaubooks.com

Available in Canada from:
Publishers Group Canada
2440 Viking Way
Richmond, British Columbia
Canada   V6V 1N2

10 9 8 7 6 5 4 3 2 1

Coteau Books gratefully acknowledges the financial support of its publishing program by: The Saskatchewan Arts Board, the Canada Council for the Arts and the Government of Canada through the Canada Book Fund.

For
Diana Worman
who chooses to find joy

PART I

Dust

CHAPTER 1

✣ ✤ ✣

MOIRA

CROWDS OF YOUNG MEN milled about the Halifax train station, kissing teary-eyed girlfriends and ducking hugs from worried mothers. I watched the scramble of limbs and luggage and listened to the boisterous talk from a perch on top of my overstuffed suitcase. Some of the men glanced my way, then quickly again. I'm sure they wondered what I was doing there, how I fit in. But I didn't. They were heading west for jobs and excitement. I was heading west because I was pregnant, because my mother insisted I spend nine months of purgatory in Moose Jaw. In Saskatchewan.

It was a Canadian province, so new I'd had to investigate where it was and how to spell its name. I'm sure Mother chose Saskatchewan because it was such a ridiculously long distance from St. John's; my *situation* was guaranteed to be hidden from the judgment of her privileged friends. Maybe she hoped to be rid of me altogether, to cut me off from my father, from my future. But while I was scared to death at the prospect of a baby and the unknown prairie, I would survive, and I would be back; I wouldn't give my mother the satisfaction of doing otherwise. The thought buoyed me, and I was suddenly caught up in the excitement I saw in the eyes of the fishermen's boys who climbed the steps of the train with me. The harvest train. A chance to reap. A chance at something better. More than the sea could offer them in 1906. More than my mother could offer me.

I wasn't entirely alone, though Mother's choice of Cousin Fred as my companion seemed ironic, if not spiteful. Fred had been in trouble since I could remember — at school, during catechism, in church. But Mother forgave him his excesses in light of mine, saying he was obviously more responsible than I. Fred had met Father and me outside the train station, where my care and my money were handed over as Mother had instructed.

There was no fanfare to my leaving, no emotional good-byes. Father looked to the distance and pretended not to notice when I hung my head over the rail on the ferry crossing from St. John's. The nausea was bad, but when he left me with Fred, the disappointment in his face and his quick, cold embrace were worse. I was already a stranger to him. He'd been so certain of my future as a doctor, one of the first female physicians on the Rock. Now he had to relinquish that idea to a new truth: I would leave a bastard baby in far-off Saskatchewan.

On the train, Fred guided me to a berth and set my suitcase on the narrow shelf under the bed. I put my black doctor's bag by the pillow where I could see it. His eyes darted about, and he rolled his new bowler hat in his hands, anxious to be rid of me.

"Stay out of trouble," I called after him. He chuckled as he swayed down the aisle and away.

I lay back against the pillow, exhausted. Out the window was forest and rock, any sign of the sea left behind. I felt claustrophobic; like the trees were keeping guard, foot soldiers for my mother. When I woke the light outside was grey. My sick stomach had settled down and I went to find the dining car. Most of the tables were filled with young men, their voices loud, excited hoots of phony laughter punching the air. Their hands fidgeted, shoulders tensing at each outburst. They had their fears too.

I hoped Fred might make an appearance and sat at a table for two against the wall. At the next one over a heavy woman sat bouncing a small baby on her lap. I imagined she was off to visit relatives and would arrive to welcoming arms and hugs for the new grandchild she brought. There'd be no shame, her baby unremarkable to anyone but her own family, free of the labels they might use for mine.

The men stopped talking for a moment to look suspiciously at another man, who showed up with a small child in his arms. They avoided meeting his eyes. I suppose they were expecting to have a good time before the months of work ahead, and a little one didn't fit into their plans.

The father was barely a boy himself, yet he seemed beaten, dark with the Irish in him, his face pounded to leather by the East Coast gales that weather them all. A wild black beard sprouted round his face, and his coveralls were patched on the knees and backside. Dirty socks poked through holes in the toes of his boots. His son's wardrobe was no better. The boy was a bundle of grey rags held together here and there by a stitch or a pin. My heart dropped for the child.

None of the other men asked the young father to join them, so he pulled out a chair at the table where the woman sat with her child. He smiled slightly at her and nodded, but the woman stood, stuck her nose in the air and looked for another seat. He yawned, grinned at his son and stretched his long legs out under the table, catching my eye and holding it. I looked away first.

I gave up on Fred and ordered soup and a biscuit. The men were quiet again, if for different reasons, as two pretty women in feathered hats and high heels came in and sat down at the table with the man and his son. They didn't speak to him, instead carried on a whispered conversation behind gloved hands, glancing at him occasionally with raised eyebrows. One of the women spoke suddenly, her words stilted as though their dismissal of him had been only a brief lapse of manners. "Taking him home to his mother then?"

The man started and glanced at his son. "Uh, yeah. In Moose Jaw."

"That's good. He doesn't look well, you know."

The boy looked to be close to two years old, his skin wan, eyes pale blue. His blond hair was wispy and untrimmed.

"He's looked like that since he was born."

His voice had become quiet and hesitant, and his eyes softened when he looked at his son, the intense black faded to deep grey. A sadness pulled at the corners of his mouth. I wondered if any of what he said was true.

"Well, he's sweet, even if he is a little pale." The second girl joined the conversation, giggling behind her hand.

"Takes after his mother," the man said proudly.

The girls nodded and went back to their whispering. But the boy's father leaned forward, eyes shining. "Sure wish we'd come out of this damn bush eh?"

The girls gasped in unison.

"I just mean," he stuttered, "that a man can't see anything, not the weather coming, or a sunrise. It's nice to greet the dawn head-on." He paused. He seemed to have forgotten anyone was listening. "Not have it sneak up on you from behind a tree."

The girls looked confused at this and then slightly amused. Embarrassed, he turned back to the window. I smiled. Greet the dawn head-on. My home was on a hill in St. John's overlooking the city, the harbour and the sea beyond. The kitchen window faced east, revealing what we could expect for the day, sunshine or fog or a storm rolling in off the water. Something clicked in my throat and I quickly finished dinner and went to lie in my berth, exhausted and lonely.

The young man had seemed so comfortable with his son. Evan was the father of the baby I carried, but he would never lay eyes on his child, never know what kind of father he might be.

When I'd finally had to admit I was pregnant, I'd wanted not to exist. Not dead mind you. Just not present for a time so I could work out what to do. But I had no idea what to do. After six weeks of carrying the growing terror myself, I'd told Evan. He loved me. He'd said so in his way. He was silent as I spoke, my voice fading as he withdrew. He nodded, pecked me on the cheek and left to give his parents the news. Doubt had stroked the spot where his lips had been, and I remembered feeling more alone in that moment than I ever had. I shook my head free of the memory, didn't need to feel more isolated than I already was in my berth on a train to nowhere.

I didn't see the father and son again. Fred showed up for the occasional bite to eat or to check on me before bed. The miles were marked by meals and sleep and nausea. I passed some of the time reading the medical texts I'd slipped into my bag, hoping to keep up with my studies, too distracted to comprehend the words. On the third night we spilled onto the prairie somewhere in Manitoba and I heard a deep voice announce Winnipeg. Passengers disembarked, bumping their cases along the aisle.

When the train resumed its chunking, I tried to sleep again, but tossed instead, shifting from side to side, nervous about our arrival, my destination a near mystery. Nowhere really. Not anywhere of significance to me. Mother had said only that her cousin's daughter had "managed" to make a good life in Moose Jaw. Or so she'd heard.

Soon I heard the murmuring of nearby passengers and the sounds of their morning preparations. I gave up on sleep and pushed up the window blind. The passing landscape was astonishing; overnight the train had left the forest, descended from the rock of the country and brought me to the vast nothing of Saskatchewan, the new prairie province with the strange name. Beyond the tracks, fields of golden crops stretched to the horizon. A few cows dotted grassed areas, kept there by wood fences so weathered and worn they appeared more an inconvenience than a deterrent. Endless blue sky surrounded the radiant hues of late fall.

"It's beautiful," I breathed.

"It's a bunch of grass." Cousin Fred scared the life out of me.

I rolled over and gasped. "You look terrible. What happened?"

His clothes were rumpled and bloodstained, his fancy hat crushed in his hands. Dried blood coated the skin under his nose, and he peered at me through red and swollen eyes. I smelled whiskey and sweat. "And you stink."

"Thanks for noticing." His voice croaked with a mix of fear and shame.

My throat was suddenly dry. "Well?"

His jaw worked, and his hands shook as he rubbed his stubbled chin. "I lost your money," he blurted and turned to leave.

"What? Someone stole it?" I sat up so quickly my head spun. "Did you call the conductor? Is there a policeman on the train?"

"No! No coppers." His face was struck through with sorrow, and for an instant I felt sorry for him. "I lost it in the saloon car. A poker game," he whispered and bowed his head.

7

I reached for the door frame to steady myself.

"I tried to get it back. That's why they beat me up. Lost most of my own too." His voice was a child's whine. "They were gonna throw me off the train; said no one would notice at night. What was I supposed to do?" There was no glimmer of hope on his face, no rescuing smile.

"All of it?" It came out a whisper.

"Except for this." He held out a fistful of cash. "Take it."

"Get out." He started to protest. "Get out right now, or I'll throw you off the train myself, you irresponsible, stupid..."

He tossed the money onto the bunk and was gone. I lay back, not moving, and listened to the pulsing roar in my ears. It was blood money, but all I had.

Evan's father had arrived at the door two days before I was scheduled to leave, looking past me to speak only to Father, saying he'd sent Evan back to Edinburgh. His son wouldn't be returning. He'd put an envelope on the hall table and turned to go. "That should see her through," he said, as though money was the only thing I'd need.

I lost my mind a little, ran after him, thumping on his back with my fists, flailing at his head. He'd turned in surprise, grabbed my arms and laughed.

"He's the baby's father," I shouted. "I won't let you do this."

"I already have." His voice was flat, eyes hard.

Father finally pulled me off him and dragged me into the house, gave me a sedative and put me to bed. My father, the doctor, knew how to treat female hysterics.

They'd all betrayed me. And now Fred too. Dear God. I lay in my berth as the roar died to a whisper. Deep breaths. In and out. I was nearly penniless, pregnant and alone but for a guardian who'd seen fit to gamble with my future. The bile rose in my throat again and I reached for the chamber pot.

CHAPTER 2

✦ ✦✦ ✦

I ARRIVED IN MOOSE JAW to a dry heat that compressed my lungs and left my throat parched. Sweaty new arrivals from across the country crowded the station. I made my way to the platform, where billboards announced jobs for everyone. A late fall, a big crop. Anyone willing to help get the harvest off before winter could make two dollars a day stooking, two seventy-five on the threshing crew. Farming words, foreign to men of the sea, yet it seemed the words had drawn hundreds with their pledge of prosperity. I caught a glimpse of the father carrying his son just beyond the platform. He spoke briefly to a constable on horseback who nodded as they hurried off, and I wondered, for an instant, where he might be headed.

Fred showed up at my elbow. Despite his injuries he was his ever-confident self. His bowler hat was perched on his head again, his long black coat and grey silk scarf in stark contrast to the work pants and boots of the boys milling around us. He'd never worked a day in his life. He stood silent in the mayhem.

"Just wire your father, Moira." He gestured into the distance. "He'll send you money."

It was true. But if Mother found out, there would be no end to what Father would endure.

"I will not give my mother the satisfaction."

"Do you hear yourself Moira? You've got nothing and you're knocked up." Others were turning to listen. "How the hell will you survive?"

Suddenly I pictured Evan's father, his scorn, and a rage flooded through me.

"This is obscene," I hissed. "You've no right to be angry or tell me what to do. You lost the money, and now I have to find a way out of this."

"Well, then," Fred blustered. "Well then, suit yourself." In a few long strides he left the platform and disappeared into the crowded street.

Moose Jaw was clearly a hub to the flat prairie stretching beyond it; the air seemed to quiver with the potential of new arrivals and new beginnings. But with little money, and fewer prospects, I was left out of the excitement and settled for a cheap room in a hotel near the station. The cash Fred had managed to hang on to would pay for only two nights.

I dragged my things through the door and fell into a chair, patting the side of the trunk to ensure my stitching was still intact. Despite Mother's searching, she hadn't managed to discover it. Before leaving home, I'd cut a hole in the trunk wall, lined it with quilt stuffing and hidden two cups and saucers, blue Coalport china, in the space I'd created. They were the last remaining pieces of a set brought from Scotland by my grandmother on my father's side. I suppose they were, on the face of it, stolen goods, but for me they were a reminder, a connection. I left them where they were. They'd be safer hidden for now.

I'd unpacked only a few things when there was a commotion outside my window. A wagon, with a small wood structure perched on top, was pulled into the crowd rushing to gather round. I got downstairs and outside just as a hush descended and the side doors of the wagon opened to reveal an array of large and small stoppered bottles, tiny leather bags tied with twine and strange-coloured concoctions in test tubes. Suddenly Fred appeared behind the counter of this instant apothecary, dressed in a stovetop hat and cutaway coat.

"Oh my Lord."

Other men began to shout slogans about the cures they could offer. Some had made a poor attempt to dress as Native medicine men, their feathered headdresses incongruent with their white skin and whiter lab coats, worn, presumably, to seduce the more conservative minded of Moose Jaw.

A young woman standing on the fringe of the eager crowd smiled at me, a small, pale child coughing weakly at her side. "Been waiting for the medicine show all summer," she said. "I plan to get some elixir for my boy's cough."

"But they're not physicians." The faces around me shone with excitement. "They're just a theatre troupe." People next to me backed away a step, raising their eyebrows at one another as though it was I who was deluded. "You're wasting your money."

The young mother glanced at me fearfully and pushed past to rush into the fray. Through the waving arms ahead, I saw Fred in the wagon dispensing remedies as fast as the others could convince the crowd of their efficacy. Trust Fred to sell himself as a salesman. Beside the wagon a sign proclaimed the group as PURVEYORS OF THE ONLY GENUINE SE-CRET INDIAN HERBAL REMEDY.

A young Native girl sat on a three-legged stool nearby. Dressed in deerskin from her beaded dress to the tattered moccasins on her feet, she wore a headband with a single feather and her dark hair hung in a braid to her waist. She gave me a bored smile.

"It's all a ruse," I told her softly. "They're using you to attract business."

She shrugged, like she didn't care, like she was quite aware she was selling the dignity of her ancestors for a few cents a day. I turned in despair to see Fred looking at me through the crowd. When I glared at him, he motioned for us to meet behind the wagon.

"What are you doing?" I asked, my voice a harsh whisper.

He looked around nervously and then put his hand in his vest pocket and struck a confident pose. "We're selling genuine Indian remedies, Moira. That's what we do here."

"We? You've been here less than a day."

"Stan says I can make a lot of money if I go on the road with him. Figured this is as good a job as any." He looked slightly apologetic. "We'll go south when it gets cold. I'll get to see some country. And I'll send money when I can."

"Fred, you're lying to these people. These things you're selling, they're not medicine. They're just some voodoo concoctions."

"There's a lot of money to be made selling hope to the hopeless."

I gaped at him. "And what of those who aren't cured and

11

don't have money left for the real doctors?"

"What? Like you and your father? Doesn't seem you can do a whole lot more for these folks than we can." He flourished his hat. "So you see – hope is worth a lot."

I wanted out of the crowd, shrank under the press of animated, expectant faces. It was an exciting diversion, the people accomplices to the lie. They wanted to be duped. Maybe Fred was right. Maybe hope was all they had left. I backed away from him.

"See you in the spring, then." Behind me, Fred's voice was tinged with regret. "Good luck."

I wanted, despite his obvious failings, to go with him, to be free of burdens, lost on the prairie where no one knew me and no one cared to. But the baby would grow and my belly accordingly. I wouldn't fool anyone. Fred's gaze was direct. Shaking my head, I shoved my way to the edge of the crowd, and ran.

Past the Station Hotel, Joyner's Department Store and the livery, I ran until I was outside town and a stich burned my side. Just into the field, I came to a huge boulder and climbed onto it to survey the few streets that made up the town, turned to take in the countryside beyond. Where was I? It seemed my life had been spinning by with little attention to me, like I was outside my body watching. Within only a few days, my pregnancy had turned into banishment and, worse, destitution. And I ached everywhere with exhaustion. My shoulders slumped. I ran my hand over the smooth side of the rock, its flat, perfect surface like the pebbles worn to a polish in the creekbed at home.

How to explain my sitting here in a hellish-hot place while Evan was at medical school, where I should have been as well? He wouldn't want this for me. He was one of few medical men who'd shown me any respect. It was Evan who had saved me from the hostility of my father's colleagues.

My face had nearly burned with embarrassment, wading through them in the crowded men's club, their black suits pressing in and making it nearly impossible to reach Father, who was deeply immersed in conversation. Their mutterings trailed behind me.

12

"Women in medicine, ha...Wouldn't let her touch the instruments in my hospital...What if it's her time of the month? Contaminate everything...Her father should know better... Reputation at stake..."

Their glaring eyes burned into my back. I was twenty, most of them over forty. Mother had insisted I wear a straight black dress, barely tucked at the waist with a high neckline. She'd gone to great pains, mostly mine, to bind my breasts tightly in an attempt to disguise any shape I might have. Hair in a matronly bun, no powder or lipstick. But the camouflage fell away under their stares. Finally I was at Father's side. Oblivious to the stir I'd caused, he beamed. "An old friend of the family," he said, introducing his friend. "No one can suture better in the whole of Newfoundland."

I hoped one day he'd say the same of me. But with the disapproval of the others thick around me, I just wanted to go home. Father was annoyed, but suddenly Evan had been there offering to escort me.

"I could tell by your face," he whispered. "Besides, if you don't leave soon, these old men may just tar and feather you."

"I don't think Father will allow it."

"The tarring or the walking you home?"

I tried to smile, and blushed instead. I'd sat next to Evan a few times in class. He was handsome enough, sharp features and dark hair that hung just slightly into his eyes so that he constantly brushed it aside. He was brilliant, answering questions with a clarity none of the rest could match. Mostly quiet, he listened to everyone with respect, just as he did walking me home that night.

"They make me so angry...'women can't practice'.... 'women are too helpless'....'women bleed.'" It was too bold. I stopped walking.

Evan had laughed. "They are archaic, I'll admit," he said. "But as far as I know, women still bleed, do they not?"

My neck was hot. "Of course, but it doesn't make us contagious, or hysterical. I am none of those things at any time and am quite capable of doctoring through any part of my...cycle."

Again the torrent of words poured out of my mouth. He was only trying to be kind.

He laughed again, more quietly, and took my hand. His level gaze challenged my defiance. His lips brushed my cheek as he whispered into my ear. "I'd like to see you again."

His father was a bastard. The word slipped into my mind and I liked the feel of it on my lips, the angry sound of it. Bastard, bastard, bastard. I sat on the rock and loudly whispered it out to the prairie, where it mixed with the rustling of the grass in the wind. Evan would come back for me. He would defy his father. As soon as the baby was adopted out, I'd go home and we'd be together.

I wrapped my arms around myself and rocked. It's not so bad, I thought. That never-ending sky offered comfort in its own way; there had to be possibilities in something so big. Running my hands over tender breasts and slightly distended belly, I ignored the skeptical voices in my head reminding me that I had no money, that I'd have to take the first job I could find in order to survive, that I had every reason to be terrified.

A lone rider approached at a slow trot from the east, growing up and out of the landscape, details of the man coming together: dark cowboy hat, green shirt, spectacles. Instead of passing by as I'd hoped, he stopped a few feet from the rock.

"Hello there." His voice was soft, yet clearly audible over the growing wind.

"Hello," I murmured, not looking directly at him, afraid it might be taken as an invitation.

"You're sitting on a buffalo rubbing stone," he said, as though I'd asked. "The buffalo rubbed against it to scratch themselves. Wore it smooth like that."

I glanced at my hand on the rock. "They must be huge."

"They were."

I looked at him more closely then. He was older, maybe thirty, his face sun-baked to deep brown, his blue eyes distorted by the thick spectacles he wore low on his nose. A misshapen cowboy hat was pushed back on his head and his boots, in their stirrups, were badly worn. His roan horse stuck its nose out and I couldn't help but touch it, laughing as the animal snorted, spraying my hands and face.

"Sorry 'bout that," he said. Then, more carefully, "Say, do you need a ride into town? I'm going through on my way back to Ibsen."

"I'm fine." I wiped my face with the hem of my skirt. "I'll walk."

He gave a slight nod. It was vaguely disappointing, his giving up so easily, though heaven knows what I would say to him. "I'm Silas Fenwick," he said and turned to go.

"Moira Burns," I said with a small wave. Jumping down from the rock I had a moment of fear. "Sir?" I called. He turned his horse back. "Are there any buffalo around here?"

He laughed a short, amused snort. "Not any more." He rode away toward town.

I returned to Moose Jaw exhausted and hungry, impatient with the rampant changes of my body. Before sending me off, Father had explained what might be expected throughout the pregnancy, what was normal and what was not. I'd have been better off had he prepared me for men – how a man could run off at first mention of the baby he'd helped create, how another could encourage such abandonment and, mostly, how a father justified sending away the daughter who loved him most.

Back at the hotel, while I was waiting in the restaurant for a supper I could ill afford, a large balding man in a faded black suit and bow tie walked with slow, swaggering strides to my table. *Pig* crossed my mind – snout, small pink eyes, tightly stretched belly – and I had to hide a chuckle behind my napkin. Without invitation he pulled up a chair and I drew back, ready to object. Up close, he seemed more a swine, and far less amusing.

"Your cousin tells me you need a job."

✤ ✤ ✤

CHAPTER 3

MR. PENNY'S BUGGY rattled into the tiny community of Ibsen. We'd travelled almost two hours, yet he whipped the horses hard the last mile as if needing to make an entrance. I'd kept my mouth shut and held on, relieved I'd had to insist only once that he allow me off to pee and retch out of his sight while he continued to stumble loudly and drunkenly through details of his grand life as Ibsen's most successful businessman.

"I own Ibsen. The general store, the lumberyard, the hotel. And everybody else owes me something." His eyes narrowed and he leered. "I like it that way. It keeps 'em humble." His Adam's apple danced with a soundless laugh.

I'd had to take the swine's offer – room and board plus one dollar a day – because it meant I'd have a roof over my head and, if I worked hard and proved myself, a job when my condition became obvious. I had to believe it. I couldn't have stepped into his buggy otherwise.

Now, leaning away from his putrid breath, I looked at my new home. Ibsen was a small protrusion of life on the flat, treeless plain of southern Saskatchewan. The dust of Main Street settled over the wagon as we moved past the grain elevator, the grocer, blacksmith and livery, a tiny barbershop. Penny hadn't mentioned if he owned these. I glanced sideways to see his eyes drooping even as he urged the horses down the street.

A saloon occupied the ground floor of a two-story building called the Ibsen Hotel. Nearby signs attempted to dissuade patrons from entering. One read, DRINKING IS THE DEVIL'S ORK, the W faded grey and lifeless like the whole town. Another implored readers to sign a petition, proclaiming ALCOHOL BE PROHIBITED IN TOWN, as though the drunken and morally impoverished of the countryside were not worthy of their attention.

"Idiots," slurred Mr. Penny. "Halfwits don't know it's rum

money built this town. Moose Jaw too."

I nodded, hoping he didn't expect an answer.

"We'll go in for a drink before I take you home."

I couldn't imagine it. "I'm really quite tired, what with the long trip and all. If you direct me to where I'll be staying, I'll just get settled."

"Third house on the left there." He pointed vaguely. "Attic is yours."

He retrieved my luggage, grabbed a passing boy by the ear and told him to help me with my bags, tossing him a coin as he turned to go. The boy couldn't have been more than ten, but he ran ahead, dragging my bags through the dust. Too tired to protest, I followed like a sheep until he stopped on the doorstep of a small two-story. It appeared Mr. Penny had built himself up bigger than his house. Inside was a mess, dishes with bits of congealed food on the table, pots on the stove. Clothing was randomly shed throughout the parlour and up the stairs. I gingerly stepped over Mr. Penny's things, the boy following, until we came to a door on the second floor that led to the attic.

"This will be fine."

His large brown eyes were so ingratiating, I reached into my purse for small change. "Thank you, ma'am." He beamed and ran down the stairs. The door slammed. It was a relief to be alone.

The attic was small and sparsely furnished with an unfinished wooden table and two chairs, a dresser and a small bed. The air was stifling and musty, though the previous inhabitant had made some effort to leave the room clean and in order. One window looked out over the street. The field beyond shimmered pink in the dying rays of the sun. Opening the window proved small relief.

Damp curls leapt from the confines of the pins I'd used to set my hair, sweat trickling down my back and under my arms. I dragged my belongings upstairs, hung my dresses on hooks on the back of the door and laid the rest of the clothes in the dresser.

Ripping the stitches of the trunk's false side, I freed the blue china from its hiding place. Holding a teacup, turning it over and sliding swollen fingers over delicate curves, I marvelled at how far it was from the life it once led. Amidst an array of beautiful things in Mother's cabinet, the Coalport had been ignored and mostly forgotten. In this place, in this room, it was precious again, made lovely by its contrast to the surroundings. I set the pieces carefully on the dresser.

Last I set the family picture alongside the china. It had been taken only months before. I'd mostly forgotten the odd quality of light in the photograph. We'd been arranged outdoors, the sun low in the west, a shadow falling over only some of the faces, while the rest were brightly lit and squinting. There was Mother in black, her face unmoved, a slight wrinkle at the side of her mouth as she tried to smile; Father, back straight, shoulders round with worry. His hat sat squarely on his head, though moments before the flash I'd tried to set it at a jaunty angle, but he'd pushed my hands away. It wouldn't have suited him anyway.

The girls were seated in front, Deirdre, the youngest, dressed in Sunday best, hair pulled back to reveal her small round face, perfect upturned nose and careless, vapid eyes. Flirting constantly, always dreaming about her next beau, she avoided being home as much as possible. The family had expected it would be Deirdre to end up in a predicament, her adventurous social outings strangely encouraged by our parents, much to the consternation of Aileen, who feared for Deirdre's soul.

Poor, pale Aileen. Her sallow complexion was made worse in the picture by the washed-out colour of the dress she wore. She smiled a weak appreciation of this small attention, but her face remained pinched, wrinkles creasing the brow between worried eyes, shoulders tightened against the onslaught of her days. She was old in the picture, made older than God with looking after Mother. Aileen bore the brunt of our mother's tyranny, listened to the unceasing complaints, worked tirelessly to run the household and nurse Mother through recurring episodes of blinding headaches that kept her in bed for days.

I felt a twinge of guilt. Aileen had suffered with me through the silence that roared around the house when I told Mother and Father of my pregnancy. For two days they closeted themselves in their bedroom, Mother's angry weeping sliding out under the door, Father's soft voice comforting her, choosing to believe her motives were pure.

"But the neighbours, they can be so harsh dear, even cruel, to people in Moira's condition. I love my daughter. I can't bear to see her scorned. She'll be back after it's adopted out. She can start again."

But when she deigned to glance my way, Mother's eyes were cold and grey and vindictive. "You will not ruin my life here. Nor your father's. We have worked too hard." She held her hand up, dismissive.

"And what have you worked at, Mother?" It popped out.

She slapped my face. Tears sprang up, though I bit down to keep from crying.

"Moira, you will leave at once."

Aileen had quietly collected my hairbrush and comb, the ribbons I wore on special occasions, my sister's eyes welling with tears at this unique injustice.

Poor Aileen.

In the portrait I sat in the middle of the family, though it always took me a moment to find myself. Are my cheeks really that full? My hair that thick and curly? I'd never noticed before how the escaped tendrils of hair framed my face in a pleasing way, how the neckline of my dress flattered my figure. White gloves were folded in my lap. I loved those gloves. They hid my hands, which I'd never loved, hands too large and easily calloused. But I liked my grin. It made me look as though I knew more than the other women in the picture: a grin of triumph at having become part of a world where I was more than the berated and ridiculed daughter of a sick woman. I would be a doctor like my father. I'd already been introduced to the sad reality of other people while on calls with him. I'd seen life beyond the walls of Mother's anger. In the picture I knew what I was. And what I was not. I would not become Aileen.

And so I vowed to make the best of Mr. Penny and this situation, went to the ill-stocked kitchen and found lard to slather on stale bread. Mr. Penny arrived after I'd retired to the attic. He made a terrific noise, cursing, dropping things. I lay stiff in the bed, covers pulled to my chin, and anticipated his footsteps, his glaring face. Instead the house grew quiet and I drifted in and out of sleep all night.

❖ ❖ ❖

CHAPTER 4

EVERY MORNING I wondered how I could continue as Mr. Penny's housekeeper. But destitution was more frightening than exhaustion, and so I hauled water to the kitchen from the well out back, a necessity consuming much of the morning. The rest of the day was spent shovelling wood into the hungry mouths of the two stoves – both stayed lit all day – one for cooking, the other for heating water and the irons. Washing his clothes the day before, I'd gagged at the sweaty stench of them. Today I would press the clean shirts.

"There can't be no wrinkles. And everything's gotta be starched." Mr. Penny was on his way out the door. "I have an appearance to maintain."

"Yes sir." I hated the ingratiating tone in my voice. I couldn't imagine how I'd save any money from the pittance he paid.

He fixed me with a hard stare. "Mind you don't steal anything or it'll be the tank for ya."

My face grew instantly hot. "Mr. Penny, I have never stolen anything in my life." I swooned with anger. "And I don't intend to start."

"Yeah, yeah. Just keep it that way." He nodded with contempt and left.

My whole body shook as I threw his wrinkled shirt on the table. The man was truly the pig I'd thought him to be. He had no right assuming such things. My father could buy his assets and more. His *palace* was a dump, his *great* Ibsen a joke, the man an idiot. I wanted to chase after him, fling a torrent of proper vocabulary in his face to show off my education and status. Instead I sagged under the weight of his insinuation, choked on a mix of rage and despair. I couldn't imagine what would happen when he learned the truth of my pregnancy, could only hope Mr. Penny remained as blind as he was vain.

Swallowing hard, I tested the iron and fought the urge to

burn a hole in the fabric. On folding the third shirt, I discovered a note in one of the front pockets that must have gone through the wash. On it was written *Annie* and *Monday*. Disgusting. The paper arched into the trash.

At three o'clock I took off my apron, straightened my hair, smoothed my dress and headed outside. People on the street nodded a curious hello and a moment of pleasure washed me clean of Mr. Penny's house. There were decent people in this town too. At the Chinese laundry a small woman eyed me from where she sat on the bench outside. She was tiny and wore a white fitted shirt and black pants with an apron wrapped over them. The Chinese were the only women I'd seen in trousers. I'd envied them in St. John's and I envied this woman too. How much simpler life must be unrestricted by corsets and layers of undergarments and overgarments.

"The doctor?" I raised my eyebrows to emphasize the question, not sure of the woman's English.

The words she offered in a short sharp tongue were at odds with the smile on her face. Finally she jerked her head toward the back of the store.

"Thank you," I murmured, aware too late of the benevolent half smile plastered on my face, the same smile my mother reserved for those she barely tolerated. As I passed the woman I turned to offer more, but she'd vanished inside. Hurrying around the corner to the back of the building, I spotted the shingle. Dr. P. Berkowski, MD.

"I'm about three months along," I informed him, stumbling over the words in my haste to get it over with. I'd seen the crucifix above the window, feared a lecture on the evils of fornication and the imperilled state of my immortal soul. "The morning sickness has abated a little, but I knew to expect relief after the first trimester." His eyes widened. I drew myself tall. "I am studying medicine with my father."

He nodded, a smile beginning to crease his hefty cheeks. "All right then, Moira, what is troubling you so much you would seek my humble advice?"

His candour was unsettling. "I have quite a bit of pain in my lower abdomen."

"Would you mind an exam then?"

When I shook my head he left me alone to undress. It was cold and uncomfortable under the thin sheet, my nipples pointed to the ceiling, the small mound of my stomach covered in goosebumps. The instruments I'd known in Father's office hung on the walls and rested on the desk – stethoscopes, scalpels, drug bottles of the trade. An odd sort of homesickness gripped me.

Every day of my life I'd watched Father rushing off in black coat and cap to the next emergency. In recent years he'd taken to helping people in the backwoods around St. John's, poor souls who could rarely pay. But he didn't mind, took pleasure instead in their grateful eyes and offers of prayers for him. "For me!" he would chuckle. He'd delivered their babies, performed their surgeries, comforted their bereaved, all without fanfare. He was a practical man. And he'd groomed me, hoping one day I might take over when he could no longer keep up the gruelling pace. Mother wasn't happy about it, displaying a muted envy at the collegial friendship grown between us, dismissing us. And Father stood back. He had, it seemed, endless capacity to put up with his wife's petty and facile nature.

"More time for his patients than his own family." It was Mother's ritual complaint.

He might have just arrived home from watching an entire family succumb to diphtheria, yet he would apologize for being late, peck her on the cheek and sit silently eating his cold supper while she spoke of the poor selection of beef at the local grocer's, told how the neighbours were fighting over the indiscretions of a certain cat, or complained no one appreciated the good work she did at the church.

"Why don't you tell her about your life? The important work you do?" I'd asked Father while on the way to deliver a baby. "She is utterly self-centred and thoughtless."

"My dear, she is your mother and I won't let you speak of her that way."

I was stung. I'd miscalculated, assumed our relationship had gone beyond his scolding protection of her position.

"But Father..."

"There are some things you don't know about your mother. And I don't intend to tell you. But she didn't have it easy. She's had her suffering. If she seems harsh now it's only because she wants so badly to hang on to what she has." We were driving up to an all-too-familiar house. Seven babies had been delivered in the tiny back bedroom. "Now let's get in there and help Mrs. McGiver. I hope she can survive another one."

I jumped down and collected Father's bags and the things we'd need – sheets, towels and Mother's rosary. Mrs. McGiver prayed the beads while in labour and was determined everyone in the room do the same. The sound of children quarrelling in the house was backdrop to Hail Mary ringing out amidst screams and groans, until, on cue with the final sign of the cross, the baby was born. I'd been there for two of the more recent births, sat and held the woman's hand, marvelled at her timing. I'd been encouraged to sponge Mrs. McGiver's forehead, to coax her to breathe and push. It was embarrassing, but I felt it my duty to offer up the occasional Glory Be or Our Father until the cord was snipped and there was a chorus of hallelujahs with the baby's first cry.

Until that last one. Another ill-conceived infant born to a woman whose faith dictated length of labour and time of birth. This time I caught the baby, a boy born with a beatific face and curly blond hair who never uttered a cry, never, in fact, learned to say one word or to take care of himself. For this one the sign of the cross came too late.

The doctor's knock was startling. I hadn't expected the tears and quickly wiped them away. He poked and prodded my belly, used an uncomfortable finger to check for cervical abnormalities, and announced he believed the baby was just fine, though I should try to eat more to sustain myself.

"And if you have these pains, you should probably avoid lifting."

I almost laughed out loud, instead whispering, "I'll try." Lifting was most of my work in Mr. Penny's employ. But I didn't want to burden the kind doctor with my sad story. He left again to allow me to dress.

"Thank you." I walked through to where he shuffled papers on his desk. "It's good to know everything is all right."

"Yes, well." He stared at his desk, absently tapping a pencil. "You know, you'd be a big help here, what with your experience." He looked at me then, compassion in his eyes. "But I really can't afford it. The damn medicine show taking people's money and luring them to their deaths. And...you're a woman. A pregnant woman." His face turned pink, his eyes averted. "I don't know if my wife would approve."

"Thank you, doctor." I wasn't at all sure it was his wife's approval that mattered. Perhaps he was just like my father's colleagues. The silence stretched awkwardly. I glanced up and his eyes met mine. "I do understand."

General Mercer's Store. The grocer's name stencilled onto the middle panel of the sign might have given the impression he was a leader of men. But a military man would have wiped the dust and stain from the glass windows and replaced the rotting wood of the door frame. A bell jangled when I opened the door and heads turned briefly. A huge black stove drew my eye, its pipes stretched like arms, one straight up, the other sideways to the wall before tracking up and through the roof. I wandered by flour barrels, cases of canned goods and mysterious wooden crates; followed the small pathways snaking between floor-to-ceiling shelves laden with everything from blankets to fabric, shiny new kettles to fancy china.

Two men sat on stools at the counter, sipping coffee and chatting with the man on the other side, General Mercer himself. Three or four women bustled around the store selecting items from piles or shelves.

"Why hello, Mrs. Berkowski. Those twins keeping you busy as usual?" The grocer's voice was loud.

She barely nodded and went about her business, but not before eyeing me with a shrewd glance. Perhaps her husband had been sincere. Whatever she'd heard about me kept her at a distance. I was new, alone and unwed, working for a man with a reputation for drink and women. I caught her looking again, judging me with my mother's eyes. I walked home to Mr. Penny's house, where I could hang my head, like she expected me to.

CHAPTER 5

DILLAN

I TRIED TO SAVE my wife from all the bad things that can happen. It hadn't gone very well so far. And then the stranger stomped in like he owned the place. I jumped up to shield Taffy from him, but he looked past like I weren't even there, to her lyin' curled up on a filthy mattress on the floor in a dark corner. He had nasty eyes, and sighed as though I was a disgusting bit of fish bait he'd like to see wriggling on a hook.

"It's Gibson," said the man, pushing past and shedding his coat and hat onto the only chair in the room. "Doctor Gibson. You're damn lucky your neighbours have some sense."

It was the burly woman next door was always asking after Taffy. Protestant. Meddling. She must have sent for him. The doctor's shirt was plastered to his back where rain had soaked through, and he shivered hard. Out the window a nor'easter was blowing. Hadn't even seen it coming. Too busy with Taffy I guess, sponging her forehead, singing softly, praying.

Gibson lit a tallow and set it on the crate beside Taffy, feeling her face, looking into her eyes with a light. "Not long for the world, I'm afraid." His voice wasn't mad any more. More weary than anything.

I couldn't say nothing, what with my gut falling to my knees. Taffy was supposed to be having a baby. I'd only thought she was tired, the baby taking its time the way Mother said a first child should. The doctor slid his stethoscope over Taffy's bulging stomach, grunting like he was surprised.

"There's a heartbeat."

He rolled up his sleeves, and before I could stop him, the bugger was looking between Taffy's legs.

"My God, the head's coming," he yelled. "Why didn't you tell me she's in labour?"

What?

"You damn Catholics. Sure know how to make 'em, and then pretend the whole bloody thing is immaculate. Like they'll just land in a goddamn crib from the goddamn sky."

He fished huge tongs from the black bag he'd brought.

"You're living in the back end of a stinking livery and you still gotta make babies." He was muttering like a lunatic. "Jesus."

He shouldn't have been swearing in front of my wife. "I couldn't find work. I..."

"Get a blanket, an old shirt, something you can wrap the baby in."

The words sent me into action. I grabbed a blanket off the bed.

"No, for Christ sake. Something clean."

Everything about the place was suddenly strange and hopelessly dirty, so I galloped around like a mental, picking up and throwing aside any piece of cloth I saw, until finally I found a towel under the washstand. Only a few stains. I turned back in time to watch Doctor Gibson reach the tongs deep into Taffy, grunting with the effort of the pull. The baby was ripped from my tiny wife. She screamed, a huge open-mouthed, gut deep, animal scream.

When she went still again I thought she was dead. Just before I could grab the doctor by the throat, she moaned real low, like the sound our milk cow made just before my father shot it, a sound like there was no way she could hold on to this world any longer. Taffy opened her eyes only once to get a glimpse of her boy. And then she turned her huge eyes on me and I all but shrank away into the floor, the world gone whirly, the doctor's voice a far-off whisper telling me she'd not likely last the night, the baby'd need caring for, he was small and sick.

Finally a shout. "Clean the place up, man. Give the child half a chance."

I didn't understand. Taffy was still, her chest barely moving under the thin blanket. The top of a small pink head and one tiny hand poked out of the towel beside her. Who was dying?

Who would live? I was like a blind man looking at the doctor. But he was stomping outside, coming back in quick with carbolic acid and a bucket. He looked around, his eyes wild, like a cat about to be skinned, and slammed the bucket on the side cupboard so hard the flaking paint flew up in a dust and the wobbly leg damn near broke off. I'd found the cupboard at the dump and brought it home for Taffy to use for the baby. It was only to be used for the baby.

"Get away from there. What the hell are you doing?"

The doctor dumped acid into the bucket and poured water into it from the pail by the door. "We're going to get this place clean so this child doesn't catch his death too."

I couldn't move. The doctor looked at me hard, grabbed my hands and thrust the wet rag into them, pushing my hands with his own, scrubbing like there were demons in the walls and floor. He had no right, barging in, hurting Taffy, ruining her things. I swung round and jumped him. He fell hard, knocking over the bucket so the water sluiced across the floor, the acid smell stinging in my nose. He just lay there in it, mad and scared.

"All right then," he said real calm. "If you want to live like this." He sat up and shrugged like he'd given up. "Your wife is going to die soon, and unless you do something you'll lose your son too. It's up to you." He picked up his things.

I didn't really notice him leave. Going to die. Pictures were flashing through my skull, beautiful Taffy, her wide-set blue eyes red from crying, small mouth and nose twisted with fear, begging to stay in Arichat, our tiny village on Isle Madame off Nova Scotia.

"This is home, where we have family." She'd taken turns between mad and yelling, or sad and whining with her lip out to there. "We'll make out just fine here. You can work with my father at the mill. He's told you he needs another foreman. And he can help out if we need it. What's in Halifax? We'll be all alone."

But that was the point. I didn't want them watching every minute, noses in the air, judging, interfering. And my family-backward immigrants and all their kids-barely surviving on a wreck of a farm. I'd brought her to Halifax so's we could find our own way. Now it was killing her.

Taffy had the typhoid. The doctor left, swearing he'd never seen anything like it, and I could only watch while her whole body shook with cold even while her face was burning up. She moaned and thrashed about, occasionally waving her hand at something in the distance, whispering at ghosts there by the door, now by the table. The stench of her was unbearable, her functions out of control. I cringed to go near her, even more with guilt at my disgust.

She would have hated the indecency of it. She hadn't even wanted me to see her scratching behind her ears for the lice. I'd shaved off my hair to get rid of them, had even soaked my head in kerosene that left it reeking for days. But Taffy would never cut her long locks, too proud, too worried of what I might think. And she never complained about it either. Only the scratching when she thought I wasn't looking. The lice was nothing compared to this.

Hours after the baby was born, Taffy was finally still, her blue eyes open and empty, blonde hair spread wildly on the flat pillow. In death she was no one I knew. Father, Son and Holy Ghost. I signed myself and figured I'd better do the same to her. I was no priest, but maybe my blessing her was enough to save her. Purgatory weren't near as bad as hell. I took the amulet from around her neck to see what prayer she might have tucked inside. Instead on a tiny piece of paper she'd scrawled, *Casey – courageous and brave.* The baby squalled and my insides crumpled up small and dead. Before I knew it I was on my knees bawling with him.

We cried together for a while, but his tiny voice insisted I pay attention, his problems were bigger than mine. Slowly he came into focus. At first I was kind of suspicious of him, felt like a cave man poking at something that might poke back. I knew babies, just not my own, and not without a woman there to take over at the first sign of trouble.

"Taffy was ready for you," I told him kind of quiet. "Stitched gowns out of feed sacks using these small perfect stitches. And cut up old flour sacks for diapers, said they'd be softer." I fingered the towel he was wrapped in. "I had to bring home any rag, anything, no matter what it looked like. And she washed them, cut them into squares and quilted them. She was a genius."

"And I was useless to her." The baby had gone quiet, just lay there, big-eyed, wanting an explanation for his current miserable situation. I'd begged for jobs, but no one wanted an unskilled, uneducated bohunk. Almost took the bottle from toothless old Ralph in the street out front. But I only had to think of my old man to chase that want away. I looked at the baby hard. "She worked hard to make this hellhole bearable for you. I couldn't do nothing to help. Should have taken the job with her father. She'd have had family around to help, women to appreciate all this." I motioned around the room and laughed. "Mind, she never said it. Told her father to piss off when he threatened to cut her out of his inheritance. Said it didn't matter; I was her husband. She was loyal, was Taffy." The baby looked bored.

As I stood looking at Taffy's body, all her efforts seemed a waste. Slowly I kissed each cold fingertip and folded her hands together on her chest, smoothed each soft eyelid over each tired eye. I drew a rough blanket over her and finally turned to the baby. It was tiny, like the small hairless kitten I'd found abandoned in a carton in an old shed at home. I'd felt helpless then too. The baby was mewling, a soft whimper. He seemed barely to breathe.

My hands felt enormous picking up the child, his soft downy head in one, the tiny bum fit neatly into the other. I swayed back and forth with him for the longest time, afraid I'd crush him if I held him close, afraid to set him down now in case he broke. His arms and legs were long and skinny, his tiny stomach stretched tight over blue ribs. Even the boy's head was narrow and pointed, his small face pinched and red, bruises starting where the doctor'd grabbed him with his tongs. Never seen anything so in need of protection; matchsticks would break with less force. It was amazing Gibson hadn't wrenched the boy in two. The thought gave me gooseflesh and I cradled the boy close, feeling his warmth through my fingertips and arms. Casey.

Why don't men prepare for anything? The dense fog parted long enough to understand what Taffy'd been doing. She didn't know anything about babies, but a million mothers before her had taught her to prepare and so she did, like life depended on it. I had waited about like a great oaf with his head up his arse. Holding this tiny thing, his dead mother only two feet away, my heart thumped with a new kind of sadness, for her loss now, the lost chance to hold him and feel what I was feeling right then.

Suddenly a new warmth flowed over me. The baby was peeing, a small fountain, and I couldn't help but chuckle a little. Casey stopped squirming, his black eyes turned toward my voice. I laid him on the mattress beside Taffy and reached for one of the diapers folded and stacked inside the small basket Taffy had secretly received from her mother. They called it a bassinet. Whatever that means. It was the one beautiful thing we owned. White lace reached to the floor while a see-through white curtain hung from a curved pole at the head of the basket to protect the baby from wind and sun.

Just as I turned back, a woman lumbered in through the door, filling the small space with her huge body and voice. "Gibson sent me," she said through the mask she wore over her mouth and nose. She only glanced at the outline of Taffy on the bed. "To be his wet nurse. Says you're desperate." She turned to holler at someone behind her. "This is the place, boys."

"What the hell?"

Two men followed her in. They wore handkerchiefs over their mouths and gloves on their hands. They pushed me away when I tried to stop them wrapping Taffy's body more securely in the blanket. Finally they picked her up and headed out the door, bumping her against the door frame on the way out.

"Wait. No." I hauled on the second man's arm.

"The doc says she's gotta go." He shrugged and hoisted Taffy so he had a better grip. "Sorry, sir," he mumbled and turned again to leave.

"Gibson even paid my first week for you," said the woman, and when I turned back, "Bless him."

She'd shed her boots at the door, and her coat was draped across the back of the chair. I could barely take all of her in. Rolls of fat smothered her limbs. Her ankles and calves were purple-veined sausages peeking out from under the huge housedress she wore. She was waiting for me to say something about the doctor's grand gift. When I didn't, she turned up her nose. "I'd say you owe him a debt of gratitude, I would." She was English. I don't like the English. "Good thing some of us'll still come and work for the likes of you, eh?"

"I don't need your help."

"Well, who's going to feed the wee thing then? You?" She laughed, pushed me out of the way and lifted Casey's bottom, taking the diaper I had still clutched in my hand and sliding it under the baby and round his legs. She pinned it, the whole thing like she'd been doing it for years. "Where's his gowns?"

I reached into the cupboard where Taffy had them neatly folded one on top of the other. They were soft against my rough hands.

When I handed her one she fingered it and frowned. "It might chafe." She looked round and let out a long, heavy sigh. "But I guess it'll have to do, eh?" She pulled his tiny arms through the holes and did up the string at the neck. "You gotta clean this place through if you want me to stay, get rid of the disease."

"My wife just..." Who the hell was this woman? "You got no right." I wanted to snatch Casey out of her arms, to protect him from this blustering whale of a woman. But the whale was right. I needed her to keep Casey alive, at least for now. No idea how I'd pay her. And if I couldn't, would Casey simply die in this godforsaken town? Not for the first time I felt a sick longing for home, mostly for my mother.

"I don't do cooking and cleaning and such. Only for the baby and myself. So you'll have to take care of the rest." She waved her arms around the room and the flabby undersides flapped like wings. Suddenly she got this sly look, her eyes all but disappearing into the volume of her cheeks. "Unless, of course, you can pay. Then things can be arranged."

"How much?"

"Dollar a day."

I was stunned, but faked like I'd expected it. "Just do it then. I'll pay." I looked at her more closely, trying to decide if I could trust her with Casey, knowing I had no choice. "What's your name then?"

"Fran Brody." She picked up Casey and began to unbutton her dress. "You get out of here now. Unless you want to watch?" Her eyebrows flicked up and down, flirting like, and she lowered her great bulk onto the bed where the imprint of Taffy's body was still warm. Casey was lying across her lap. "Scrawny thing, isn't he?"

Scrambling to put my shoes on, I rushed to the door. She called out, sounding almost sorry. "Gibson paid those two to come get her. Says they'll have to burn her, 'cause you can't afford anything else."

I slammed the door behind me so the horses in the livery jumped. One pulled back hard on its halter.

"Hey!" The stable hand ran to calm the mare. "What the hell's the matter with you?"

I reeled out onto the street, almost stumbling over Ralph lying in the warmth coming from under the livery door.

"Fucker." He spit it at me.

I must have looked half mad, 'cause he pulled back into the shadows when I turned on him. And then I ran. Hard. Pumping my arms and legs 'til they were rubber, 'til my breath came in great gulps, 'til I decided crying wasn't gonna get me far and Mrs. Brody was a piss-poor substitute for a parent, 'til I found myself back outside the livery, girding myself for the battle to come.

The livery boss took one look at Casey and offered me a job.

"We stick together," he muttered, Irish accent thick. "Only for a few months, mind."

His pity was embarrassing. I worked like a dog to make

up for it. Don't know he ever noticed. The whole time I was there he ducked so's I couldn't see his face, but the pity never left it. Getting up early with Casey, I learned to change diapers and keep the boy happy until Mrs. Brody showed up for the day. In the evening I went for a pint with other working men just scraping to provide for their families. Heading home after, it felt almost a normal life until I got to the door, where Mrs. Brody was always impatient for her pay. Then I'd hold Casey on my knee, tell him stories of Taffy and Arichat. And every night before I conked on the bed, I'd touch the cedar box I made to hold my wife's ashes.

"I'll make it better for him someday, Taffy. I will."

Eight months later I was still forking horseshit, every cent spent to keep Brody. But I was feeding Casey more mashed potatoes from my own plate and doing more of the cleaning and washing at the end of the day. Brody always had an excuse.

"Oh look at my feet, so swollen from chasing the boy all day."

"He never quits. I can't even keep up with the diapers let alone the cleaning."

She didn't do much more than watch Casey. And on the way home I'd hear her hollering at him as though the boy's sole purpose in shitting his diaper was to irritate her. And when I'd get there just wanting her to leave, she'd putter about, picking up the few toys I'd managed to find for Casey, asking about *my* day as though it were the most interesting thing she'd heard. Made me wonder if maybe she was worse off than me.

Finally I came home one night to Casey screaming, tied in his crib, diaper soaked and dirty, every bit of food gone from the cupboard. And a note.

Sorry to leave, but the pay wasn't enough. Your son can survive without me now. Gibson found a new orphan for me to raise.

She had written *good luck* at the bottom, like one of them PSs, like the wish was only something she thought of after, like she thought she should say something nice.

It was the word *orphan* that sent me back home to Arichat. Sure Casey didn't have a mother, but he sure as hell wasn't no orphan. A father's gotta be worth something in the mix even if he isn't so good at diapers and cuddling. I was learning that too. Had to. And if I was honest, I'd have to say I was glad. I knew more about my boy at six months old than my father knew about me in twenty years. But I needed a real job and Casey needed some real mothering, so I headed home to show my father what he'd never given me.

Only he'd gone off to Sydney, to work in the coal mines. It suited me just fine.

"Your father refuses to come home." Mother sounded proud, like this alone would redeem him, like he was finally proving why she'd stayed with him all those years. It was a shock to see her. She looked like hell. Skin looking for bones to wrap itself around, that's all was left. Even when things were at their worst- a new baby hanging on her, little ones with croup, Da drunk and ugly – her eyes always had a spark. But when I got home and hugged her tight, there was only the skin. Until she saw Casey; he lit her up with laughing and crying all at once.

Almost a year I was a dockhand, loading and unloading the few ships still stopping in our small harbour. Casey grew, Mother teaching him to walk, to say a few words, his young uncles and aunts spoiling him every day after school.

I hardly recognized Da when he finally came home. He was like the ivy my mother tried to keep alive in our shack where the sun never reached, his body hunched like brown, curled leaves, his arms and legs the spindly vines. His face was pinched and black with soot in the deep creases. And he was old. He coughed and hacked, bringing up the black shit and wheezing afterward, hardly able to catch his wind.

"It's almost the end for me now, boy." His breath was hot and rank. "I wanted to see my grandson before I go."

Da nudged me and nodded at the four other children crowding around the bed where Casey was putting on a show, making faces at his audience. He went outside, stopping to lean against the table when another hacking fit caught him. I shivered and stood up just as Mother swooped in on Casey.

"Come on, little one, let's see if you can go on the pot before your nap." She was nuzzling Casey's neck, kissing his nose and cheeks while he flailed at her for interrupting his fun. "He's figuring out what he has to do." She laughed and disappeared into the curtained-off bedroom.

I found father on the sagging front stoop, rolling a cigarette with one hand and holding a bottle to his mouth with the other. He looked at me hard and for so long I felt skinned, like my pelt was hanging from the rail, him waiting to devour my raw insides. The hair on my neck prickled. Finally he flicked his ashes into the shrubs beside the porch and pulled on the bottle again.

"You should've taken better care of Taffy." The voice rattled from his chest. "You'll never get anything from her old man now."

Oh he knew what he was saying. Knew it would send me at him. His bony figure blurred to red, my breath coming too fast, shoulders heaving. I was on him in two strides. "You bastard." I grabbed his arm and wrenched it behind his back. "That's all that mattered then? Her family havin' money?"

He tried to lurch away, the cigarette falling from his lips. "Don't hurt me, boy." His voice was pleading, pathetic, and I saw how very small he was. "I didn't mean nothin'."

I pushed him away.

"But they owed it to your grandfather, bless his soul. Taking his land, sending him over half-starved from the famine." His voice rose and his bent body uncurled, his finger stabbing the air.

He gave me a long hard look as though I had something to do with any of it. And finally I saw what he'd been waiting for since I could remember. Since the time I was a wee thing listening to him whine and wait for *those bastards to give him a chance*, to lift him from the muck hole he was wallowing in.

He suddenly leaned over the porch rail, spitting blood, hanging on the door frame to steady himself. And he was pathetic, not just because he was scared and sick, but because he'd wasted his whole life in waiting for it to start.

"Taffy was right," I told him, not too harsh. "I could have worked at the mill. Probably would have enjoyed it."

37

"But you left."

"It wasn't no handout either. I would have made something of myself."

"Why didn't you then." He sneered. "Chicken? Too pansy?"

"You prick." My voice went quiet, a huge weight of sadness resting on my chest. "I left because all you wanted was a ticket out of this hell hole."

"Yeah right." He tried to sound mean, but the meanness was leaving him. He saw that I knew.

"Nobody owes you a life, you sorry bastard." I opened the door and looked back. "You don't deserve one."

It was the last time I saw my family. Da had forced the decision between the poverty I knew and a dreamer's chance at something better. Casey and I were both orphaned, so in the late fall of 1906 I laid ten dollars on the counter and bought a ticket on the last Harvest Train heading to Saskatchewan.

CHAPTER 6

THE TRAIN WEREN'T SO BAD, but for the three days of hard slat-
ted seats, bad food and nervous women. My God, you'd think
they'd never seen a man hold a babe before. Buggered off
soon's I came near their precious wee ones, like my boy had
some kind of contagion. Then some other dames, asking after
Casey, so I yammered away and they could laugh at the bohunk fresh from the sea. But those weren't no good girls hiding behind their fancy gloves. And their shoes. Taffy would've
laughed. They wouldn't have lasted a minute in the rock and
mud of Arichat. It was the shoes that proved it. Only bad girls
wore heels like that. They'd have given me a roll if I'd asked.
Not that I would, seeing as how I'd just lost Taffy and all.

But the other one, the one with curly hair and sensible
shoes. Not real pretty, but handsome. Don't know what a decent girl like her was doing on a train full of men. She looked
on, smiling like she knew about me. Women like her know
things, things like my being a bloody liar, and Casey's mother
being dead, and it being all my fault.

Casey slept most of the time. The hum of the rails seemed
to lull him. Couldn't get off the train in Toronto, even when
the conductor came up and said it was okay. The uniform
made me nervous. Figured I must have done something wrong
to get his attention.

"It would do you good to stretch your legs. It's a long trip."
He was a nice enough fellow. "And the little one could use
some fresh air. You've lots of time."

I shook my head. The crowd out the window was huge,
so many people my throat went dry and my chest pounding
so I figured they could hear it out there on the platform. No
way in hell I was exploring with so many watching. The train
pulling out again was a relief. There was nothing expected of
me now except to ride, and I finally dozed in fits and starts,

waking at Casey's every move, every time the train lurched. I
knew we'd be snaking across the Canadian Shield. My mother had taught me geography. She loved it, poring over maps,
pointing out the continents, the oceans and Ireland, where my
clan come from. That night, somewhere in Manitoba, the train
rolled onto the prairie.

The other men were up all night. I pretended to sleep
when they went by to take a piss off the platform outside.
They were loud and ugly, their voices carrying through every
time the door was opened between cars. I'd seen such men
in Halifax: far from home, no women to keep them in line. A
few months earlier I might have laughed at them and maybe,
if they weren't too far gone, have joined in.

Near dawn we stopped at the Regina station. A scuffle
broke out down the corridor, but I didn't move, didn't want
to risk getting involved. Then a roar of men's voices shook
the air and I had to take a look out the window, careful, like
a detective, Casey pawing at me to let him see. Five or six of
the men were hanging off the side of the train. They shouted
encouragements to a drunk who'd come out of a tavern near
where the train was stopped, and he lurched toward a beautiful
horse saddled and tied out front. The horse was a prize. The
man staggered in front of it while it reared up on its rope with
nostrils flared and eyes wild. Just missed getting a hoof in the
head, the idiot, until he finally got the rope in his hand and a
foot in the stirrup. He swung himself up and rode the terrified
thing out of sight behind the train. The men shouted, jubilant
at the daring of another to steal such a fine animal. The train
started moving and it was over, the men staggering off to bed
to sleep off their whiskey. I held tight to Casey.

What changes when you're holding a kid you fathered?
Do your gonads suddenly shrink 'cause they've proven their
worth? Or maybe they swell at the idea of what you've done?
Maybe that's what makes you a man. Or maybe it's you know
how men can be and it scares you that something so innocent
might see what his father's capable of. I felt like a ninny for
being nervous, protective and pissed off on Casey's behalf.

It never fails. The moment you fall into a deep sleep after a restless night, the sun comes up to shine in your eyes. That and Casey wailing for his breakfast. I dragged my head out of the fog and stuck a cup of sugar water in Casey's greedy hands. His face twisted like I was trying to poison him, and he babbled on, mad as hell at the lack of milk. He kept glaring at me from over the rim, but settled into the crook of my arm like always. The sun was higher. Out the window, great fields of wheat and grass stretched to the horizon, like beautiful waves bowing to the wind. My throat closed up with a homesick lump.

✠ ✠ ✠

We arrived in Moose Jaw to a heat I'd never known.

"Hey, Casey," I picked him up and wiped a shirt sleeve under his runny nose. "Maybe we've died and this is hell then?"

Police met us on the station platform, setting suspicious eyes on each of us, asking after anyone who'd seen the man who stole the horse at Regina. They passed me over quick when Casey started fussing. Stealing a man's horse was low, almost worse than stealing a man's wife I figure, but I wasn't saying anything. I was too afraid to get involved. I grabbed our things and hit the road as soon as they let the barricade down. A member of the North West Mounted Police looked me over real slow from his perch on a broad grey gelding.

"Hey. You. With the kid."

I turned back terrified. "Me?"

"You're the only one carrying a kid."

"Yeah."

"They're looking for workers on a crew in Ibsen, couple hours' ride south." He looked away over the barricade again.

Under my shirt I could feel my sweat go cold. "Uh, thanks."

He didn't look at me again.

It was hell, hitching rides with a little one. You'd have thought I was carrying a live skunk the way people wrinkled their noses and drove their horses a little faster as they went by. Finally I had to leave Casey out of sight in the tall grass at the side of the trail until a wagon slowed. Then I'd quick grab him and hoist us both up onto the back until they kicked us off. Some let us ride. Some didn't, cursing all bums and delinquents, as though I was some kind of representative.

Finally a driver stopped of his own accord and a woman's hands reached down to take Casey. They were a husband and wife, maybe fifty years old, a flash of smile between them when they made room on the seat for me. She reached behind to a basket and pulled out a cheese sandwich and jar of milk.

"Thanks." The bread melted in my mouth.

"Looks like you've had some hard luck," she said.

I nodded, looking down at the holes in my boots and the bundle of dirty grey clothes that was Casey.

"Going to the crew?" her husband asked, sizing me up with his one good eye. The other wandered to the left a little, so I wasn't sure where he was looking. I took my chances on the straight eye and spoke to it.

"I was told they were looking for men in Ibsen."

"Yeah, so they say." He thought for a minute. "But watch yourself. There's some of those outfits don't give a damn how they treat ya. Look for a big guy named Henry. He'll steer you right."

"What will you do with this little guy?" The woman shifted Casey on her knee and smiled down at him. "You're a sweet thing, aren't you?"

Casey mumbled through the sandwich he chewed.

"Well, ma'am, I don't know." I was thinking quick so she wouldn't think me an idiot. "I was hoping the farm women would watch him while I worked."

She laughed and shook her head. "Oh Lord, those women won't have time for another little one underfoot. They'll be too busy cooking for the crew and tending to their own." Her husband looked at her, she raised her eyebrows at him and he nodded. "It's none of my business, but where's his mother?"

A lump rose in my throat. No one except Doctor Gibson and Mrs. Brody knew how bad Taffy's death had been. The memory was like a sore that had mossed over, ugly with festering, but hidden from everyone, so saying it out loud was like ripping off a scab. "She died of the typhoid the day he was born."

The woman's eyes went soft, concern creasing at her forehead. "Oh Lord." She held Casey too close and he squirmed to get away.

"I tried to make it in Halifax, but there was no work. We was practically starving and Taffy pregnant and then..." My voice broke and I hated myself, because part of me enjoyed the telling and the sympathy it brought. Part of me wanted there to be a clean white scar where the wound was. See it the way these people saw it. But when I ducked my head to fake tears, all I could think of was the part I wasn't telling where it was my fault.

"Don't you worry...?"

"Dillan."

"Dillan. This little fellow can stay with us while you work the harvest."

"I'll make out okay." My hands unclenched and shoulders relaxed even as I protested. Someone else to worry over Casey, to figure out what he needed, to be responsible.

"Nonsense. Look, we're Mr. and Mrs. George Miller. You come have supper with us, ask about us in town if you like, see if we're trustworthy enough." She glanced at her husband and laughed out loud. "The boy will be fine."

I liked her. She was straight-on, looked at you when she spoke, and her eyes were kind. "Yes, I believe he will be. I'll make it up to you, Mrs. Miller. I promise."

When we got to their farm, I washed up and helped Casey do the same. Mrs. Miller's fried potatoes and salt pork were like honey on my tongue. She bounced around her small kitchen, talking of her garden, her husband's crops, laughing with Casey as she tickled his naked belly and washed him clean of the livery and the train and the past. The boy and I slept like we were dead, wrapped in a feather tick on a bed of straw in the barn. And in the morning, Mr. Miller squeezed my shoulder and pointed me toward town.

"The crews are assembling at the end of Main Street," he said. I reached for Casey, struggling in Mrs. Miller's arms. "Gotta say goodbye."

Strange feelings tugged at my belly when I hugged him – relief he'd be cared for, scared witless for him at the same time. Relief too, at being alone in the world again, the strange combination of freedom and fear you get on entering a pub where no one knows you or anything about you, the sense you will have to make it on your own legs. I'd used Taffy's story to my advantage. Casey too. But now I'd have no excuses.

"Go now." Mrs. Miller looked at me sorrowfully, took my hands and squeezed them. Her hands were like my mother's hands, hard with life, gentle with love. "Go and work out your grief. Then you'll be ready to raise this young thing properly."

I couldn't tell her it wasn't grief keeping me poor and hopeless. The grief was easy compared to the guilt. I handed Casey to her and walked away slow, looked back and waved. Casey wouldn't understand this leaving. How could he? I turned back at least twice, and finally started to run, faster and faster until the wind drowned out Casey's cries, until my lungs were bursting with the great gulps of blue sky burning them.

CHAPTER 7

I REACHED MAIN STREET, Ibsen, and slowed up. Main Street, it turned out, was the only street and made up the whole of the business district. A few shops, a livery, hardware. Small spurs of homes sprang from this hub. That was it. Back home people lived in town, close to town, on embankments, hills, rocks and valleys. But this flat little place spread across two streets and then just stopped to make way for prairie. In Arichat a person had to make an effort to spy on his neighbour. There'd be no need of spying here. Just look down the street and you'd know everybody's business. The whole place was cracked dry and hard.

At the end of Main Street, a ragtag bunch of men had assembled. Men like me. Most owned nothing but the shirts on their backs and the boots on their feet. Some wore strange hats that must have come from places I'd never even heard of. It was a guilty kind of joy pumped up my chest as I got closer. I was a man again, with no child to make me weak or single me out.

A great beast of a machine was set on a flat wagon, draft horses harnessed and ready. A line of wagons and bunkhouses were hitched to mules, donkeys and oxen. Climbing on the machine and hollering at everyone to "look at this big fogger" was a squat-looking man with a thick neck, and forearms looking like they could crush anything. He glared at me and my stomach somersaulted.

"What are you looking at?" he shouted over the commotion around him. His voice was slurred with a heavy accent I didn't recognize.

My tongue was thick. "I'm just...uh..."

"Listen to the fuckin' mental. Just stay out of my way, you little..."

A large hand gripped my elbow and steered me toward the line of wagons.

"Never mind him then. He's a horse's ass." The voice was heavy with an Irish brogue. The hand belonged to a huge man with flaming red hair and beard. "Name's Henry. First time with the crew then?"

It was more a statement than a question. I nodded.

"Just stay away from Gabe." Henry nodded slightly toward the man who was swinging like a monkey from one wagon to the next, hollering at everyone he saw. "He's an idiot, but you gotta feel sorry for him, poor bugger." He shook his head. "Waiting for his chance two years now, but he hasn't got a hope in hell of getting any land. He's Polish, or Ukrainian, maybe Russian for all I know."

I must have looked stunned.

"No one's gonna give him the time of day, especially the land office. Government wants to keep folks like him out as long as they can." Henry looked at me like I understood, so I just nodded. "But he's a stupid bugger too. Doesn't help his chances, acting like he does. Don't know his arse from a knot in a pine board. But he can work. I'll give him that." Henry pulled himself up so he towered over me. "Now what might you be good for?"

"I don't know, but..." I decided I'd better sound like I knew something from a pine board. "I'd sure like to get on the threshing crew."

"Ha!" Henry boomed. "Wouldn't you though? You'll start pitching like everybody else. Work hard and learn fast and you'll move on to the machine soon enough, 'specially since the harvest is so late. Maybe get to drive a wagon."

"I'll do my best."

"Yeah. One more thing." Henry gave me a sidelong look. "Where're you from?"

"Arichat."

"Good. I got a second cousin from there. Good." He walked away.

I trailed behind feeling foolish until a wagon rumbled by and I jumped in. I grunted to the men already in the back and pretended to doze with my hat pulled down over my face.

From under the brim I recognized some of the men from Halifax. Thank Christ Gabe wasn't with 'em.

The weeks of harvest were a blur. A new farm every few days. Men dropped off and others took their places. The sweet smells of harvest made my eyes itch and my nose drip like a leaky bucket. Even my ears itched. On the inside. Henry told me it was the dust, said a good rain would dampen things down and take care of it. Sometimes I slept in a bunkhouse on a thin mattress, sometimes in a hayloft, the loose straw giving comfort to my aching back. Exhausted and sore, I'd have slept hanging from a tree, grateful finally to sleep without dreams or regret.

I was one of two pitchers, forking the heavy stooks onto a wagon that took them to the threshing machine. After three weeks of the endless rhythm of stab, lift, heave, pitch, Henry finally told me I'd be getting a better job. But I didn't want one. Sure I suffered with itching and snot and aching joints, but I liked the predictability of the work, the smells, the feeling I was doing something that mattered. And the urgency of it; the whole crew checked the sky as though it might fall down around us, racing billowing black clouds that grew and threatened for miles, running to get the field done because the next storm might be bringing winter with it. The work kept Taffy locked away somewhere.

We ate four times a day: breakfast, lunch, another meal in late afternoon and yet another at the end of the day. And the Scotsmen brought *crowdy* to the field, a mix of oatmeal and water they claimed would give me energy. A *refreshment* they called it. It tasted like wet sawdust. Otherwise, the women of the farms cooked for the entire crew as well as their own large families.

It was a cool evening and we were camped in a circle in a field not far from the farmyard. The farmer looked exhausted, his wife worn out. Still, she beckoned us to join her family and enjoy harvest ice cream. She poured salt over packed ice surrounding the bucket of cream, then turned the crank until the little ones crowded around her hollering, "It's thick, Momma. Momma, it's ready." Momma insisted on a few more minutes of cranking before declaring the ice cream fit to eat. It was cold, creamy perfection. I held it on my tongue to save the taste there as long as I could before it dissolved, and I swallowed it along with the dusty rawness in my throat. I smiled at the woman whose name I couldn't remember. Mary or Kate or Frieda. There'd been so many farm wives.

Gabe sat a little apart from the rest of us. He'd been staring across the fire toward the house. All through the harvest, I'd said nothing to him, staying away from him as Henry advised. I only watched as he convinced a big French guy to join a poker game and then cheated him out of a day's earnings with an ace up his sleeve. And I minded my own business when I saw him pocket a gold watch at the general store in Benson. I watched my back and slept with my moneybelt under my head. I'd no plans to get involved.

From beside the fire I could see the farmer's daughter, a silhouette standing in the open doorway of the house. I'd seen her earlier, guessed her to be thirteen or so, dark hair pulled into two long braids. She'd stared right back at me, innocent, like she didn't know her skin was clear and her breasts made a small rise under her shirt – temptation to a lesser man. She was fresh and beautiful. Like Taffy...before... Gabe was looking at her with hard eyes. There was a sudden chill on my skin.

Behind me someone tuned a guitar, and the farmer started singing cowboy songs about love and losing love and horses and dogs. We all sat quiet, listening, embarrassed by it, the western tunes strange to our eastern ears.

And then Henry gave us a Celtic dance on his harp, and two or three from home stood up, stepping kind of awkward-like, until everyone was clapping and hollering "faster, faster." The moonshine appeared, and soon the strangeness was gone, and we were all flushed and homesick and happy, the evening mild, a light wind keeping the mosquitoes away, the dust of the harvest hanging in the air and the taste of ice cream faint on our lips.

Without really looking, I saw that Gabe was gone. The door of the house was empty, too, and I searched round the fire for the girl's face. I worked hard to keep down the bad feeling rising in my throat. Standing and slowly stretching, I started toward the yard. It was stupid, giving in to the bad feeling, but my legs just took me. I needed some time alone anyway. The moonshine made my head fuzzy and the dark of the night made it worse, like I was walking sideways and uphill.

"Hey there." I patted one of the horses in a pen near the barn and crooned to her like she was a woman. "Nice night. Aren't you a beauty then?" Fear was growing to dread, my breath coming quick and shallow. There was no one in the barn. Where were they? I stopped and looked around at the black night, and shook my head. This was crazy. Gabe probably went back to camp, the girl to bed. Maybe they were both back at the fire. And I was a fool.

And then I saw them at the back door of the house. He pushed her and she stumbled into the porch, the door closing behind them. I crept closer until I was just outside, my whole body rigid with listening, fists clenched, head pounding like my heart had leapt up there into my brain.

"Where's the key?" Gabe's voice was loud through the door.

"Please don't," she whispered, and then sucked in her breath, crying out a little like she was hurt. "Pa won't be able to pay the crew. Please."

Son of a bitch. He was stealing our wages?

"Another fucking word and I'll hurt you worse. Where is it?" Gabe was breathing hard.

"Ow, don't." The girl yelped. "On a hook under the coats, right there by the door."

There was shuffling near the door.

"You tell anyone," Gabe said, the words slow and hard, "an' I'll come back and burn your house down with your ma and those other brats inside."

"Leave her alone." The words growled up from my throat. I hadn't known they were there. I'd been so afraid, I'd forgotten to plan. "Leave her alone," I said again, louder, and kicked open the door. Gabe had the girl's arm pushed up behind her back. Her face was filled with pain and fear and tears. He was rooting in a strongbox on the floor with his free hand. He flashed surprised and ugly eyes at me, let go the girl and lunged, but I was already running out into the dark.

He tackled me at the edge of the wheat field, landing on top of me, his arm across my throat. He fought like an animal, scratching my face, hammering my stomach, my kidneys, my head. I landed only a weak punch or two. I hadn't fought much, didn't know how to protect myself, how to hurt him back. He was standing over me, kicking at my groin and back. The pain exploded in my chest and I heard a cracking sound, my ribs under his boots. There was shouting in the distance and suddenly it was over, Gabe running away, Henry's huge arms lifting me and carrying me all the way back to the farmhouse, the girl mute beside her mother and sisters, who suddenly switched their attention to me. I saw her through one swollen eye as she turned away, flushed and suffering.

She helped her mother nurse me, coming only at night when the lights were low, never looking me in the eye. She kept her head down, her face frowning while she changed the dressing on my eye and rewrapped the bandage round my ribs. I was useless to help her, the pain too great. Useless in other ways too. Gabe hadn't got all the farmer's money. We were all paid. But the family would do without 'cause of Gabe's thieving. And I didn't tell anyone who done it, told them it was too dark to see. Didn't tell them how Gabe threatened the daughter so she kept quiet too. Both of us had seen what was in Gabe's eyes. Both of us were too afraid to speak.

Finally, one night, I tried. "He's an evil man."

Her frown deepened, pulling the corners of her eyes with it. I started to tell her it wasn't her fault. She shouldn't be afraid to walk in the daylight. But I couldn't find the words. Who was I to counsel anyone? I left her home as soon as I could walk a few paces without pain. My harvest was over.

CHAPTER 8

MOIRA

"YOU'RE AN EMBARRASSMENT. You lied to me and now I can't trust you." Mr. Penny's voice was loud, rumbling about the small room he fancied as a business office, the volume of his accusations threatening to make them true. "You will no longer work in this house."

I'd known this moment would come. I was almost five months on and had just endured a Christmas as lonely and bleak as the winter landscape. And all the while I'd worried only about how I'd respond, rehearsed language measured and eloquent, proof of how very respectable I was so he might, on sober second thought, ask me to stay on. But the words fled.

"Please, sir, I'll be destitute. I've nowhere to go."

"Well, that's not my problem now, is it?" He looked contemptuously at my belly bursting its camouflage. "Maybe you should have thought about that before you got yourself in trouble."

Myself.

"I'll stay out of the way when you have guests." The words tripped over each other. "I mean, I can set out the tea. And then stay in my room. You could do the shopping. No one would know."

"People are already talking about your bastard." He slunk out from behind his desk to stand beside my chair, the fingers of his hand closing over the back of it close to my neck. It seemed the hairs on his knuckles must be gently reaching for my skin. I shuddered. He snorted, his eyes heavy on my head. And I wanted to smash his smug face, pictured with satisfaction his soft, fleshy nose disappearing behind the force of my fist.

"You have until the end of the month," he said with a self-satisfied nod.

"Oh no." I quickly calculated the days and how much money I might save before then.

"You stay any longer and the gossips are gonna wonder if I'm keeping you on 'cause its mine."

I didn't know if I'd heard correctly until I looked up to see his suggestive grin.

"Yours," I snorted. "Wouldn't that be a sweet revenge?"

"What?"

"I could drop them hints, keep them guessing."

"You wouldn't dare."

"Why not?" Reckless abandon filled the pit where fear had boiled for weeks. "I've got nothing to lose." I thought it was true. A laugh rolled up and out of my throat and the tension slipped from my shoulders.

Mr. Penny's small, confused eyes narrowed to slits.

"Don't worry though." I stood to face him. "I could never let anyone believe I'd have anything to do with a fat, sweaty..."

His puffy skin turned red.

"Stinking..."

His body trembled with rage.

"Swine," I shouted.

His stubby fingers clenched into fists. "Get out." His voice was murderously soft. "Now."

✣ ✣ ✣

The money in the jar would pay for two weeks at the rooming house. My *suite* was tiny, a cot and bedside table almost filling the space. Narrow wooden shelves hung on the wall above the bed. Cracked white paint flaked away from the walls and windowsill, while outside the grimy second-floor window was the most impressive array of grey backyard outhouses.

"And the bath?"

The scrawny, grey-haired landlord pointed down the hall. "You share with all the women on this floor." He was surprisingly sympathetic. "It's all I've got for what you can pay."

"It'll be fine." Mr. Penny's hate-filled eyes still loomed large. "Just fine."

The shelves were small, so I sacrificed more practical items in order to display the blue china pieces. They gleamed in the drab room. My clothes hung on hooks on the wall, the family picture taking up most of the space on the bedside table. I wanted them near me, to see them, especially my father, on waking every morning. The cot sagged under my weight, the mattress hardly thick enough to hold down the warped plywood it rested on. My few possessions cluttered the small space, incongruent yet heartening.

A tenuous sense of well-being was invaded by sounds from the house – shuffling feet, squeaking bedsprings, chairs pushed away from tables. A moment later a knock startled me and I froze. I'd wanted to sit in the relative quiet and disappear, perhaps until the baby arrived. Who could be bothering me already? A weight of impatience and dread rested between my shoulder blades.

The knock came again, a little louder. Heaving myself up, I lifted the hook out of its eye and slowly opened the door enough to peek out.

A young woman stood in the hall, eyeing me through the opening.

"Hello. My name is Annie." She glanced past me as though expecting someone else. "I live in the room down the hall. Third one on the right. I guess we're neighbours of a sort."

She was a tall blonde with sky-blue eyes, tiny nose and full round cheeks that tapered into a small dimpled chin. When she smiled her mouth opened wide, sending pleasing wrinkles to the corners of her eyes. I swung the door a little wider just as a bell rang downstairs.

"That'd be supper," said Annie.

Oh Lord. I wasn't ready to meet the people who belonged to the sounds. Panic rose in my throat.

"We can go together." She made to leave. "You should wear your coat. It's even colder in the dining hall than up here."

"Oh, thank you." Breathing deep, I straightened my coat, trying to smooth the bodice over my belly.

Annie watched patiently. "Ready then?"

"Yes." The door swung shut, banging against the frame. There was no way to lock it against thieves.

"We have to trust each other in this place. We're all in the same boat."

Her ability to read my mind was most impressive. I followed behind like a child glad to have a friend. "My name is Moira."

"I know."

The dining room was a larger version of the tenant rooms, the walls bare, a mottled green faded to grey. Two small windows let in shafts of the dying sun's light. A few women sat on benches pulled up to a long plank supported by sawhorses. Plates of food were set out along the table, and Annie found two spots beside a lanky girl, her long bones covered by wan, loose skin waiting to be filled with flesh. She rubbed red hands together.

"This is Lynn," said Annie. "Lynn, Moira."

We nodded at one another. As we sat down, the bench wobbled a little and Lynn laughed. "That always happens."

I couldn't look up, pretending instead to concentrate on the plate in front of me, while trying to catch a peek at the other women. I ate mechancially until Annie nudged me.

"Pretty bad, eh?"

The plate came into focus. The food was base and minimal: a small mound of mashed potatoes, no gravy, and a tiny sliver of salted pork. Loaves of bread and bowls of lard were spaced the length of the table. Other girls were breaking chunks off the hardening loaves and slathering them with the greasy mess. I didn't dare reach further down and across the table for the bread sitting in front of two women whose eyes hadn't left my face.

"Bad? Ha! Might as well be in jail." Lynn's nasal voice was pitched at the level of a small rodent. At the sound of it, the other women smirked and turned their attention to each other.

"My mother would probably be happy to hear that." The words popped out of my mouth, an offering to these strangers. Lynn and Annie leaned in, their eager faces yearning for a good story. I was unbound by their openness. "Well, this pregnancy seems to have assumed criminal proportions to her. She's Catholic and stiff." I opened my eyes wide and clasped my hands in mock prayer. "And pious. She'd probably like the idea of my being in a correctional facility."

We laughed together, the sudden release of tension making me giddy.

"She's only ever cared about what the neighbours think." One hand on my hip, I flung my head back and used my best operatic tone. "Simply scandalous, Moira. Mrs. Fenwick will be most appalled."

Giggling erupted from the two girls, and others at the table looked up. I lowered my voice. "She wouldn't care that my body seems to be sucking the life right out of me. And I'm swelling everywhere, belly, breasts, not to mention other parts." The others howled at the face I made. "I have to run to the outhouse every five minutes. And you should see my belly button." The girls' eyebrows arched. "It's stretched so flat, it's all but disappeared. Gone!"

Their laughter filled the room. The other women scowled and threw agitated glances our way. Shushing Lynn, my voice sank to a whisper, exhausted by what I'd revealed and the release of tension held too long.

"And I laugh and I cry, all in the same breath, because it feels like I'm going to be forever fat and tired and hungry and poor..."

Afraid I might burst into tears, I stood quickly to go. Annie jumped up in alarm, pushing Lynn out of the way. Grabbing my elbow, she steered me back down the hall and up the stairs to the pitiful room that was now home. She pulled a handkerchief from her sleeve and brought a drink of water in a filmy glass. I blew my nose, holding the wrinkled square of cotton there longer than necessary, embarrassed that my new neighbour might think me completely insane. I gulped the air, rushing to fill lungs starved by weeks of fear. Annie sat on the bed beside me, still holding the glass.

"Thank you."

"They have a hold on you, don't they? Mothers, I mean." Annie was thoughtful. "It never goes away."

"I know. But she's never allowed even the least mistake. Let alone this." The rise in my dress was like a beacon.

"Well that...," Annie's laugh was short and bitter, "is more than a mistake."

We sat in silence for a short time.

"What's it like?" she asked.

"Well, if I let myself think about what's happening in there, it's actually quite amazing." And it was. Every day my hands ran unbidden over the growing mound that was the baby. "To think this little thing is just making itself at home in there, kicking and elbowing its way around with no thought to my comfort."

"Were you sick?"

"Yes, the first three months were terrible. I was sick and exhausted all the time. But lately I've been feeling better." I tried to smile.

"I lost one." Annie's voice was impassive, her face expressionless.

"Oh Annie, I'm so sorry."

"It was for the better. I was already living here. This is no place for a child."

"No, I suppose not."

"Although it would have been nice to get that glow." She paused. "Like you have now."

Her smile was encouraging. We sat quietly, not touching but close, her warmth helping me to settle into my glow. After a time Annie stood up, put the glass on the night table and walked to the door.

"You'll be all right." She looked back as she left. "You're smart. Just keep out of the way and don't ask too many questions. We'll get you a job or something soon enough. Good night."

I lay back on the bed and smiled with relief.

CHAPTER 9

My dearest Aileen,

Well, Mr. Penny fired me for being pregnant. Though I am destitute, I am happy to be out of his employ. I have found a rooming house for the meantime and a new friend named Annie. She has been wonderful. But the other women are like none I've ever met. The backwoods people of Newfoundland may be ignorant and superstitious, but these women are crass and vulgar. They are arrogant about it, too, as though these are enviable attributes. They walk between rooms barely dressed and lounge at one another's doors smoking and chatting like they haven't a care in the world. But they do. None has any better room or food or any more money than I. And men coming and going at all hours of the day and night. I don't even want to imagine. These women seem to pass every day in this degradation and not expect any more out of their lives. It's really quite sad…

What would Father think of this new housing arrangement? He'd always encouraged me to witness the *real world*, the ways in which people survived, or not. Except for Annie, those who peopled my world in Ibsen didn't appear to hold much promise. But then neither had the world offered much to those in my father's life, those sick and destitute I'd met while travelling with him.

We'd been called to a lumber camp once where a man's leg had been cut off when a tree fell the wrong way. Despite the gruesome prospects, I'd been excited. It was the first time I was allowed to ride to a case and to bring supplies of my own. I felt the picture of a country doctor, complete with black bag and coat. Father was distracted, gazing into the distance.

"When I first came here," he mused, "I thought I could convince them to turn to God in a new way. If I could heal their bodies, maybe they'd give me their souls too." The lines etched in his face bore testament to his efforts. "I was young and idealistic. But it didn't take long to realize the only thing I might be able to do was save them from themselves."

I hadn't known yet what he could mean.

"They don't often want a doctor. They're very suspicious, think we practice some sort of devil's work. 'Leave it to the Lord.' I hear that all the time."

"But surely when they see what you can do?"

"It doesn't work that way. You've seen how isolated these people are. Forgotten by the rest of the world. I sometimes think they believe they're not worth saving." He stopped to turn the collar up on his jacket. "They're like the detractors of Job. Think somehow they've brought their misery upon themselves. That they don't deserve help."

"How can people be so stupid?"

"Don't ever say that." His voice had been sharp. "They are ignorant, yes, but not stupid. I've seen each of these people do the work of ten men. Women included. They improvise and invent. They are quite remarkable." He didn't seem to be speaking to me any more. "Not stupid at all."

A shout from ahead interrupted us. The approaching rider went straight to Father. "What's the girl doing here?" He eyed me warily.

"She's my daughter and my assistant." Father's tone took the rider by surprise. I drew myself up tall.

He hesitated only an instant before riding off, calling back over his shoulder, "Camp is just a half mile ahead. He's in the first shack on the right."

"Shack all right," said Father, tying our horses to the rail alongside the building. The whole thing looked like it would blow over at the wind's slightest provocation. Collecting my things from the saddlebag, I ran quickly to follow close behind Father, trying to avoid the stares of three men.

The man who'd met us was explaining, "His daughter. Won't go anywhere without her."

I was grateful for his help until I looked up to see him

raise his eyebrows, a suggestion in his eyes. The others snorted. Catching my glance he made a lewd gesture at his pants. I gasped, instantly wishing I hadn't. The men laughed loudly, and Father turned back to see my red-hot face.

"Moira."

I rushed to his side and promptly gagged at the sight and stench in the shack. The man's leg was gone from just below the knee. He was lying on a plank two feet off the floor, his upper half covered with a thin, dirty sheet. From the stump of his severed leg a yellow-green infection had spread to above his knee. His face was whiter than the sheet drawn to his chin, shining with sweat though he shivered uncontrollably. I'd started to shake.

"I did what it said in the book here." A voice boomed from behind us, so I jumped out of the way. "Name's Ivan. Only one here that can read. So I brung this book with me. It says to let his blood. So I did. Right above his knee there."

Ivan pointed to somewhere near where the infection had spread. His hands were huge and filthy. All of him was huge and filthy. Most striking was his large bald head, shining like a lamppost. His wide grin was filled with black, rotting teeth. He looked around with pride, enjoying his newfound role as camp medic.

"Bloodletting. Dear God," muttered Father.

"Says here it will 'eliminate the cause of disease.'" Ivan sounded out each word as he read. "Any imbalance in the morbid humours: blood, yellow bile, black bile and phlegm." He looked up. "I figured that oughta cover it 'til you got here."

"Thank you, Ivan is it? We'll look after it from here then." Father gave me a long look, as though grounding himself, then nodded at the man on the bed. "Just talk to him and wipe his face now, will you?"

When the sponge touched his face, the man opened his eyes and grabbed my forearm with shocking strength. He squeezed harder as Father probed his wound, until I could barely feel my fingers, until I thought I might lose my arm too. I had to distract him.

"What's your name then?"

"Beaver."

"Now what kind of name is that?"

"Not my real name." Each word was a clipped breath.

"Try breathing deeply. More oxygen. It'll help with the pain." I wasn't actually sure if it was true for anything but childbirth, but I had to say something. Slowly I worked my arm out of his clenched fingers. "What's your real name?"

"James. I don't want to live. Tell the doctor to give me something to make me die. Quick."

"We can't do that." The request was not uncommon, death seen as the only ready solution to end the pain. "You just have to hold on until we get you fixed up. You'll be all right." His face was anguished. "Do you have a family?"

James started to cry. "You let me die, damn it." He tried to push himself up on one elbow. "She can't marry nobody else if I'm still alive. And then who'll provide for them?" He looked about wildly, frantic to make himself understood. "I can't work without my leg. You let me die. It's the only way. They'll starve..." His voice drifted as he passed out. I looked to Father, tears pressing against my eyelids.

"We can't do anything about it now, Moira."

We amputated above the knee to stop the infection. There'd been no chloroform, no cocaine for James. Father hadn't received supplies from Edinburgh for weeks, and so the men held James down as Father began to saw. James woke, his screams finding their way around the leather strap in his mouth, filling the room, searing into my head to rest behind my eyes. The psalms Father had badgered me to memorize through every idle moment would not come. I closed my eyes to the scene and pictured our fine drawing room.

"Oh Lord, reprove me not in your anger," I started. "Nor chastise me in your wrath. Have pity on me, O Lord, for I am languishing: heal me, Oh Lord, for my body is in terror: My soul, too, is utterly..."

Ivan retched and his vomit stained my boots. I tried something less morbid. "When I behold your heavens, the work of your fingers, the moon and the stars which you set in place – What is man that you should be mindful of him, or the son of man...?"

James finally passed out and I sighed heavenward, thankful for whatever benevolence might be out there. All three men ran out of the shack, clutching their hands over their mouths.

We applied a poultice and bandaged the stump. James woke to the vision of his new life cursing, screaming he wanted to die, since we'd killed him anyway and his whole family too. This last was directed at me, his eyes wild, frightening. The men urged whiskey down his throat until he passed out again. All night I held his hand and sponged his face, visions of a skeletal family accompanying me in and out of consciousness. We emerged from the shack exhausted, the sun just beginning to burn off the morning fog. Father left written instructions with Ivan. Looking back I could see Ivan's lips moving, slowly sounding out the words. He would take James back to his family as soon as James was able to travel.

The ride home was long and cold. My stomach clenched at the thought of a dirty home filled with howling children waiting for their father to bring home money and food. Instead, he would come back disfigured and useless.

"I'll see if the church can help," Father said absently, then sighed. "It'll be all right, Moira. We did everything we could."

The letter I'd been writing lay on the table in front of me along with the memory of James's fierce, shattered will to do the right thing, even to die. Sitting now in this horrid place, I remembered with vivid clarity what I'd been too preoccupied to notice that morning on the way home from the camp – the countryside had displayed a frightening beauty, and the granite and limestone outcrops loomed over us as we rode by, the bright green mosses and contrasting red berries a stark contrast to my own plainness, my failure to help the legless man heard in the whispering sound of the waves.

Suddenly covered in goosebumps, I climbed into bed. Such

a rich landscape and the degradation of the people so complete. How could anyone succeed?

From my bed I could just see out the window. Past the outhouses, the moon rose, a perfect globe lighting the sleeping homes of Ibsen. Silhouettes of horses, barely distinguishable except for the occasional tossed head or flicked tail, melded into one as they tucked into each other against the cold. The real world. The expansive landscape and huge skies of the prairie had not proven any more friendly than the forests of home. My world had become dark and foreign, peopled by characters as deeply haunted as James. My being here was unimaginable, yet here I was.

Tomorrow I would start as helper cook downstairs, a way to earn at least part of my keep. Annie begged the job from the landlord on my behalf, appealing to his kinder self on account of my being pregnant. Blowing out the bedside lantern, I huddled under the covers and fell into a troubled sleep.

✥ ✥ ✥

CHAPTER 10

A DOOR BANGED somewhere down the hall. Not again. Every night for three nights they'd screamed at one another, coming home late from the Ibsen Hotel, each accusing the other of absconding with her beau. It was hard to believe either of them could actually attract a man.

"You stay the hell away from him." The voice belonged to Katy, a tiny woman with long dark hair, a hooked nose and cold grey eyes. Diminutive, yet frightening.

More noises in the hall were followed by a sudden thud against the wall. Slowly I opened the door and poked my head out. Lynn was lying on the floor, limbs askew, blood pouring from her nose. Throwing the door wide, I stepped out to help her.

"Get the hell back in your room," Katy hollered from behind me. "This is none of your goddamn business. You want I should belt you one too?" I turned, but could only gape at her. Katy suddenly shouted, "Boo!"

A short scream leapt from my mouth and I scooted back into my room, latching the door and leaning against it. Katy's laughter followed, and suddenly I was shaking. What did I owe Lynn anyway? Just days before, she'd accused me of stealing her boots, as though I would steal anything, let alone ragged old boots from a stranger. Annie said to pay Lynn no mind, that she was a good person, her mind a little fragile. Especially since her mother's necklace was stolen, the only remaining piece of a set she'd been pawning to feed herself. Still, I resented having tried to help her.

When it was quiet, I poked my head out again. Everyone was gone. I felt like a turtle, afraid of anything but its own shell. I had to see Annie. At least she understood this place, the women, how to get what she needed and stay out of trouble. As I crept down the hall, my belly preceded me, conspicuous even under my housecoat.

We'd agreed on three quick knocks. But in my distracted state, I forgot to wait for the appropriate reply and shoved the sticky door open to slip in.

"Moira, no!" I heard it just as the door closed.

A man's bare and hairy backside greeted me, Annie on all fours in front of him. They were on the bed, the man in paroxysms, tufts of pubic hair and dangling breasts visible between their two sets of legs. I couldn't move, didn't know if the man was aware of me yet. I stared in shock until Annie twisted around to peer at me, took one hand off the bed and waved wildly toward the door, gesturing at me to get out. Spinning back, I grasped the bent nail serving as a latch. Too large for the frame, the door stuck. I gave it a yank. The latch slipped from my fingers. I tried again. In that eternity the door finally opened. Glancing back, I saw the man turn, and our eyes met. His were cruel and unwavering. It was Mr. Penny.

I was not a turtle. Dashing down the hall, feet thudding, I scrambled into my room and banged the door. Mr. Penny could easily barrel through the weak latch. All my senses strained to hear him, the vision of his backside and eyes burning my eyelids. I felt dirty, a co-conspirator, Annie's look so normal, as if I'd simply walked in on her at an inopportune moment, like an "oops, pardon me" would suffice to absolve me of the sin of bad timing.

But I knew what I'd seen. Vomit filled my mouth and I rushed to the wash basin. Soon the dry heaves quieted and I sat down on the narrow cot. The house was quiet: Mr. Penny probably gone, Annie cleaning herself up. I remembered the note I'd discovered in his pocket and shuddered. I'd become the friend of a whore. How could I have let that happen? How could Annie let it? I hadn't allowed myself to believe she might be doing what the other girls so obviously were. And with such a pig. But then they were all pigs.

I felt a kick on my left side as the baby rearranged its limbs, seeking a more comfortable position, maybe finding its thumb. This was the world it would be brought into. I was sick again, rinsed my mouth and threw the whole mess out the window. Desperation constricted my throat and tightened my stomach. I had to leave, but was so hopelessly alone. Afraid to go. Afraid to stay.

For the first time since leaving home, I longed for Mother, the realization shocking. She'd been so harsh, yet it was her cold, reasoning voice that could bring the world into perspective. I needed her to convince me that somehow this would turn out all right; I'd survive pregnancy and poverty and parturition, and I'd be able to feed and clothe this child and find it a good home. But now I had no one, the isolation overwhelming.

When sleep finally saved me, I dreamed that Evan peered at me from Annie's bed, his embrace tight around my friend, who became only a stricken stranger. The dream transformed Mr. Penny's mocking face into Evan's. The transformation did not change the cruelty in his eyes.

✠ ✠ ✠

"How did you think I afforded to live, to stay here?" Annie looked at me like I was at best naïve, at worst an imbecile.

After days of avoiding her, I answered the familiar knock at the door, fearing a three-headed monster. But it was the same Annie, blonde hair pulled into a girlish ponytail, eyes bearing just a hint of sadness.

"Well." I closed my eyes against the tears threatening. "I don't know. I thought you were different from the other girls, that you worked somewhere else. Maybe family money?" It sounded ridiculous.

"Hmmph." Annie snorted. "Not all of us are so lucky."

I shrank back. "Wait a minute. I've got nothing from home. Nothing."

"Yeah, but you know you can go back. When that baby is born...," Annie gestured at my belly, "you can go back to Mommy and Daddy and all the comforts of home."

"I don't know that I want to."

"Well, I don't have the choice." Annie's glare dared me to argue. I lowered my eyes.

"It was the shock." Shame filled my chest. Annie was the first person to react to me without judgment or dismissal, to give real comfort. Yet I'd been only marginally aware my friend might have her own sad story, and she might need compassion in return. I'd been frantically sorry for myself while Annie's terrible reality moved on unnoticed and unacknowledged. I was not a good friend. Quietly, I went to the door and pulled her into the room.

"How do you manage..." I blushed and hurried on. "What about diseases? And so many women die in childbirth. It's so dangerous for you."

"We have our ways," Annie shrugged. "Condoms made of linen or animal gut. And there's a new thing called a womb veil. As though a veil is all it takes." Her laugh was a short bark. "And I use a douche I make up in the kitchen."

I gasped then, like a little girl. How had my father kept such basic things from me?

"Lynn thought she was pregnant a few months back. We used pennyroyal to induce her." She looked up then. "It's okay, Moira. We all know what to do."

"But Annie, is there nothing else you can do? Nowhere to go?"

"Not that I know of."

"But you're smart and beautiful."

"What does that matter out here?" Annie was less angry, more resigned. "Look, I'll be fine. I am what I am. I'm not unhappy." A weak smile flitted across her face. "It's not bliss. But mostly they treat me well." At my flinch, she repeated, "But I'm not unhappy."

Hugging her, I whispered into her hair, "But I wish you could be blissfully happy."

"Maybe I choose not to be."

"I don't know if it's about choice."

"Sure it is. Like right now." Annie grinned. "You're choosing to be my friend despite what you know."

"Yes."

"But you could choose differently and then you'd never know what I found." She laughed mischievously. "I found a job for you."

"Oh my goodness." I could hardly breathe. "Where?"

"You could be a dollybird."

✤ ✤ ✤

CHAPTER 11

"WHO KNOWS, you might snag a husband along with the job."
The homestead officer's name was Walter. He was dressed in
a black suit and bow tie, a sheen worn into the knees of his
pants, the collar of his white shirt slightly frayed and grey. My
ears turned hot.

"She's not looking for a husband." Annie came to my rescue.

"Well, with her condition and all, she might do worse."
Walter surveyed me with a calculating eye, as though I were a
heifer he might be considering at the local fair.

"I just need a place to see me through," I said sternly.
"Nothing else."

"Whatever you say." He bowed ceremoniously. "I only need
your name and particulars and we'll do the paperwork. Won't
cost you a thing."

"Oh, I'm sure it'll cost somebody," Annie murmured behind me.

Walter forced a smile, looked out the dirty window of his
small office and shuffled some papers on his desk. "I've only
got one prospect might take a dollybird. Flaherty. Young fellow
from the East Coast."

At least he was from home. It was a slight consolation; perhaps
we'd share at least a common background in good manners.

"Found the kid a piece of land. He's coming in tomorrow
to make it official. He's only getting a chance 'cause the pow-
ers that be would rather have him out there homesteading
than the bastard from Eastern Europe what applied." Walter
shrugged when Annie clucked her disapproval at his language.
"That one's getting a piece of land two miles south, all carved
up with ravines, lots of stones and scrub. It'll be perfect for
him." Walter laughed laconically. He was a grotesque man. He
would sell his mother.

"And when do I meet this man, Flaherty?" I asked. "To

decide if he's appropriate?"

"Appropriate?" Walter roared with laughter. "It'll be him choosing whether he'll take you. Not the other way round."

The idiocy of the whole plan struck me. I was going to the middle of nowhere with a complete stranger to play house. A dollybird. I backed away. Annie touched my elbow. When I turned to her she looked wise beyond her twenty-two years.

"I don't see you have much choice, Moira," she said quietly. "There's a contract you'll sign. He has to live up to it. You're not his slave, just his housekeeper. And if he hurts you, you can leave and he has to pay you for six months. Walter told me."

I didn't trust Walter, but I had to trust Annie. She was right. There was no other choice. "All right then."

Walter held the paper for me to sign. "The way the weather's warming, your man will be wanting to go soon. You'll be his in no time." He winked as I lifted the pen.

"Not likely." I marched out the door.

"I'll be fine," I reassured Annie when she caught up to me outside. She had to get back to the rooming house for an *appointment*. I tried to smile, called, "Thank you," as she rushed away, turning briefly to grin and wave.

I desperately wanted to believe everything would indeed be fine, that *my man* would at the very least be a decent human being whose intentions were as honest as my own.

"Well, hello there Moira," a man's voice called out behind me. It was Silas, the rider from the buffalo stone. "So how is it I find you in Ibsen?" He fell into step alongside me.

I owed him no explanation but quickly told him of leaving Moose Jaw shortly after meeting him, for employment in Ibsen. It all sounded so respectable when I left out the part about Mr. Penny and the brothel.

"Mind if I walk with you?" He took my arm and glanced down at my belly protruding through the buttons of a coat grown too small. "I see you're pregnant."

It was stunningly inappropriate, and I thought to tell him, but just then the honey wagon rattled by, pulled by a stringy mule driven by a young man. Several children followed, calling after him, taunting him with rhymes about his dirty occupation. He was clean-shaven, but one of those dark men who appear to have stubble ten minutes after they've shaved. A rim of black hair was visible beneath his cap. He looked vaguely familiar, but I couldn't place him. I'd seen the wagon from my window in the rooming house, and witnessed, too, these same children, their shrill voices rising an octave when he emerged from the outhouses carrying their buckets. Sometimes he tried to spray them a little as he swung the bucket up and over to dump it into the tank. I wished for his success. The children deserved a little of their own medicine. But he seemed only to be playing with them, and they ran screaming then, threatening with little conviction to tell their mothers, calling him names – *shithead, pissman* – their voices drifting away as he moved on.

We stopped to let the wagon pass. "Hey Silas," the man waved, and Silas gave him a nod. I saw a child's small foot sticking out the end of the seat where he must have been sleeping beside the man.

"Now there's a sorry fellow. Only job he could get," Silas said as the wagon moved down the street. He lifted his hat and ran long fingers through thinning hair. "Sounds like he's had a pretty rough time of it. Wife died of typhoid right after the birth."

"Oh Lord." I imagined his poor wife shaking with the cold, the delirium of her fever. I'd seen it before. Victims of it, everything inside purged from every orifice until their bodies were mere shells. "The stench of typhoid is unbearable, you know."

Silas raised his eyebrows and frowned. My neck and cheeks went hot.

"No, that's not what I mean. It's just an observation I've made." He stopped walking. "No. You don't understand. My father's a doctor. I was his assistant." The words tumbled out. "In fact I was planning to take over his practice before...well. Never mind." I hurried away. "I have to be going."

"Moira," he called behind me. I turned briefly. "Anything

I can do?"

I shook my head. What could he do? Let me be a doctor? Do real work? Live a real life? I walked quickly back to the rooming house where I boiled cabbage for women who led foul lives. While the baby kicked harder and deeper with every day, I would work and wait for my only chance to be somewhere else, someone else.

CHAPTER 12

DILLAN

I'D HAD MY FILL of moonshine. It was Silas brought it, brought the rotgut to this abandoned place, the dark sod shack I found after my ribs healed from Gabe's beating. People had stopped asking about the thief, bought my story of the dark and not seeing his face, thinking I was some kind of hero for trying to stop him. No one else knew about the girl being there, and we were both keeping our mouths shut.

"It helps chase those demons, boy." Silas nodded at the jar in my hand.

What did he know of demons? He'd showed up shortly after I moved in, said he was a neighbour, said he could help a little, introduce me to people in the community and such. So far I was still on my own. But between tending the neighbours' livestock and driving the honey wagon I was making ends meets, feeding Casey okay. Didn't need nobody to take care of him either. He came with me to do the cow chores and then slept on the wagon seat while I dumped the foul buckets of them could afford to pay someone to deal with the stink coming from their prim asses. I was glad Casey was too little to understand what those young foggers were saying to me. Taffy wouldn't have liked him to see his old man put down. And I didn't want him getting no idea that was a proper way for kids to act. Casey would learn respect. I'd make sure of that. The Millers had been good to him. He'd grown, his cheeks fattened up a little. Mrs. Miller even cried a bit, handing him over and quick wiping her eyes like she knew it was silly. Just couldn't help herself. I looked over at him sleeping by the stove in a small bed fashioned out of wooden crates. Casey did that to people.

But I was getting all trapped up by the dark of winter. Couldn't sit still any more, my whole body aching for the sun. The shack was about a mile from town on a bit of a knoll. I liked it when I first saw it. Looking out the window over all that grass was just like looking out over the water at home. Bad choice for winter though. Windy as hell. The cold nosed around the sod in the windows and the snow blew in drifts against the door so every day I had to dig us out. So bloody cold. Casey slept with me so we could trap our heat. Even so, every morning the blankets were frozen to the end of the bed and iced under our noses where our breath froze. Kindle the stove to a roar, thaw the water and our bones, a little porridge and off for the day. When the snow blew hard we might as well have been a hundred miles from anywhere. On those days I could only keep the stove lit and hope the storm let up before the water run out.

Looking out now, I could see a huge moon, the cold hanging in the air, beautiful like I imagined diamonds might look.

"Holy Mother of Christ." The moonshine whirled in my head. I leaned against the wall for support. "Godforsaken hellhole."

"It doesn't sound like you left anything better behind." Silas was always telling me it wasn't so bad a winter. He'd seen worse. He took a swig from the jar. Seemed immune to the stuff.

"Things were better there in some ways." A dog or a coyote loped across the moonlit snow a hundred yards from the window, then disappeared. "Family, for one. The Flaherty clan watched out for one another. Everybody knew each other, the whole works transplanted into Cape Breton, following the first ones who came after the famine. They always talked about it."

"So you were born here?"

"Yeah, but you'd not have known it. Didn't speak a word of English until they made us go to their schools. I was maybe seven or eight." Children were cruel back then too, taunting; the teachers almost as bad. "We spoke the Gaelic. But you know it's funny. Each area had its own. It was so bad me and my wi...Well – people could live fifty miles apart and not understand each other."

"She wasn't from your town then."

He was a nosy bugger. "There was always the fiddle. Who needed to talk?" I smiled remembering. We knew how to have fun. 'Come to the ceilidh,' they'd say and every house would show off the talents of them that lived there. "My mother loved the ceilidh."

It was the only time I saw her laugh and stand up a little straighter. She'd stooped over with years of caring for all of us and worrying after my Da. But at a party she'd draw up tall and sing or play the fiddle a bit. Mostly she danced, stepping quicker as the night wore on, looking younger, even pretty. I'd be embarrassed and proud at the same time, watching from the floor with all the other kids, wondering if this woman was another person and my real mother was back at home bent over the stoves, pushing damp hair out of tired eyes.

"She didn't drink," I said to Silas, and glared at the jar in his hand. With a head full of my mother, the moonshine was wrong. She left drinking to the men, who only came inside when the jug was empty and sat watching with stupid grins, or passed out in the corner, or worse, joined in with their laughing too loud and cursing in front of the kids. My Da was one of them, and all the warm feeling I got from watching Mother would turn bad.

"But my Da made up for it. Figured himself a regular troubadour, spouting the words of Robbie Burns as though the bard was one of his own. When he was drunk he forgot how much he hated the Scots."

Silas's moonshine had fogged me over so I could barely see, forgot I was talking to him. But the memories were clear enough.

"My father is a bastard."

"Oh?"

"She'd tell him, 'Please Aiden. Let's just be going home now. It's late for the little ones.' Saving him his dignity. Not like Mrs. Hennesey, pulling her husband out by the ear, cursing him with every pinch, everyone laughing behind. Or Mrs. Dunhanley chasing hers out with her purse." I laughed and Silas looked amused. I wondered if I had been as pathetic on those nights as her three boys, sullen and pimpled, trailing behind.

"I don't know why she cared about his good name," I said, Silas just watching. "He'd stumble around, puking in the bushes, moaning about his sorry ass, how we'd be better off without him."

It was true. But it suddenly felt like I'd said too much. Until I said it out loud I could pretend it wasn't what everyone knew and thought, could tell myself the town was wrong about my father, and the rest of us too. But far from home, drunk and lonely, it didn't seem to matter who knew. And telling it felt good.

"I grew up in a dump," I said. "Barely hanging on, buildings leaning right out over the coulee on the edge of town."

I heard myself saying the edge of town. It was the edge of the world. The house was a two-room shanty. Four of us slept in one tiny lean-to room off the kitchen. If you needed to piss in the night, you'd crawl over the others yelping and groaning, the same when you came back. The main room was the kitchen, where my parents' bed was tucked into the corner, three feet in the air on pine blocks. Underneath was a box-like crib pulled out for the two youngest to sleep in. And there always seemed to be baby sheep or pigs in the house. Mother hated it, but Da said we couldn't let them die of cold. It seemed an odd thing when only weeks later we'd butcher one of them that we'd saved.

"If I'd have stayed, I'd have done something with that place."

"What'd you leave for?"

I didn't want to answer. Casey snuffled in his sleep. The boy's hair floated around his head, his face like an angel's in the glow from moonlight coming through the window. His right thumb was resting limp on his lower lip ready to comfort him. There was a knife-sharp twist in my gut. I'd like to think it was love, but I never knew for sure after Taffy. I grabbed the moonshine, took a swig and another, coughing hard and finishing off the jar, waving it at Silas.

"I've gotta get a place of my own. Walter says he has a good piece of land for me. All I have to do is go in and sign the papers. Don't know that I trust him though. Like he's not telling me something."

"They usually give first chance to those who've farmed before," Silas said.

"Yeah, well. I learned to stook and thresh and every other bloody thing they asked for on that harvest team."

"There are others who have waited longer," he said, his eyes like razor points behind his thick glasses. "Worked harder too."

I knew it, but it was easier to begrudge someone else than figure out how to pull myself up. My head was buzzing.

"And there's the boy." Silas jerked his head in the direction of the crib. "You're gonna need a woman out there for Casey."

"I know, damn it. You can stop pestering me."

"Just saying, I don't think you know how hard it's gonna be."

"Oh shut up, you lumpy old man." I smashed the jar onto the table and watched in surprise as glass sprayed across it and onto the floor. Casey started howling. "You get him. I gotta piss."

Silas shook his head. "How the hell do I know what to do with this?" he muttered, walking over to Casey, who had sat up and was rubbing his eyes.

Silas bent and tried to wrap the rough blanket around Casey, picked him up and held him to his shoulder. I seen his face soften against Casey's hair and heard soothing noises coming from his throat. When I stomped out the door, Silas was patting and rubbing the boy's back as though he knew exactly what to do. I staggered to the side of the barn, sending the shadows of the horses into a skittish dance.

CHAPTER 13

BY THE TIME I went to sign for the land the next day, Walter had already found me a woman to go with it. A dollybird. Said he wouldn't give me the land unless I took her with me 'cause he was responsible for my making a go of the homestead, counting on my success to help him keep his job.

"I've heard some of these women are only too happy to become wives," he said. He sat at his desk and smirked up at me.

"I'm not looking for a wife."

"Okay. But you have to sign these papers so it's all up to snuff. And there's only a small fee."

He was a shit of a man.

Walter looked out the dirty window. "Look, you won't make it without a woman. Not with a kid out there."

"I know." I wanted to turn and walk out, but it was as though one foot was already snared in a trap. "Somehow I thought I'd just get a homestead. Never figured it all out."

"Well, figure it out quick. The weather's warming up and others will start asking about that quarter." He looked at me hard. "I might even have to give it to that bastard Gabe, if you can't decide." His eyebrows shot up as though I would be solely responsible for this travesty if I made the wrong decision. "This here's the last piece of decent dirt this year. And you need the dollybird." He shrugged. "But it's your choice."

"All right. All right. How do I get fixed up with her then?"

"Already done. Just have to sign here. Hope she can handle a miserable young bugger."

"Yeah, yeah."

I pulled my hat down to cover my face when I stepped out into the street. I'd showed up in this town alone with Casey and right away chose to ignore the sidelong glances, the women whispering as though I didn't know their gossip was about my motherless child. And now this plan, this dollybird.

There'd be more talk, the town so small an outsider was their only source of entertainment, proving those from elsewhere could never measure up. Then again, why would this place be any different from Arichat?

I wasn't even sure I cared, the infernal cold winter making me crazy to get out of my shack, out of Ibsen. I wanted land, to be my own boss, crazed and selfish and greedy for expecting anything at all, yet wanting it all the more. Wanting too much was how I lost Taffy. The memories were always lurking, creeping over me like a harbour fog, clouding up every thought until I couldn't move. If I hadn't made her go to Halifax, if we hadn't committed the most mortal of sins.

At the Ceilidh I'd watched the dance and clapped along or sat looking at my scuffed shoes, embarrassed as Taffy's father wished me to be. Until Taffy danced by, her slim white legs flashing. She fixed me with a smile that raced over my skin and fluttered in my stomach; the crowd, her father's glare, all of it gone. She loved me. She was quiet and gentle and sweet and she loved me. My throat ached watching her.

We left without a word to one another, just looked across the room and nodded, time to go, as though we'd agreed to something and there was no going back. Outside near the back porch, we grabbed hands and ran towards the harbour. The wind was loud and driving, a storm coming off the water. We stood looking out over the edge of the rock. It was deep dusk, that time when the black of night hasn't quite come down, but nothing has the shape it takes during the day. Everything was just shadows dancing against the rocks. The waves crashed below, roaring in the darkness.

Taffy was afraid. So was I, if I'm honest.

"This way." I leaned in close so she could hear, smelled her damp hair, felt her ear against my lips. She looked at me excited, eyes shining, face specked with spray. "There's a cave." I grabbed her hand tight, pulling her along the edge of the rock.

It wasn't a cave, only a hollowed-out face of stone worn smooth by water and wind and sand. We tumbled in and Taffy looked around, brushing the hair out of her eyes.

"It's beautiful in here," she sighed. "And what's this?" She pulled an old grey wool blanket from a crevice.

"It's. I..." My face was hot, but my teeth were chattering.

"Were you expecting someone then?" She spread it on the ground and sat down, tucking her legs underneath her and wrapping her skirt around her knees. A proper girl.

I didn't know where to look, what to say, so I finally thumped down next to her. "I've come here since I was a kid. Spent hours watching the waves."

"With other girls, I imagine." She flicked her hair out of her eyes to laugh at me.

Just Rebecca, but we were little kids wondering about privates and how they worked, curious and disgusted at the same time.

"I like to get away from the racket at home." I didn't want to tell her of Da's endless, miserable act of dying. Taffy thought he was charming, *though a little rough around the edges*. She didn't know the half of it.

Taffy shivered and I slid my arm around her. We'd sat the same way on her father's porch swing, rocking while we talked. It was different alone in the storm. There were choices we were making that could change everything. She was tense, waiting for direction, putting me in charge. I wrapped the blanket around us. When she looked up, I kissed her damp forehead, tasted the sea spray, nibbling bit by bit, her eyes, her nose, her cheek and neck, soft and smelling like flowers. Her breasts were small and firm, her cold nipples reaching out to my tongue. She moaned, slipped her hand around the back of my neck and pulled me close, finding my mouth. A warm current ran from her lips to mine and through my gut. I was so hard I could barely move.

"But what will we do?" She was suddenly stiff, her big eyes staring into mine.

For an instant I pulled away and gazed down into her trusting face. She loved me. My chest swelled with the power of it, being a man making anything possible.

"We'll get married," I whispered into her mouth, "and go

away from here and be very, very happy."

All night we lay wrapped in the scratchy blanket, clothes twisted around us, whispering and touching. Rain pooled in hollows in the rock and the waves beat against the rock below. Toward dawn the wind died and the sky lightened. She started to fidget, pushing fingers through her tangled hair, straightening her skirt and sweater. She seemed to want to be somewhere else. Suddenly she turned on me.

"Dillan, what will we do now?" Her eyes were getting misty, her bottom lip quivering. "I love you, but my father..." She began to cry quietly.

Being the man was suddenly less powerful. I was supposed to make her feel better, but the same doubts had started swatting at my head. "We'll be all right, Taffy." I helped her up, brushing the hair back from her face and the grit from her skirt, feeling more like a father than a lover. Taking her arm, I walked her out into the dawn. "They don't understand. And your father, well, I'll handle him."

It was what I had to say, but Mother's voice was ringing in my ears. *Don't do it Dillan. God sees everything. Just pray for strength to fight the temptation.* And Da. *Sure it feels good boy, but you don't want to be saddled with no baby. Just keep your pants on.* I didn't want my father in my head. The water was sparkling in the sun; the wind was only a light breeze now. Rain made everything fresh, colours stronger. Looking down from the rocks, each stone and pebble was clear against the bottom of the harbour, magnified by light on water. We walked home, pretending. But the light made all the difference.

I wished she was beside me now on this godforsaken prairie, walking this unfriendly street with her head high, saying fog off to all who had doubted. We'd made a mistake, but she didn't deserve what happened, her father cutting her loose, the filth of Halifax, being dead.

Suddenly the frozen ground came up to meet my face. I

was a half-mile from home.

"You son of a bitch."

The familiar voice froze my balls hard, fear making it hard to breathe. I waited for the boots to land.

"You think I don't know what Walter's done? Givin' you my land so I'm left with that piece of shit to the south. Won't grow nothing."

Slowly I stood to face the man who'd beaten me senseless only months before. Gabe was less bulky now, the skin around his jaw slack, muscles all but gone. His filthy pants were tucked into high-top boots, and his stained coat had buttons missing. He glared at me. His narrowed eyes were like my Da's after a binge, glazed and drunk, his real self somewhere just beyond, eyes that could be slobbering in self-pity or beating you. Gabe stumbled closer and I stepped back.

"You think you're better than me? Like Walter, that bastard." He swayed slightly.

"No." I stopped. He didn't recognize me. "I'm just taking the piece he offered." I shrugged like it was nothing. "There's no need of fighting here. I'm going home."

"Yeah run away, you little prick." Gabe laughed a short barking sound. "Like you did from your wife."

"What?" My neck bristled. I turned slowly, fists clenched.

"Left her behind. Whole town's talking about it."

"You don't know anything, you drunken ass."

"Maybe I do and maybe I don't. All I know is you got the land meant for me, and you better watch your back." Gabe staggered away, turning to shake a dirty finger in the air.

He was a liar like my father, saying anything to make himself bigger, making me feel small. *Gabe* was the bastard, stealing a woman's savings, threatening a girl. He'd beat the shit out of me but somehow managed to make me feel bad all over again, mentioning Taffy like he knew about my guilt. Maybe I got his land, but screw him. If I'd have told what he did, he wouldn't be farming at all. He'd be in jail. I didn't want to consider how that just made me a coward.

I was half froze by the time I got home to find Silas feeding

Casey broth and biscuits with cheese. I'd asked Silas to watch the boy so's I could see Walter. Casey smiled through a mouthful of biscuit and waved his empty tin bowl at me.

"There's enough left here for you," Silas said.

I sat down heavily. Casey was sweet. I loved him. But if I was honest, I was tired of him too, of trying to do everything for him and find money to live. Just so tired.

"So you got your land then?" Silas asked.

"You ever hear anything about guys taking on a dollybird?"

"A little. Supposed to help them get set up for the wife and kids coming, or just help out if there's no woman around." He laughed. "Heard of a guy left his wife where she was 'cause he got to liking the dollybird better."

"Walter's got one for me. Hell, I don't know if it's a good idea."

"Well, have you found anyone willing to be your new wife?"

"Ha."

"Then the dollybird is a good idea."

I threw my hat on the floor beside the chair and ate some soup. For a while there was only slurping and chewing and Casey grunting as he forced a huge fart. Silas looked at him, laughter in his eyes.

"Do you think it's a sin?" I asked.

"Shittin' at the table?"

I couldn't help but laugh. "No, me taking a woman out there."

"Suppose it depends on what you plan to do with her." Silas raised his eyebrows.

"Nothing. But my mother, well, she'd say the temptation'd be too great. That it's a sin even to think about it." I stuffed the last of the bread into my mouth. "So what happens if she's a looker, and I'm thinking about it all the time and can't do anything about it?"

"I guess you'll go to hell after dying from a hard-on."

Silas was no help.

"Look," he said, "If the only thing on your mind when you take her out there is her looking after Casey, how can it be a bad thing? If something happens after you get to know her, you'll have to make your peace with it then." He stuffed a piece of bread in his mouth. "And you know, God isn't as pigheaded as some mothers can be."

"Hey."

"I'm just saying. There's a lot of sinning going on in the world. I don't think the Almighty has time to worry about what *might* happen." He put his hand on my shoulder. "It'll be fine, Dillan. You gotta trust things will work out. Or you'll spend your whole life slopping someone else's hogs and hauling someone else's shit, thinking you're safe but wishing you were somewhere the hell else."

"I don't even know her name."

"The only thing that matters is she's good to Casey."

Casey had fallen asleep in his chair. He looked up through hooded eyes, smiling at the mention of his name, and drifted away again. I reached to hold him, wanting to hold him through the rest of the winter, to feed cows, dump piss-pots and hold Casey until spring, until we could go home.

PART 2

Air and Light

CHAPTER 14

MOIRA

I RECOGNIZED HIM the moment I stepped through the door to Walter's office. His beard and moustache had grown back a little, though now his hair was shorn, but he was definitely the driver of the honey wagon, the man the children had taunted. He held a child, a small boy, and, as I watched, swung him effortlessly from one hip to the other like an experienced mother might, then stood swaying back and forth, the child's head resting on his shoulder. I was relieved and angry at the same time. A child meant the man and I would not be alone in an empty house. But a child also meant work and mothering, something I didn't feel much capable of. He reached up to brush blond wisps of hair out of the boy's eyes and caught me watching. And then I knew him from an eternity before. He was the single father on the train.

A flush spread, darkening him from the base of his neck to his hairline. His eyes narrowed and moved from my face to my belly. At seven months I was bursting out everywhere. He looked up again, bewildered, sudden panic in those eyes. I glared, daring him to look again at my belly. He didn't.

"Well, Moira, there you are." Walter's bow tie was askew, hanging to one side, his shirt unbuttoned at the throat. The office was stuffy, the windows sealed despite the fresh spring day outside. Walter came around behind me to close the door, as though to avoid the possibility of anyone attempting escape.

"You never said anything about no baby coming." The man's eyes never left my face.

"Well he didn't tell me I'd have a child to care for either." I nodded at the boy.

"I don't need another mouth to feed."

"I hadn't planned to be a nanny."

"Whoa there." Walter held up his hands and laughed hollowly, then cleared his throat. "Okay, so you didn't know everything. But would you have showed up if you did?"

The man's eyes shifted to his son and back to me. He shrugged then as though he just wanted to get this over with, except it wouldn't be over any time soon. I shook my head.

"Exactly." Walter stepped behind his desk and pushed his glasses up on his nose as though readying himself to deliver a grand elocution. "Face it. You're both in a predicament and you need each other. So let's just get through this."

The room was silent except for the child's snuffling.

"Moira here only wants a roof over her head and three square meals," Walter said.

My neck grew hot. A man like him could reduce my life to this.

"And Dillan," Walter pointed, "needs someone to watch the kid and take care of the house so he can get his farming done." He leaned in close to me and whispered loudly, "Doesn't know shit about it, so we don't want him distracted having to raise the boy."

Dillan flushed at this report of his inadequacies trumpeted for my amusement. The boy was trying to climb his father's torso, and Dillan swung him back to his other hip.

"It's perfect," said Walter and, seeing he had the advantage added, "mind she won't tolerate no advances from you, young stud." He winked at Dillan, who looked like he wanted to melt into the varnish of the floor. "A simple business arrangement is all."

"Oh for heaven's sake." I looked hard at Dillan, rolling my eyes to indicate Walter was as much idiot as saviour. "Let's go."

Dillan followed me out. I climbed up to sit on the seat of the wagon while he quickly hoisted the boy up and loaded my possessions. Walter was still talking, reminding us of the conditions of our commitment. Dillan clambered up, grabbed the reins and whipped them over the back of the small mule hitched to the wagon. And we were off, relieved finally to escape Walter's incessant, embarrassing chatter. We rode, both of us ramrod straight on the seat, his knuckles white on the reins. The boy sat stiff between us, glancing up first at his father, then furtively at me, inching away when I tried to smile down at him.

After a long silence, I sniffed hard. "I guess we were both lied to."

"I suppose so, then."

We stared straight ahead. He shifted on the hard, uncomfortable seat. His sidelong glances grew longer and I sat upright under his stare, hoping to appear confident, maybe even stately. Perhaps he expected a dollybird to be needy, or contrite, especially one in my condition. I wouldn't give him that satisfaction.

The narrow trail was mined with rocks, the cart lurching into the air as the wheels jumped over them. Before long, my back and neck were stiff from anticipating the next jarring spasm. The mule seemed awfully small to be forced to haul even the meager contents of the cart.

The silence stretched.

Dillan continued to eye me, though not directly. Whether he was still coming to terms with the fact of my pregnancy, or my being there at all, I couldn't say. The tension from him grew, bloated questions hanging about.

Suddenly he looked hard at the child. "His name is Casey."

"Nice. How old are you?" This last was directed to the boy, who shrank even further into his father's side. But it was a relief to speak, and the release of tension caused a strange weight in my chest to push my words out fast and breathless. "I'm quite sure I will have a girl. Her name will be Shannon Louise." Why was I telling him this?

"After your mother, then?"

"No!" I said it too quickly, harshly, my jaw set.

He looked surprised, but thankfully didn't inquire further. Silence again.

"Walter is really something, isn't he?" I ventured.

"He's an ass all right." He glanced over quickly and blushed.

I nodded. At least we agreed on that point. I wanted to ask him about the rest of the agreement, what he expected of his home-stead, of me. And what of his son? But it stunned me to silence-the colossal insanity of our being together on a wagon, heading god-knew-where. It was as though my very nerve endings were searching the air for the answer to who he was. He seemed civil enough, but in the past my instincts had proven sorely lacking.

"The Scots are pigheaded Englishmen with an accent."

"What?"

"Like Walter. They take over wherever they please as if they have a goddamn right to everything."

I laughed then, so Casey had to look at me, puzzled, allowing himself a small grin.

"Where," I sputtered, "did you hear that?"

"My father." Dillan laughed. "He doesn't like Scotsmen much."

"And what about Scotswomen?"

"He never said, though I think he'd pay no mind to where a woman came from."

"I'm Scottish. Or at least my father is. I'm from St. John's."

"Yeah, I know. I could tell from your accent."

"And you?"

"Irish. Nova Scotia."

Answers only led to more questions, but we knew too little. It would be improper to ask.

"Excuse me, but could we stop by that bluff up there?"

"Why?"

"I um." Good Lord, did he have no manners at all?

The mule made his way toward the trees at his own pace, but I couldn't wait and stood up. "I have to go now!" Clench-ing my jaw, I scrambled onto the sideboard before the mule was stopped.

"Whoa!" he said, but I was already climbing down. "Okay, okay."

I did my business out of sight, only a shrub and wagon between a total stranger and myself. Squatting there, holding my breath, barely able to go with the tension that clenched my whole body, I tried to relax, looking at spring around us.

Buds were barely forming on the few scattered shrubs. The tall grasses, yellowed and brittle from the long winter, showed a hint of green at their base. Cowpies dotted the trail, some disintegrated into powder under the wheels of carts that had passed before us. Flocks of brilliant white snow geese and their darker Canadian cousins pointed uneven arrow formations north. Two or three pair landed on a dried-up slough nearby, keeping one suspicious eye on the wagon. I heard Casey laugh and finally stood to see him pointing at the geese.

"It can't be helped," I said, climbing back in. "My father says the only thing to do when pregnant is go with whatever comes. Quite literally, I suppose."

He snorted. "Your father an expert then?"

"Well yes. He's a doctor. Graduated from the Royal College of Surgeons in Edinburgh."

"Well then. What are you doing..." He stopped briefly.

Maybe he realized it was too soon, or that the question could mean anything: here with him, here in the new province of Saskatchewan, here and pregnant.

"Here?"

He was a surprisingly straightforward man.

"My father came to Newfoundland to help the ignorant Catholics."

"What?"

"A sort of missionary post, you know."

"Wait a minute." He held up his hand. "It's not like Catholics are a bunch of savages to be saved."

"No, no. But you should have seen them on the island. Not ten miles from St. John's, living in filth you can't imagine, no idea really and no medicine."

"Maybe they had no choice," he said quietly.

I considered this a moment, then blurted, "They wore charms, for goodness sake. And when we showed up to help, some of them even chased us off. Said they couldn't trust our magic. Magic! Can you imagine? It was so stupid." I stopped, blushing. "No, not stupid. Just ignorant."

Silence again, broken only by the creaking of the cart and

Mule's plodding footfalls.

"We had charms," he said quietly. "There, around Casey's neck in the amulet. It was his mother's. I made it."

It was a tiny cross, made of cherry wood and wreathed in a flock of minute doves. His hands on the reins were big, detached from the rest of his body by ragged cuffs, and wrists that were bony and small. They had the harmless appearance of bear paws. That their careful crafting had fashioned something so delicate gave me pause. Such sensitivity surely pointed to something in his character.

"It's beautiful," I said.

"We prayed every day the baby would be born healthy, not like so many of them little ones that never stood a chance."

I looked down at Casey. "Well I guess it worked."

"Yeah." He smiled vaguely. "But I should have been praying for Taffy – my wife." He nodded. "Guess I forgot all those aunts and cousins and other women who died having babies. People said it was God's way, but everyone grieved the poor motherless tykes."

"I'm sorry. About your wife I mean." There was a long pause. "Could the doctor do nothing?"

"Hmmph," he snorted. "Doctors! Didn't help my Taffy none. Beg your pardon, but they mess things up bad before they do any good. Heard all about their operations; patients nearly always winding up as dead as they would have been without them."

I couldn't help but laugh. "Surely you don't believe that?" But his eyes were neither amused nor doubtful.

"Saw it myself. An uncle. Watched the green and yellow pus fill up his lungs after they opened him up." He shuddered. "He died in a hell of a lot more pain than if they'd just let him cough himself to death."

"But a person has to try. If death is the only certainty, then every attempt should be made to find an alternative."

"If you're meant to go." He shrugged and raised his eyebrows.

How could anyone be so cavalier about death? Ready to argue the point, I glanced up just in time to see Mule veering off the path. "Look out," I shrieked.

Dillan hauled on the reins, but Mule kept walking. He was about to cross a small creek when he stopped suddenly, pitching us all forward. Dillan clambered down and grabbed the harness, trying to pull the animal across the water.

"Whip those reins over his back. Hard," Dillan yelled.

"I know how to drive a cart. I drove my father all over the countryside."

"He couldn't drive himself, then?" Dillan whacked Mule's shoulders and hind end, but the beast wouldn't move. "Mac an diabhoil," he berated the animal under his breath and finally cuffed it about the ears and nose.

"This is some horse," I said quietly, trying not to laugh.

"It's a mule and he'll do just fine." He held his head a little higher.

"Yes, until you get yourself stuck in a bog." The laughter rolled out of me. He looked like he wanted to smack me too.

He waved his arms at the acres and acres of grass. "Do you see any bogs around then?"

"No, I suppose not. Still, he did manage to find the only water for miles." Suddenly I had to clench my jaw to hold my bladder. I dropped the reins and scrambled off the wagon. "Turn around."

"Holy hell," he muttered as I disappeared behind the wagon.

When I came back he had taken the harness off Mule and tied him so he could reach the grass alongside the ruts that were the road. "I think he just needs a rest. We'll stop here awhile."

"Here?" I was incredulous. "But we've no shelter, no fire."

"No outhouse," he said and his eyes went wide, like he wanted to suck the words back in with his breath.

The urge to protest evaporated. "No outhouse," I smiled.

Casey called to us then and we both moved toward him. Dillan lifted him from the wagon, and I reached down and lightly rubbed his back as he gazed at me with sleepy eyes. "It's all right. We'll get you warmed up and find something to eat now." It seemed a surprisingly natural thing to do. Dillan was watching; his face relaxed into the barest hint of relief. Maybe this was all he wanted from me.

✣ ✣ ✣

CHAPTER 15

AFTER WE'D EATEN and fed Casey, Dillan finally coaxed Mule across the water with oats from the feed bag in the wagon. The trail finally smoothed out and the swaying wagon lulled Casey to sleep. I felt myself nod off, but kept one half-open eye on Dillan. The fingers of his right hand relaxed on the reins, and he massaged the muscles at the back of his neck. But his eyes were worried, passing back and forth over the unchanging landscape: dead grass with a hint of spring green, blue sky lightly ribboned with clouds stretched to the horizon.

A short distance ahead a graveyard loomed, in it a huge white crypt, probably eight feet long and six feet wide, and standing three feet high. Around this monstrous thing were small head-stones, the lesser of the family relegated to the underground. Dillan had started to fidget, leaning forward, his mouth open.

"It's a mausoleum," I offered with a yawn.

"What?"

"A mausoleum. You know, like the Greek ruler who built a permanent shrine to himself. My father figures he was just afraid of the dark. Maybe that was this poor soul's problem." I yawned again and then dismissed my own words with a wave of my hand. "He was probably just afraid he'd be forgotten out here once everything grassed. That he'd be just like everyone else."

"What are you talking about?"

"That tomb we just passed. Didn't you see it?"

"Yeah, two miles west and we'll be home." He was sitting straight, shaking a little. He caught my surprise at the word home and turned away still smiling. "What were you saying?"

"Never mind."

Mule plodded in silence while Dillan perched at the edge of his seat. I scoured the land around us, but could see nothing to indicate any change, no distinctive feature from this side of the wagon to that.

"We're looking for a stick then," he offered. "Just a small piece of cut lumber to show us the edge of the homestead."

Casey woke up. "You're almost home," I whispered in his ear. He giggled. I nodded and said to Dillan, "It will be good for him I think."

"Yeah."

We peered into the distance, Dillan hunched further forward in an undeclared contest to be the first to see the marker. He was so excited. I wanted to let him be first. But competition is hard to ignore, and soon I was gazing as intensely as he. I saw the stick. Casey and I stood, balancing against the seat, and I pointed toward it, hollering.

"There it is. Don't you see it? There." Jabbing again, and waving my arms as though this would help his vision. "Right there."

And then he saw it, a smile creasing his face. He took a huge breath, his chest swelling visibly. He whooped and laughed like a fool, like the surveyors' stick marked more than just the corner of a piece of land. Casey's eyes were wide and he started to squirm, his father's excitement contagious. Dillan dropped the reins, took Casey and swung him into the air. "We're here, boy. We're home."

"Home," the boy said quietly. It was the first word I'd heard him speak.

As we passed the stick, I sat down again and Dillan put Casey between us. Glancing from one side of the trail to the other, I searched, but everything – the near, the far – was exactly the same: flat, barren and treeless. We'd worked ourselves up for this. A laugh came out in a snort.

"It's not that bad."

"I'm sorry. It's just that...well...if I don't laugh..." I was surprised at the lump in my throat. "I might..."

"Oh Jesus," he said.

Despair, too, is contagious and the muscles around his mouth started to twitch, his nose flared. If only there were more trees, a creek, something. Nothing was distinguishable except the stick. Mule had slowed and was barely moving.

Dillan whipped the reins across the animal's back. "Get up there." He set his face, refusing to let my disappointment ruin his moment.

My stomach curled into a knot, and I tried to smother my fear. He was right. This was real and we had much to do in order to survive. I would have to keep my fears hidden.

"We'll set up the tent," he said. "Get the boy settled. Find some water. There's only enough in the barrels there for a few days." He motioned behind us in the wagon.

I straightened up. "Maybe we should just let Mule find us a bog." I tried to grin.

He smiled back, grateful I think. Ahead, a lone elm tree spread its old worn branches, stretching up as though to beseech the heavens.

"There, that old tree. It's a sign." He pointed. "We'll set up there."

Small birds with white bellies flitted in front of us on the trail and finally flew up to scold us from the tree. A fox, bushy red tail flowing out behind him, ran a short distance, looked back and smelled the air, then ran again. Dillan stopped Mule and helped me down. Under the tree was a large rock and beside it, tucked under its sheltering face, were tiny purple flowers just starting to open, their petals covered in soft down.

"Crocuses, I think." I breathed the words out. "In town, they were talking about crocus season."

"Well, I think they're a good sign too," Dillan said. "We'll set up here for now. At least the tree will give us a little shade in the afternoon once it leafs out."

It was midday and the still-bare branches threw a criss-crossed pattern of shade. The air was deliciously warm, the cool morning dew burned off in the new heat of a cocky spring sun. A meadowlark trilled its scale in thirds on the way up, quick and chromatic on the descent. The sound burst through the silence. Dillan closed his eyes and breathed deeply as though he were purging winter, or something worse, from his lungs.

"What are you doing?" I tried not to laugh.

"Don't you feel it?"

"The wind?"

"Well that too, but...well...the newness. Spring, I guess. The air is so clean. It's like everything just woke up and washed."

I wanted to understand, but if there was beauty, it was blanketed in isolation. I stood there, breathing it in, and smiled. Maybe I felt it a little, smelled what he smelled. I waved my hand at the emptiness around us. "It's just so big."

He turned to unhitch Mule. The wind was picking up, the dead grasses rustling. "We better get that tent up before it gets too windy." He busied himself. "There's an old man in town. Told me about winds kicking up dust so thick you can't breathe."

I didn't want to hear the terrible musings of some crony and went to the wagon to let him enjoy what he appeared to think might be his last peaceful moment. Among the provisions I found bread and some soup I'd made in the boardinghouse kitchen. We ate a little and unloaded the wagon. I felt strong helping in that way, as much as I could, with no expectation that he be chivalrous, just two people doing what needed doing. It reminded me of how it felt to work side by side with my father, a kind of freedom in having no awkward assignment of roles. Casey toddled circles around us, tripping over small hazards, happy to be out of the wagon.

Dillan pulled the tent out from the rest of our things and sized it up, trying to hold down one section of the canvas while puzzling over another. By the time we figured out front and back and where the posts should be positioned, the wind had grown, threatening to rip the tent out of his hands. I tried to help, but soon felt like a flag waving at the end of its pole, hair flying wildly around my face.

"This won't work," he said. "We'll have to do it in the morning when the wind is down."

"And what until then?"

"Sleep on the ground I guess."

"Oh Lord." He watched me, trying not to react as I let go a huge sigh.

Dearest Aileen,

Today I sense a freedom I haven't felt in months. Maybe silence is liberating. No, not silence, for I hear crickets chirping like an insect symphony, the crackle of our small fire providing an inconsistent percussion and the wind blowing like reed instruments in the background. Always the wind. It is not silence, but an absence of sound, of people, in the space out here.

I am lying under the wagon on a bed of blankets with a lantern beside me. I have Casey with me. He is Flaherty's small son. I hear him sigh quietly from time to time. It is a rather peaceful scene, if bizarre. Bizarre, but at least not terrible...

Casey whimpered in his sleep, found his ever-willing thumb. The wagon offered at least a primitive shelter from the elements, a small protection from the dark world. I felt an affinity for the boy, sent out into a world where he appeared to have survived more by sheer grit than good care.

He was an unnaturally quiet child. When I helped to change his clothes he didn't fuss, though his pale, thin body was quickly covered in goosebumps, and he shivered long after he was dressed. And he never gave any indication of hunger, yet he gobbled down the potatoes I boiled and mashed with a little water and salt. The newborns I'd helped deliver made more noise in their first few hours than Casey made all day. I couldn't help wondering if he was normal. His light blue eyes were bright enough and inquisitive about the new face I presented. The calm knowing in his gaze was unnerving. It made me wonder what he'd seen.

I looked across the fire at Dillan spreading his blankets for a bed. It was a comfort he was there, distant enough I needn't worry about his intentions, close enough to protect us if necessary. He was a mystery, darting about, looking for all the world like a willing idiot who hadn't an idea what to do next. I feared if someone were to yell *run*, he would, without a clue as to his destination.

But he appeared tough and athletic, jet-black hair in fast-growing curls, the permanent shadow of stubble adding darkness to an already swarthy complexion. His face was thin, with a long, bony nose and high cheekbones. It was his eyes that really drew attention, slate grey, set far apart and huge, with unnaturally long lashes for a man. They forced a person to look into them, like you might see something about the world in those eyes. Maybe that's what his wife had seen.

The next day would be our first in the tent. Dillan said it would be our home until a house could be built. He said it was very large, leaving me to wonder if it would be large enough, the air around us crowded with tension, the huge expanse of land and sky reduced to a pinpoint.

Dillan pulled off his boots as I watched, then lay down and covered himself. It seemed intimate even from a distance. I wondered what he was thinking, if his mind was reeling with questions and secrets, as mine was. A coyote sang in the distance. Another answered not far away to the east, and soon a chorus of yipping laughter filled the cool night air and sent a tingle up my spine. Casey's eyes were wide, listening to the song. Pulling him closer, I tucked the blankets around us.

"You all right then?" Dillan called softly from across the fire.

"We're fine. I think he'll go back to sleep."

"Okay then." There was a long pause. Dillan must have fallen asleep just like that. "Good night, my sweet boy."

For a moment I wasn't sure I'd heard it, but I had, the soft voice of a father. The outline of Dillan's body glowed red through the flames.

From under the wagon I could see stars filling the sky from one horizon to the other. Earlier the sunset had been achingly beautiful, and just as it became a pink memory, a brilliant orange moon emerged, glowing huge against the night. As it rose it grew smaller, fading into regular moon colours again.

People in Ibsen had told me the prairie was harsh and unforgiving, and I'd be lucky to last the winter. But perhaps it was instead a kindred spirit of sorts, its obvious failures pocking the surface for the world to see: the slough dried up before the ducks could hatch their eggs, the would-be trees stunted into shrubs, the fledgling grasses destined always to wait for the sun. My failures simply blended in.

CHAPTER 16

I WOKE TO SHOUTING and kicked at the twisted blankets, scrambling out from under the wagon and banging my head on the sideboard. Casey wasn't there. Dear God, I'd lost him already. The sudden awakening tilted the world and my eyes blurred, but finally I spotted the boy beside Dillan at the fire. They were scooping oatmeal straight from the pot. Dillan must have seen me sleeping. I might have been drooling or snoring – Aileen always claimed I kept her up nights with my snoring. Mortified, I smoothed my hair and straightened my skirt.

"Well hello, Silas," said Dillan. "Want some breakfast then?"

Silas? I came around the wagon to see him tying his horse to the tree.

"Not if you cooked it."

They both laughed, and relief quickly released the tightened muscles of my bladder, sending me scrambling for a place to go.

"Damn." The profanity surprised me as much as the men. "Don't look."

"Moira?" Silas's look was incredulous before he turned away.

Squatting beside the far wagon wheel, I hoped the long grass would hide me as much as possible. What was he doing here? I emerged to find their backs toward me, shaking with laughter. So now I was the butt of their jokes. My heart sank even as anger welled.

"Mules. Sometimes I think it's not being able to breed has made them stubborn. I mean, wouldn't it make you ornery if you never got screwed?" Silas's face turned crimson when he saw me. "I'm sorry, Moira."

"I've heard worse. My father had a mule once. Said it was hopelessly handicapped by sterility." I laughed, then blushed, Dillan's eyes like the silent, confused eyes of the villagers at home when they failed to understand what was said. I looked at Silas. "What are you doing here?"

"You two know each other?" Dillan asked.

"Yes, we've already met," said Silas. "And it's you who's come to help this young bastard out of his woes is it?" He looked at me hard. Dillan snorted and went to get the tent.

"Yes, I'm a dollybird." I said it quietly. "I've agreed to help Dillan with Casey for the time being."

"I had no idea you were that..."

"Hey old man," Dillan interrupted. "Why don't you help me get this tent up?" He had the poles out of the wagon and spread the canvas over the ground. "Hard to tell which end is up."

"That could be said for a lot of things." Silas glanced my way.

We busied ourselves for the rest of the morning. The men pounded four posts into the ground, wrapping the tent taut around them. I chose a spot for the firepit, strung rope for a clothesline, chased Casey back to our small camp when he strayed too far. The shouts of the two men bounced through the air as they hollered instructions back and forth. Silas laughed when the wind whipped the tent out of his hands. Dillan cursed when an errant hammer hit his thumb. There had been no such friendly give-and-take in my mother's house, the seriousness with which one worked taken as measure of character and godliness.

Finally I sat on the ground and leaned against the wheel of the wagon, Casey drooping against me, exhausted by the free rein he'd had to explore his new home. Silas was tying the tent tightly to the posts, his movement fluid and sure, wiry frame leaping lithely from one task to the next. He wore a cowboy hat, and a fringe of dark hair poked out from beneath the band secured tightly around his head. The distortion of his thick glasses made his eyes sharp points of blue, and it was difficult to see whether he was looking at me or beyond. He caught me watching and came to sit down.

"You should rest. We'll get this done. Then you can have that tick." He jerked his thumb in the direction of the wagon. "And a proper place to nap."

"Oh, but that's not my bed." I didn't want him to know how little I owned in the world.

"Well it is now."

Wondering how Dillan would feel about that, I smiled at him. The wind gusted and I spit strands of hair out of my mouth and sighed.

"You'll get used to the wind," he said.

"I thought maybe I was. But then I catch myself gritting my teeth." I rubbed my aching jaw. "And my shoulders are tensed up around my ears all the time."

"It's because there's no shelter. Nothing to break its path."

"Like my mother's oration on the merits of the church. You only wish for a moment's peace."

"Ha." Silas shook with laughter, his face open and turned to the sky, while the wind threatened to dislodge his hat. He was a man of great intensity.

We finished the tent and moved our things in. Turning around, I bumped into Dillan. We both mumbled excuse me, turned around and bumped again, strangers in a slow dance, unsure of the steps. I tried to anticipate where his feet would be in order to avoid stepping on them. In spite of ourselves everything was finally arranged.

"I'm going to see where there's water on this place," said Dillan with a look at Casey, who'd fallen into a stupor on the tick. "You'll be all right?"

"Yes." I said it more quickly than I'd meant to, relieved to have him away.

Silas looked in after Dillan was gone. "This will be comfortable for now, eh?"

"Yes, thank you." Wiping my hands on my skirt, I followed him outside. He was tacking his horse, and suddenly I didn't want to be alone, the thought almost paralyzing. "I hope he finds water," I chattered.

"Can't believe Walter didn't tell him where it is. If there is any."

"Dillan didn't ask?"

"He was in a hurry," said Silas.

"I'm beginning to wonder. He seems so excited to own this piece of dirt, but he hasn't mentioned anything about the actual farming." In the distance Dillan rode away on Mule, bouncing in time to the animal's slow trot. "Maybe he doesn't think a simple woman would be interested."

"Well, I think you're anything but simple." His eyes searched my face. "I imagine you're a different sort of bird than what Dillan expected." His face wrinkled as he grinned. "Sorry."

"I've been wondering about that. Dollybird. It must have been coined by a man; they want a dolly, perfect and beautiful, without a blemish or a past." My fists clenched. "Something to toy with and then discard, something that doesn't demand anything from them."

"And the bird part?"

"An Englishman, I'm sure, assuming anyone who chooses to do this must be peculiar." We both laughed. "Although I could see where a person might be inclined to think that."

He paused a moment. "Some people will think the worst. I suppose I'm surprised myself."

"No more surprised than I," I said hotly. "But did I have another choice, given the circumstances?"

"It's none of my business really."

"No, it's not."

He finished tightening the cinch on his saddle, swung his leg up to the stirrup and mounted in one fluid motion. I'd never known anyone so at ease in his body. "I'm sure you'll do just fine," he said. "You'll need patience to handle him though."

"Casey?"

"Dillan." He tipped his hat. "I'll be by to check on you in a couple of days if that's okay."

"Of course."

I was alone now except for Casey. I looked around at the tent, at my few belongings still scattered on the grass, so small any significance they'd once had was lost. They were like footnotes in a book, the landscape like an empty page I was about to mark with my story. It would have to be a big story to have any meaning at all in this expanse. If the thought was daunting, it was also liberating. The only person in charge of writing it was me.

CHAPTER 17

"WRITING A DIARY then?" Dillan asked, startling me as he threw open the tent flap.

"No, a letter to my sister."

I was sitting on one of two rickety chairs at an old wooden table arranged against one wall of the tent. Dillan had seemed mildly offended when I'd laughed and called it the dining area. I'd strung a rope to curtain off one end of the tent for a little privacy. Dillan had agreed with Silas's generosity in endowing me with the feather tick. I imagine he didn't actually much like the idea, but would have been too embarrassed to insist a pregnant woman sleep on the ground. I hated to be indebted, but my aching back held sway over pride. The tick now rested on a plank set on four stumps. They were a little uneven in height so I rolled a bit toward the door, but I wasn't about to complain.

"We'll need to conserve kerosene."

"Oh yes, I suppose." I reached to lower the flame and cringed, my quick reaction an implicit agreement that my writing a letter was frivolous and wasteful. Maybe it was. I hadn't heard a thing from home, and now I wondered if their letters could ever reach me in this isolated place. "Did you find water?"

"No." He pulled his suspenders down from his shoulders and turned his back. "I'll be off to bed then."

"Oh, well." With the mess of our things around us, the absence of privacy was more striking than I'd anticipated. "I'd better get out of your way."

"Suit yourself."

I couldn't stay at the table and watch him prepare for bed. It was humiliating. But apparently he had no such sentiment. He started to take off his shirt. I left the lantern on his side of the tent and furtively watched his shadow through the fabric of the curtain. He was tall, his muscles long and lean. Dillan had a physical strength about him that Evan had not. Father would have said Dillan had the physique of a featherweight boxer. I was suddenly aware of staring at the shadowed movements of a perfect stranger preparing for bed. I blushed and turned away.

"You ready then?" he asked.

"Yes, you can turn out the lamp."

Undressing in the dark, conscious of the moon's glow through the canvas, the silhouette it might provide, I quickly pulled on my nightgown. The print was washed out, the bottom edge and cuffs tattered, the whole thing baggy and unflattering. But what did that matter now, in this place? Gingerly resting my head on the pillow I'd stolen from the boarding house, I relaxed a little and pulled the blanket up to my chin. The evenings were still cold and my nipples, darkening and expanding with pregnancy, hardened as my frigid fingertips brushed against them. My hands ran over my growing belly, at rest beside me like a great ball of flesh, an entity unto itself. I lay on my side with one leg crossed over the other in search of relief for my back, more exhausted than I'd ever been in my life.

"Thank you," I said quietly.

"For what then?" His voice startled me. He could have been right beside me. I laughed out loud. He was right beside me, the facade of a wall there only to assuage my sense of decency.

"This tick." I turned toward his voice in the dark. "I don't think I'd sleep at all without it. Besides making me have to use the outhouse all the time, pregnancy is just damn uncomfortable."

There was a pause. "Taffy never complained." His voice was low as though the mere utterance of her name was cause for solemnity.

"Well every pregnancy is different." It came out peevish.

"No, I think she just didn't want me to know it hurt. And I was too stupid to get it." The bitterness in his voice was painful. "She always wanted everything to be perfect for us, even when it was terrible."

"That's not such a bad quality sometimes." It might have saved us from Mother's constant complaints over the slightest inconvenience.

The darkness swallowed us again. Maybe talking about his dead wife was too hard, the emotions too raw. The silence was vaguely disappointing; speaking into the dark was comforting, the words captured and safe. Casey was snoring lightly in his crate bed. We'd managed to create at least a temporary home for him. I touched my belly again and the skin rippled as the baby moved. Only a layer of fat and skin, the baby curled up just beyond. That close, but the darkness sustaining the child was a world removed from my own. The possibility of my loving this creature seemed remote at best.

"And what of the father, then?"

I jumped again at his voice so close. Normally his boldness, the ease with which he delved into private matters, would have been appalling. At home such questions would have been met with the sniff of an upturned nose, scorned as uncultured and uncouth. But his question seemed ordinary, even obvious given the situation, and he had asked without motive.

"Studying in Scotland. His father sent him away."

"Oh?"

"We weren't married. Though you must know that... Otherwise I'd be with him and not..."

"Here. A dollybird."

"Yes, exactly."

"And your parents, they sent you away?"

"My mother." I scowled into the night. "She couldn't stand what the neighbours might think. Not my father though. He'd have kept me home."

"Even so, parents get disappointed."

"They only judge."

"You can't live in a family your whole life and not know what your parents will do when you get yourself in trouble." His voice floated around the tent. "Say you were caught stealing? You knew they'd tan your hide, send you to take the stolen goods back and then off to confession."

"Oh yes, confession." I snorted. "A very convenient thing, that."

He didn't say anything and I was afraid I'd offended him

again. "But a baby too soon?" he said finally. "Now that's their greatest fear. 'Cause you can't send it back."

I thought of Father wanting me to take over the practice, knowing a baby would make it impossible.

"And you can confess, but maybe your parents know your confession's just a lie. Maybe they actually understand why you did it, a love so strong." His voice was frightening in its intensity. "And it scares them that you know that feeling, and you're too young to know it, and now it will tempt you like the devil tempting Jesus in the desert. They know you'll be fighting it your whole life, one way or another."

"Good Lord, relations between a man and a woman are a natural thing." I didn't like where he was going.

"Natural yes, but a sin too. That's what makes it so hard to resist."

"This is crazy Catholic nonsense." I sat up and shook my head. I thought I'd left my mother at home. What was I supposed to think of him now?

"Did you not feel anything then? No great excitement and then the greatest remorse?" His voice dropped to a gruff whisper. "Were you not in love with it and scared to death at the same time?"

With Evan, with the idea of love? I couldn't answer for the tears squeezing their way out. I lay back down, pushing my face into the pillow, hoping he would sleep. I couldn't let him hear me, vowed never to speak of this again. Soon his breathing was even and deep. I was awake long into the night, listening to the sounds of the prairie around us, rustling grass, the creaking branches of our lone tree, and Casey and Dillan snoring in syncopated rhythm.

CHAPTER 18

DILLAN

SOMEHOW I'D MANAGED to piss off Moira after only two days together. I hadn't thought our talk would have shattered anyone's world. She didn't tell me anything I hadn't suspected. I only wondered how she'd ended up knocked up and alone on the bald prairie. And with me. She sounded educated all right, like those few who wandered Arichat, never quite fitting in, all that learning making them strange, addled a little by books teaching them every goddamn thing except how to get by amongst their own. And Scottish to boot. I'm not my Da, but I don't like the Scots much either. I don't know if I was more riled that she was pregnant or her being one of them.

Breakfast was silent except for Casey snuffling through his porridge. I was finishing off some hellish black coffee when Silas rode up in his wagon, the wind whipping the hair around the face of the old man beside him on the seat.

Moira came to stand just outside the door of the tent with me. The old man jumped lightly off the wagon and followed Silas toward us.

"This is Moses," said Silas, a warning in his voice.

Moira mumbled a greeting and turned away, handkerchief to her mouth, shoulders shaking. I was sucking in my cheeks, trying to keep from laughing. Moses could have been the real thing; long white hair shooting out from under a crumpled cowboy hat and a dirty grey beard hanging down to his belly. Stooped in the shoulders, his grey clothes hung from him like he'd shrunk away. He carried a stick, the handle about three feet long, with a forked end, the tines each another foot.

"Moses is a water witch."

Moira coughed into her hanky. "Excuse me," she gasped. "I have to get Casey."

Moses nodded, but said nothing.

I thought Silas had lost his mind. "A what?"

"He can find water anywhere, you dumb ass. Now stop staring and let's go."

If the man could find water, I'd let myself believe he wrote the Ten Commandments. Only other solution would be to take Mule and the wagon to fill up barrels in town. It'd eat up at least a day a week. I pulled on my boots quickly and joined the two men.

"I don't know exactly how," said Silas, "but the stick tells him where the water is."

Moses grunted, nodding hard, and walked to the base of the tree by the tent. He took the tines of the forked stick in his hands, pointed the long end ahead of him and started walking. I followed beside Silas and saw Moira a short distance behind. Casey was running circles around us all. Moses walked a few hundred paces in straight lines from the tree, first east, then west, then south.

"I told you the tree was a sign," I called quietly over my shoulder to Moira.

"Well he hasn't found anything yet, now has he?" She stood with hands on hips.

"Moses has only been wrong twice," said Silas. He fell back to walk with her. "And those times they hit huge boulders under the surface and couldn't go on. So he may not have been wrong at all."

About a hundred yards north of the tent Moses stood stiff suddenly, his head cocked to one side, eyes fixed on the end of the stick. It was bending to the ground, pulling his hands down with it. He turned to the right and the stick straightened, back and the stick bent, turned to the left and it straightened again, back and it bent. It was some powerful force down there arching that stick toward it, Moses just the guy who knew how to hold it right. I shot a look at Moira. Her eyebrows were raised, lips pursed. Moses did one more dance with the stick and my head bobbed along with the gentle arching that offered up the earth's secret.

One final time Moses checked the exact spot, laughed, then looked around as if he'd forgotten we were there.

"There she is. Dig there."

And I dug for days, scaring myself a little with how I couldn't quit. I dug first with a shovel to start the hole that narrowed into a kind of tunnel. Then at eight or nine feet, when I couldn't throw the dirt out of the hole any longer, I borrowed a windlass, a long rope wound onto a sleeve with a crank at the end. I'd fill buckets at the bottom, jump out and crank them to the top, dump them and send them back down. I worked from sun-up 'til evening, when I couldn't see to dig any more. And then slept like I was dead.

"My God, Dillan," Moira called down after the third day. "What if Moses was wrong? What if he's just crazy?"

"Silas wouldn't have brought him." I looked up from the bottom of the hole, panting. "Look, if you don't want to help."

She didn't say anything for a minute. The sunlight was blinding until her shadow covered the hole. "It's just I've never seen such work." She sounded worried. "You must be exhausted."

"We'll hit water, Moira. We have to."

That was it. We'd find water or we'd be back in the frozen shack on the hill. By the fourth day it was too deep for me to keep climbing out of there. I couldn't ask Moira to help; the work was too heavy. So I asked Silas. I'd fill the metal bucket to overflowing, yank on the rope and hear the crank squealing like a pig above me as Silas pulled the bucket up. My whole body ached, arms like rubber, back on fire with the constant bending and lifting. At fifteen feet, clay gave way to sand and gravel and I didn't notice the pain any more. My heart was exploding with excitement, pumping faster, tricking my body to work through the agony. At sixteen feet, the soil and gravel turned to mud. A few more plunging shovels full and water was seeping over my boots.

"I did it." My voice echoed hollow in the hole, surprised. My legs near crumpled underneath me, but I kept digging faster, to get as much dirt out as I could before the water got too deep and I had to get the hell out of there. "Silas, hurry, get it up quick. There's water." I shouted it loud. "We've hit water."

Moira's shadow closed over the hole and her excited face appeared. "You've done it?"

"Yes." I stopped a second and smiled at her.

I was a mess coming out of there, a ball of mud and sweat with a few tears mixed in. She was hugging me before I was all the way out of the hole, laughing, her head thrown back. I jumped out and we danced a jig, arms and legs flying until we almost crashed on the ground, her grabbing at her belly.

Suddenly she stood straight again, like she'd just remembered who I was, remembered Silas was there. Casey was watching us like we were the craziest things he'd ever seen, the can he'd been using for a shovel limp in his hand. Getting up, my knees and back pret' near exploded with pain, I grabbed him and swung him in the air.

"We'll make it now, my boy." We were grinning back and forth like mentals. Casey giggled 'til he turned red. "We'll make it."

Moira smiled.

✥ ✤ ✥

CHAPTER 19

"VIRGIN SOIL IS BROKE with a sulky plow," Silas told me. It'd been a week since Moses found water, and now I could finally turn to figuring out the farming. "It's heavier than a regular plow, breaks it up better. But you'll need two horses to pull it. You're lucky there're no trees and stumps on the place. Should make it a little easier."

We were outside the tent listening to Moira chattering with Casey inside. Two plow horses. So far the only animal I owned was Mule.

"Where am I gonna get the money for horses?" I raked dirty fingers through my hair.

"I'll lend you a plow and my animals if you'll promise not to work them more than a few hours a day and treat them well."

"You don't have to do this, Silas."

"I know that." He nodded toward the tent. "But they need you to make a go of this place. Just take my offer."

I broke my first ten acres — the homestead agreement said ten acres the first year — watching the grass turn into huge lumps of earth, the plow skidding off when it hit hardpan, throwing me damn near off the seat. But I'd bring the horses back and start again, and slowly it was done. Each night I fed Silas's horses up good, brushed them down 'til they shone. He trusted me with them. Nobody'd ever trusted me with anything, let alone their workhorses.

Each evening Casey waited at the tent door, excited to see me. Moira would have him fed and ready for bed so I could play with him a little. If I was honest, I'd have to admit I missed caring for him myself. I'd done it 'cause I had to, but losing it made me sad, a kind of space opened up. I didn't belong any more, not in that spot where a woman lives in a kid's life. But it was right she was caring for him, the truth being I was too busy keeping my head above water with the farming. He was better off. Moira was a strange bird, but Casey seemed to like her right from the beginning, so I wasn't about to complain. Made me wish for Taffy though. She'd trusted me. I'd fought for her and won. And now spent all my time wondering if she'd have been better off if I'd lost. Here was Moira, alive and making a life. If Taffy'd stayed home, there'd have been shame, but she'd be a mother, maybe a wife. Or – maybe her father would have sent her away and she'd be like Moira, in some crazy place between a home and hell.

Being busy was a relief, saved me thinking too hard about it. After breaking those first acres, the next job was to ribbon the soil into furrows for seeding. I had a little money saved from the honey-wagon pay, and spent it to buy a used furrow plow from two brothers a mile east who looked at me like I'd just walked out of the bush. But no matter. It was the first piece of equipment I'd ever owned. Every time I went by it I had to stop and walk around it, running my hands over the wooden handles like they were thighs on a woman, testing the fine edge of the ploughshare.

In the field I gripped firm and followed behind, watching the blade ripping the clods of earth into tracts of mallow black dirt. It was finally real. Until then I'd just been a kid playing, pretending at being a farmer, the neighbours grinning at each other like there was a joke between them and I was it. But the plow made my chest swell, the fresh smell of dirt mixed with spring air kicking winter from the lungs, throwing out the dank stuff of the old winter shack that had got into my veins, chasing the events of the harvest out of my bones. My own place. My own air.

Silas had let me borrow a horse again, this time a lone furrow horse that knew more about plowing than I did. Nelly walked exactly so as to keep the furrow straight, needing hardly any guidance from me. After three days, it weren't so exciting as it was boring, and I got to excessive thinking. Silas had warned me. The *politics of plowing* he called it, too much thinking leading to questions, leading to meetings about marketing, freight rates, elevator organizations. He'd got himself into a grain growers' association, was getting involved in local politics. I didn't know what any of it meant and didn't give a fug either.

Truth was I felt like I was drowning in the little I'd learned and everything I hadn't yet. A few potatoes at home were one thing, but acres of wheat, well it made my chest tighten up again at the thought. I was doing everything Silas told me, but feeling like a blind man doing it, reaching ahead just far enough to touch the edge so I didn't fall off some sort of crazy road I'd started down. And I still had to get a house built.

Silas was the only one to help. He seemed to enjoy giving advice, teaching me. The others grunted answers, looking like if they said more they'd be giving away some kind of secret that might just put me ahead of them. I learned to ask without getting excited, to keep the hope out of my voice, asking like their answers didn't really matter, like I didn't run home and borrow some of Moira's paper to write them down so's I'd remember when the season was right. Some of the men spoke as though I were addled, their wisdom wasted on me, but they still went on, enjoying the audience that usually gathered. They were the real assholes. But it all helped, the tidbits coming together so I began to understand the theory of dryland farming, even if the details were still a little murky.

Moira didn't appreciate any of it. Walking her around the plow, I'd point out its furrow depth and width, how much I expected to be able to get done in a day. She didn't seem to care, nodding even when I knew she hadn't heard a thing, hurrying back to the tent the minute she could escape.

"Yes, that'd be a good idea." She nodded when I announced it was Red Fife wheat we'd be growing.

"They say it needs a long season, but it's early yet."

She was looking right past me, not listening.

"They say it can't be beat for hardness of kernel and flour strength." Not really knowing what it all meant, it still felt good to know the right words. "If we can get it planted in the next couple of weeks, we should be okay."

"That's good then."

Following the plow was hot and sweaty, and I was thirsty,

lips dry, mouth full of grit. Spitting hard, I was suddenly mad. What the hell did it matter what Moira thought? I didn't need her blessing. Only it was nice to share things, tell someone about the day, about the decisions running around my head, like saying them out loud would make them good. But to hell with her. I couldn't make her care. The next day I would go to town and pick up the seed and then begin to sow. My lungs almost hurt from spring air laced with the smell of fresh dirt and horse manure.

All at once I was on the ground with my nose in it, and my head pounding hard where the handle of the plow had knocked it. The furrow horse was looking back at me lying there gasping. She snorted and stomped her foot, impatient with the delay my broken skull was causing.

"Oh shit." I rolled onto my side.

Silas had warned me to watch out for large rocks heaved up by the frost. "If the plow hits 'em, it'll buck like a son-of-a-bitch." He'd thrown his arms around wildly, his head tilted forward, eyebrows furrowed like my field. I'd laughed. "Don't laugh, you bugger. I'm warning you. It'll throw you right off your goddamn feet, or worse."

Judging by the pain in the side of my head, worse had happened. I got up slow, holding my head to stop the world spinning, and went to unhitch the horse from the plow. The harness dropped off her shoulders and head.

"Go home now." Slapping her hard on the rear end, I lowered myself to the ground to wait for help.

"Probably a concussion. But if you didn't lose consciousness, you should be all right." Moira sounded pretty certain. Nelly had run straight home to Silas's place and he was there when she rounded the corner. He guessed the rest and found me, brought me home and dumped me on Moira's tick. My tick. She pressed and prodded, and once she'd cleaned up the cut, poured a little antiseptic on it, making me yelp so loud Silas raised his eyebrows. They seemed to be enjoying themselves.

"Don't be a baby now. I've seen a man lose a leg and complain less."

My ears grew hot. "Well it still hurts like hell."

"I know. Now just hold still."

She started stitching and I sucked in my breath real hard to keep the tears back.

"Are you sure there's nothing more?" I held onto my head when she was done. "God, it's pounding."

She shone a taper in my face again. "If you cracked your skull or hurt your brain, your pupils would be huge and you'd be vomiting and falling asleep."

"Oh well, sorry then, Doc." I glanced at Silas, who was amused at something. "What?"

Silas scratched his head. "It's just you'd think a guy would be grateful he wasn't about to die."

Though the pain was shooting behind my eyes, I laughed and couldn't stop. "It must have been funnier than hell to see it. One minute I'm daydreaming about what a great farm I'm gonna have." I swiped my hands over my face. "And the next, wham, I'm in the dirt. Great farmer!"

Silas and Moira started to chuckle.

"Poor Nelly. Couldn't figure out what happened. Probably thinking..." I lowered my voice, "... 'What's the poor bugger doing down there?'"

No one could speak for laughing. Slowly I got up off Moira's bed and made it to a chair at the table. Casey woke up hollering and Moira went to get him.

"So you learned something from your old man, eh?"

"I guess so." She looked back at me with raised eyebrows.

"We could use a doctor around here," Silas said. "Berkowski's in Ibsen, but he's so busy he doesn't get out to the farms much. Sometimes I don't think he wants to. I know lots of families..." He frowned. "Well, the doc just didn't get there in time."

"I don't know." Moira shook her head and rubbed her huge belly. But I could tell she was thinking, her voice getting excited. "I'm almost due now. I don't know how much I can do."

I couldn't believe she was actually considering it.

"I'd drive the wagon. You wouldn't be alone." Silas was rubbing his hands together, the idea blooming right up there

116

in front of his eyes. Moira had her head cocked to the side, picturing it too. I was looking from one to the other, getting mad.

"Wait just a minute," I said. "She's supposed to be helping me, remember."

"How much help do you need?" said Silas. "As long as Casey's looked after. You're a grown man. Fend for yourself."

Moira gave a short laugh and I glared at her, turned away and then couldn't help myself. I turned back. "How the hell am I gonna get any farming done if she's running all over the countryside playing doctor instead of watching Casey?"

They both fixed me with a stunned look.

"Oh don't worry." Moira's voice was bitter. "I won't be playing. I'll be right here with you, being the good little dollybird you ordered." Her look made my balls wither. She stormed outside, Casey looking after her surprised.

Silas was watching me real careful, but he didn't say a word. I didn't want to know what he was thinking, what the question hanging between us might be. Past the throbbing in my head, I knew he was right. I could manage. But it wasn't right him coming here and starting things that messed with my life. It wasn't right. I turned away and heard the tent flap fall closed behind him.

"Shit."

CHAPTER 20

MOIRA

My Dear Aileen,

We've got water and what a relief it is. A person can't know how important it is until you've had to ration and save. And Dillan is downright happy. I think the well helps him believe in a future here, at least for Casey and himself. I'm not quite sure where I fit in, given the circumstances. It's so awkward.

I'm hoping to become a bit of an on-call doctor in the area. Last week I treated an abscessed tooth with cocaine solution and two days ago was midwife to a very young woman, just a girl really. She was scared out of her wits, naturally, but she listened and she and her baby girl are fine. It was a much simpler episode than any of Mrs. Mc-Giver's deliveries. Nevertheless it was a nice challenge...

In spite of Dillan's childish outburst, I'd gone doctoring a few times while he finished seeding. It felt good helping people who had no one else to turn to, their appreciation the familiar kind shown to Father back home. I took the tokens they offered, the odd bits of money or food, remembering Father's observation that those in poverty hated to feel indebted. Father might have been proud of my efforts had he known of them. Silas seemed to be. He drove me to wherever I was needed.

Riding beside him now, I looked up at the barren farmyard he'd brought me to. The barking of an emaciated black dog broke the silence, a quiet both eerie and incongruous with the cheerful April morning. The dog ran circles around us, tail thumping a greeting despite his desperate state. Silas went quickly up the steps to the door. I hung back; it was too quiet, too dark, the curtains drawn against the sun. Silas knocked lightly, opened the door and reeled back with a gasp. The smell of ripening bodies attacked us, seeping through holes in the flimsy masks we wore. As we entered, I tried breathing through my mouth, but only succeeded in adding an acrid taste to the cloying assault on my senses.

Just inside and to the left of the door, a man and his son lay clutched in each other's arms on a narrow cot. They were dead, their bodies stiff and stinking. Stopping to draw a breath at an open window, I pushed the curtain back to find the sill wreathed with flies awaiting their anticipated feast. Bile surged to the back of my throat and I forced my feet forward to a larger bed where the rest of the family lay. A mother and two small girls had been consumed by diphtheria.

"They were probably sick within days of each other," I whispered to Silas following behind.

"No one knew," he said quietly. "Old Frank down the road saw their jersey wandering in the field with an udder full to bursting. He came to check. When no one answered he got scared and came for me."

"And you're not scared of anything."

Silas shrugged. "We got the shots."

Father had warned of the virulence of the disease. He'd tried to quarantine people and force them to receive antitoxins, but most resisted. Even the sight of their own dead family members was insufficient persuasion to overcome fear and superstition. Dr. Berkowski had, with the understanding he would not be held responsible, injected both me and Silas. He'd agreed the science on antitoxins was sound, but still seemed relieved and a little impressed at my willingness to attend to those farm families afflicted. But in the house the disease lingered in every breath we took. The injection, the mask – they were suddenly all too little for something so violent.

"It's too late." I turned to bolt.

Silas caught me. "It'll be all right, Moira."

"Their blood's poisoned, carried it to their hearts and lungs.

It won't be all right." Anger was a calming agent. I took a moment to look around and discovered a small girl gazing at me through death-drunk eyes.

"She's still alive." I hurried to the bed and pulled her away from the bodies around her. I sat with her on my lap in a kitchen chair. She had huge, startlingly pink eyes rimmed with white lashes. They stared out from a ghostly pale face surrounded by granny-white hair. Though she was not more than five years old, there was an ancient quality in the albino features that were sunken with fever and exhaustion. A cough seized the girl until she was almost blue. She heaved a little, coughed again. Gathering her in my arms, I held her upright to make breathing easier and through the thin nightgown felt her bones, fragile as the delicate bluebells wilted in the vase on the night table.

"Mommy," the girl whimpered, tucking herself into me.

Silas was across the room closing the mother's eyes.

"It's okay, honey. You'll be okay." Whispering it into the girl's silky-fine hair, I rocked her gently back and forth, surveying the room, tears threatening. Dear God. In that instant I wanted to pray, but there were no words for this. God was nowhere near this family.

"Don't cry," said the girl, momentarily lucid. She cast about the room until her eyes landed on her mother's body. Slowly she looked to where Silas was bent over her dead sister. He looked up at that moment, trying to force a smile from his slack mouth, but his face was stitched with grief, belying what he knew, what even the tiny waif in my arms knew.

"It's all right." Her voice was small in the room. "We're going to be fine. Soon."

There was nothing to do but wait, rocking her, whispering soothing words into her cold ear. Silas busied himself covering the bodies, opening windows and tidying up a home that would be burned before the sun set. Finally her head lolled back across my arm. She'd joined the rest of them, the small house now a family morgue. The weight of her frail body grew as though what had buoyed her in life was expelled and replaced by solid matter. Maybe soul is simply air temporarily travelling through a person, escaping in one last breath to search for the heaven everyone speaks of. The light had left her, something in her eyes become only vapour. I lay the child down and covered her. I didn't know her name.

Through a haze of tears I could see what had until that moment been the girl's home. A pail, half full of water, sat on the floor by the door, a tin dipper hanging just above it. Clothing of various sizes hung neatly from hooks on the wall beside the bed. The table was set for five, as though the mother's faith in the ordinary domestic patterns of her life could save her family.

Pushing myself up, I set the girl with her mother and sister and pulled the blanket back over them. I couldn't speak except to mutter familiar words, "Rest in peace. Rest in peace. Rest in peace."

"I couldn't do anything," I said. Silas's arm seemed the only solid thing in the room as I sagged against it.

"Nobody could. At least you tried."

"Yes. But they're still dead."

Daylight was another assault on our gaping, raw senses. The sun was on the west end of its ancient arc, sending our shadows stretching long ahead. A slight haze rendered the world insubstantial and slightly lazy, too drugged with spring to care about the family it had just released.

We were silent walking to the wagon. Silas sighed deeply. "They're somewhere better now."

"I think my father attempted faith." I shook my head. "He would come home from something just like this, and sit in his study in a big overstuffed chair, his head bowed over the Bible. But I never saw him actually read it. His eyes were always closed as though his comfort came from the solid weight of those words in his hands."

"Maybe it gave him strength, knowing all that faith went into those pages," Silas said.

"I don't know how it could."

Father had seen misery like this almost every day. When he was doctoring he held his body erect, kept his step light, as though confidence alone could save lives. The neighbours thought him aloof and distant, if awe-inspiring. But listening to the suffering of others slowly diminished him, his certainty ebbing away with each death, reminded he was not God after all. And worse, perhaps God had abandoned him. Slumped in his chair, Father wasn't awesome, only human, slightly afraid like everyone else, searching something old and distant and beyond logic for answers he'd already been given in everything he'd studied. While he couldn't embrace my mother's Catholic zeal and absolute faith – her need to evangelize and fend off her own fears – time had also stolen his belief in the rational sciences. He was left with nothing.

"Everyone needs something other than themselves, Moira." Silas startled me.

I wanted to believe like my father once had, to be as certain as my mother, but if there was a God, he wasn't with me or the little girl who just died. I had science, medicine. If more people understood the possibilities they wouldn't be waiting around like this family, praying for some higher power miraculously to fix things.

"But in the end we have to rely on ourselves," I said.

"That girl in there. She wasn't waiting for God to save her. Only to take her home."

The white-haired girl, her life probably already made difficult by the distinction of her pigment. I wanted to throw something. "That girl died because people are too ignorant to accept help in this world. Don't you see?" I found myself standing with feet apart, hands on hips. "There were other choices for that family. If someone had gone for help, if someone had known. Antitoxins. That's what might have saved them."

"All right, Moira." Silas's hand was on my arm. "I only think life is sometimes easier if we accept what we can't change."

"Dillan says things like that. And he acts like it's all fate. I think people have to take control of their life, their destiny."

The house was a dark silhouette behind us. Silas helped me into the wagon and jumped in, flicking the reins over Nelly's back. He was silent for a moment. "But even you don't have control over everything. You're here. They sent you here."

"My mother did."

"And do you want to go back to her? What about your father?"

"There are others. I have a sister, Aileen. You'd like her. Very practical."

Silas waited. I felt awkward, like I owed him an explanation, but where to start with a family so strangely ordinary.

"Aileen doesn't have any dreams," I blurted. "She lives in my mother's world and doesn't expect anything else of her life. As though that's all she can hope for."

"Don't we all hope to be like our parents? Until they disappoint us. Then we want more." He lifted the front of his cowboy hat to scratch his head where the band had plastered his hair to his scalp.

"I want to be like my father. He's a good man."

"I'm sure he is."

I lightened my tone, shrugging to brush off his opinion. "I'm only saying he would have kept me at home."

"But he didn't."

We headed home in silence. My head was pounding, back aching. I was exhausted and sad and, in those few honest moments between waking and sleep, I understood that Silas was right. Father could have kept me home, stood up to Mother, forced Evan's father to let his son take responsibility. My throat constricted with fear, my loneliness complete. I dozed off, barely conscious of the welcome warmth of Silas's arm around my shoulder, the comfort of resting my head on his chest.

We were approaching the tent when I woke and quickly moved away from Silas. "Sorry, I'm just so tired."

"You have a right to be."

Dillan had lit a lamp and its glow threw a silhouette of him at the table with Casey on his lap. He was feeding him supper. The scene reflected the warmth of a family. At least the little albino girl had that much in her short life. I didn't want to get down from the wagon and smiled sleepily at Silas.

"You're a good man too."

"No. I've just lived a little longer. And I've learned something about acceptance. I lost a wife and child to smallpox."

"Oh no. I'm so sorry." I thought of the bodies we'd left behind. They'd be burned along with their house and all its contents. There would be no trace left, the family consumed in flames to reassure those fearful of suffering a similar fate. The girl and her family would be forgotten, their passing marked only by a small cross. Silas had stood over the same scene with his own. I couldn't imagine what he might be feeling.

"It was a long time ago," he said, stopping the wagon in front of the tent. He was silent for a moment, then suddenly jumped from the sideboard and helped me climb down. "So maybe that's why I hang around. I want to help you." He blushed. "And maybe I can help Dillan with Casey. I don't know."

My feet hit the ground and a sharp pang shot through my lower belly. I was grateful for the certainty of pain, a dependable reminder of existing in a less than dependable world.

"I do know one thing," he said. "You shouldn't be giving this baby away."

I'd been adjusting my skirts and reaching for my bag, but stiffened at his words, breath stopped. "If I keep this baby" – every word was drawn out – "it will be because I want to, and not because I feel guilty or ashamed."

Silas's face was open, challenging but friendly, reminding me that, for whatever reason, he cared about what happened to me. It was more than I could say for others in my life. My shoulders dropped. "Dillan has enough guilt for three people, and it seems to be killing him."

"Guilt or conscience? They're different you know."

"Of course." I didn't know.

"Guilt is what others make you feel. Conscience is your own."

He jumped back into the wagon and grabbed the reins, ready to whip them over Nelly's broad back. He drove away leaving a heavy space where his words had been.

✣ ✤ ✣

CHAPTER 21

THE NEXT FEW DAYS were sultry. The locals said it was unusually hot for the end of April. As far as I could tell, I hadn't experienced a usual season yet. I wondered if normal existed. Ironically, the wind had stopped when we most needed it. The air barely stirred. Hanging laundry, grateful now for even the slightest ripple of a breeze, my every movement was heavy, my swollen feet and ankles lumbering under me almost out of sight, body swaying to its own fat rhythm. In a moment of abandon, I took off my shirt, hanging it on the line alongside the sheets pinned there.

I could only imagine the picture – half naked and heat crazed, feet planted wide, arms outstretched, belly protruding from under a shelf of ever-growing breasts I had to wrangle into a huge bra every morning – and laughed. Casey smiled up from where he played in a small area of shade provided by the tent. The baby gave a tremendous kick to my groin. I winced and cursed small feet impatient to stand on the ground and join the dry, hot dance we struggled through every day.

"Only two or three weeks," I whispered to it, hardly believing it myself.

Casey suddenly hollered, "Daddy!" and was running toward Dillan, who emerged from south of the tent only a few yards away.

He'd seen me, but pretended he hadn't. Turning away, I pulled on my shirt, buttoning it quickly. Dillan went along with the charade, loudly teasing and tickling Casey, making a show of the attention he was not paying me.

"I found a lake over on the next quarter," he said, coming closer only when I turned back to him. "We could go there and cool off a little."

"Oh yes, let's. It's so hot out here." I reached for Casey. "And this poor thing has hardly moved all day."

"I know who owns it, guy named Gabe. Worked with him on the harvest. But we'll have to be careful he doesn't see us." He was surprisingly vehement. "You don't have anything to do with him. He's one of them."

Before I could ask what he was talking about, Casey was squirming out of my arms and pulling at my hand, and we were off. The *lake* was a large slough smelling of earth and water, wet cattails and long reed grasses. The surface was beginning to slime over with green algae encouraged to grow by the heat of the sun. I held back, watching Dillan strip down to his grey underwear. He was a shockingly hairy man, dark spirals whorling around his chest and navel. At ease with his body, he stood as though my watching made no difference to either of us. It was slightly insulting, his being oblivious because pregnancy rendered me less female in his eyes, less interesting or interested. I wondered if he'd have been so quick to undress in front of me if I were not in this current state.

"Well just go ahead and jump right in," I called, annoyed at the shrill in my voice. "I'll bring Casey."

He was already far from the edge of the slough, swimming with strong quick strokes, his head bobbing and then, like an otter, disappearing with a quick splash, only to reappear closer to shore. "I'll take him if you want."

"Maybe for a little while."

He came to me, dripping, hair plastered to his head. I caught myself peeking at the bulge in his underwear as he strode forward. Embarrassed, I tried to stop, but it seems the more one tries not to look at a thing, the more the eye is drawn to it. It was the dark of night when I was with Evan, and everything had happened so quickly... And Father's convoluted explanations were no better than the one-dimensional pictures displayed at the conference or in my anatomy classes. He'd delivered the information in scientific, even mundane, terms and references. But it was the change in his voice, the clipped and overly analytical, slightly shrill tone that gave him away. He was lying, protecting me from something the rest of the world was privy to. It had to do with men and women and how they behaved with one another, with all the subtleties of growing up.

If he'd only let me in on that part. Perhaps I wouldn't be standing on the edge of a Saskatchewan slough, looking at a near stranger in his underwear, far away from the men I had trusted. Dillan stood as if suspended in the water, a torso with outstretched arms. I jumped a little, laughing an embarrassed laugh, and handed Casey to him.

Glancing around, I undressed to my skivvies and rushed into the water. My bloomers floated up forming white lily pads around my knees, then my middle, and suddenly my belly took on a life of its own. It wanted to float, to reach to the surface of the water and drift like a huge ball pushed by the breeze. As I lay back, my hair rose light and buoyant, fanning out in every direction. I closed my eyes against the sun and relaxed, giving in, floating. The water was dirty, but its coolness refreshing, stripping me of the ugliness of the day. I abandoned myself, forgetting for a moment my aching back, the endless headaches, the shooting leg pains.

I'd been so sure of my choice. The baby would go to a good home and I back to mine, to the life I'd enjoyed – studying, helping my father, avoiding my mother. Eventually Evan would return and our reunion would be a vindication. I had no need for the kind of guilt Dillan carried around. If Evan and I had been allowed to love each other, the baby would be ours. That I'd been coerced to make other choices was not my fault; that I couldn't love the baby was not something I could change. My conscience was clear. I wanted to tell Silas as much.

It was amazing he'd broached the topic at all. But in the isolation of the prairies, conversation so quickly became personal. Small talk was like dust, easily blown away by the wind. The prairie insisted words carry meaning, that people ought not waste them. Intimate cares of life, then, seemed reasonable fodder for discussion, a backdrop, really, to the overwhelming demands of the elements. Guilt or conscience. Damn Silas.

The clouds passed overhead, small and wispy, offering little hope of shade or rain, shapes constantly changing in their slow westerly progress toward whatever fate awaited them. I wanted to float like a cloud, destiny determined by wind, a cloud that might become furious and terrible, or dissipate into nothing.

Casey shrieked. Struggling up, I could see Dillan holding the boy out of the water while he screamed and pointed to his leg. The muddy bottom met my toes and I pushed myself toward them, conscious my belly was indeed still with me, its bulk pushing slowly through the water.

"What is it?" I hollered.

"It's a leech." Dillan was almost as frantic as Casey. "I can't get it off."

I reached them just as Casey's screaming reached a new pitch. "Hold him now. He has to hold still. There now, Casey, it's all right. See, it's gone."

The boy held his arms out and, when I took him, buried his face in my shoulder and wet hair. I crooned to him and over Casey's head saw the fear in Dillan's eyes dissipate. Only a leech – no danger really – but a fierceness in Dillan nonetheless. We struggled up the muddy, slippery side of the slough, and I sat Casey down on a flat rock, using my bloomers to wipe blood flowing from a small spot on his calf.

"Let's see now. Just a little mark is all. You didn't let him get much, did you?" I kept my voice low, coaxing the anxiety out of him.

Casey grinned and shook his head.

"I think the ruckus you made scared that thing so much it just pulled its head right out to see what was going on."

The boy laughed and jumped up, running to Dillan and lifting his leg so his father could see the mark.

Dillan pretended not to see it. "Where did he bite you? I don't see anything." He kept at it until Casey was giggling uncontrollably. "All right then. You want to go back in?"

Casey's nod was noncommittal. He climbed Dillan's torso as the water deepened, until there was nothing to do but let his feet dangle in the leech's murky home. He examined his legs every few seconds as though vigilance would protect him from something that happened so obviously by chance.

"Hello there."

A young woman stood only a few feet behind me, already down to her bloomers. She was tiny, short, with fine features and small hands and feet. Large brown eyes dominated her face and her hair hung down in two long braids. She was a beautiful elf.

"I see you've found the swimming hole. Only one for miles around. Was that you screaming? I guess the water must feel cold on a day like today. It's best just to dive right in. It's so-o-o-o refreshing." And before I could reply, the girl ran into the water and dove under the surface.

"Wait." I rushed after her until I was in to my knees.

Dillan came out of the reeds at the pond's edge with Casey in his arms and ran straight into the girl coming up for air.

"Hey," he started. The two stood staring, eyes wide, mouths open in perfect Os. Suddenly they turned to rush away, she swimming back toward me with strong, fast strokes, Dillan pushing hard against the water to disappear again into the reeds. Casey looked past his father's shoulder to the strange woman whose arms furiously wheeled her away. A chuckle rose up from my stomach and exploded into a laugh. The girl came up for air a couple of feet away.

"It's just" – I tried – "the look. On your faces. Oh my." The girl waited until I could speak again, a small grin on her face. "My name is Moira," I finally managed.

"Oh I know that." She smiled broadly, wrung out her braids and coiled them into a bun, neatly tucking the ends in at the top. "Everybody knows who you are."

"But I've only been here a short while." It was disconcerting to know strangers were speaking of me. "I've hardly met a soul."

"That doesn't matter. You're new," she said, as though that were sufficient explanation. She leaned in close, water dripping from her chin. "I'll share a secret."

"Oh please." A comforting warmth spread through my chest.

"They're going to have a sodding bee for the two of you." She nodded conspiratorially toward where Dillan had disappeared. "You know. To build you a proper house. The whole countryside is saying what a shame it is a young mother with another on the way is living in a tent. They figure your man is too busy trying to farm to think about a house right now."

"My man?" I looked at her, then toward the pond. "Oh. Dillan. You don't understand. He's not my..."

"It will be wonderful. Everybody comes. And it's a little like Christmas. The women will make things for you, nice things you might need for the house. Or for the baby. You know, blankets, curtains for the windows, things you might not already have."

We had fetched our clothes from where they lay in the tall grass beyond the water's edge, pulled the dresses over our heads and adjusted wet underclothes.

"They're doing that for me?" It was all a bit dramatic. "But they don't even know me."

"Doesn't matter. People know how hard it is to make it out here. They want to make it easier. Besides, I think they figure the more families homesteading, the more services we'll get in town. And a sodding's a good excuse for a party."

"Party?"

"Of course. Later, when the work's done, there'll be music and dancing and food. You wait and see."

"A real house would be lovely."

She tied a kerchief around her head. Looking up to the prairie beyond, she muttered under her breath. In the distance a rider sat slouched in his saddle, head tilted to one side.

"Gabe," she shivered, and motioned around us. "This is his land. It's not a very good piece. He's been telling my father how Walter promised him a better quarter and then gave it to your man last minute."

"Oh dear."

Carla shuddered. "Anyway, I have to go, but it was very nice to meet you, Moira."

"The pleasure's mine." It sounded so formal. "Wait. What's your name?"

"Carla. Carla Schmidt."

"Goodbye Carla." I hated to see her go. I hadn't realized how much I missed the companionship of my sisters.

"Who in the hell was that?" Dillan asked as he emerged from the reeds.

"Carla."

"Well you could have got rid of her a little quicker. Casey and I've been fighting off the damn leeches while you two went on."

I laughed and raised my eyebrows. "Well it doesn't seem to bother you any that *I'm* standing right here."

He blushed and silently handed Casey over, quickly struggling to pull his clothes on over dripping underwear. He took Casey from me and wrapped him in a blanket. I scrambled further up the bank to collect our things. The sun quickly evaporated the water from my skin, leaving goosebumps in its wake. My neck prickled in a peculiar way, and I turned to see Gabe still silhouetted against the sky. The man returned a long look before pulling his horse around. Carla was obviously disturbed by him. And now this business with the land. Maybe that's why Dillan wanted to stay away from him, to avoid a confrontation. I forced myself to wave a little and turned, shivering, to rush back to Dillan. Casey was already asleep in his arms. I ignored the question in Dillan's eyes and began to walk home, back to the tent where the curtain would conceal us from one another again.

CHAPTER 22

DILLAN

I SAT UP ON ONE elbow, stunned with sleep. It was voices outside the tent that woke me, and I looked across at Moira standing and looking out the flap. Someone called out, "Hello in there." And then a woman's teasing song, "Come on out you two. We've got a surprise."

"Must be the sodding crew," Moira said. She was looking pleased with herself, eyes shiny, excited. "They've come to build us a house."

"What?" I jumped up, hopped on one foot and then the other, pulling on pants, suspenders snapping hard over my undershirt. I was outside in seconds. "Hey, what the hell is this then?" A couple of the women frowned.

There were more than twenty people standing there looking at me, smiling kind of silly, like they knew something I didn't. Men and boys were carrying shovels and blades. They were all dressed alike, work pants tucked into tall leather boots, suspenders over shirts with sleeves rolled to the elbows. The women were a wave of housedresses, their arms loaded with picnic baskets and parcels. Little girls were jumping up and down, their pigtails bobbing. They looked past me, trying to catch sight of Moira. Someone had brought a dog, a red-coloured retriever running around as excited as the kids. I started to shake, too nervous to look at anyone properly until I recognized Mrs. Miller in the crowd. She grinned wide and nodded at me like I should say something.

"We figured it's about time you two had a decent house." It was Mr. Miller, standing with his arms folded across his huge chest, his good eye fixing to look right through me.

"Especially with a new babe coming soon." His gaze wandered to Moira, his face going soft into a smile, like she was the damn Virgin herself.

"I don't know what to say. I'm, I mean we're..." The stuttering wouldn't stop, so I did.

"Me and the missus homestead not so far from here." A tall man stepped out from the crowd, long arms and legs propelling him forward. He clapped me on the back and waved toward the crowd. "Wanted to get here sooner, but had to get the seeding done." He glanced at Moira. "The whole countryside's here now, ready to help you and your little woman."

A strange ping went off in my head, but before I could figure out what it was about, Mr. Miller was there beside me, making things happen. He pointed to tall, lush grass not fifty yards away. "That slough bottom over there is about perfect for good sod. Lots of roots. Helps to hold it together when it rains or the winds get up."

The men took the furrow plow to the slough and soon the sod rolled up in a dark coil behind it. They brought the strips to higher ground, where other men had constructed a wood frame.

"Make sure that sod's about four inches deep."

"And cut those lengths a good two feet."

"Use that sharp spade so the ends are straight."

"Grass side down, you idiot, or it'll rain as heavy inside as out."

The men hollered back and forth, setting each layer of sod, lacing the corners and filling the cracks with leftover chunks. Mostly I stood and watched, feeling useless, running from the slough back to the growing house, grabbing a spade only to have someone take it from me. They were quick. Each of them knew his small job, working toward something bigger. They were at ease, efficient, knowing each other in a way I'd never known other men. The suspicion I'd started with melted away with the heat of the day. I saw Moira a couple of times, chatting with the other women busy setting out lunch, chasing after Casey when he got too close to the work. She smiled real big at me.

By lunchtime the sod house was half done. Walls, a small

porch, a front door hanging at a bit of an angle 'cause the sod weren't sturdy enough yet to hold the wooden door frame and hinges. It needed windows cut and a roof built. The sky was clouding up right quick and the men didn't want to take time to eat. But their women stared them down until we were all sitting on blankets on the ground eating bread and lengths of sausage and fruit pies. Cellar-cold milk from Mrs. Miller's Jersey washed everything down. Even the dog was finally taking a break from tearing around.

"It'll be about twenty-four feet long." The tall man was beside me again. I was feeling groggy from the food and sun. "There won't be no partitions, but at least you can have a little privacy if you put your bed at the other end from the little ones." He elbowed my ribs and winked at the women, who blushed and looked offended, but weren't.

My breath left me quick. Their faces were laughing, Moira was blushing and Carla was looking at the ground. Mrs. Miller caught my eye and glared, shook her head in a warning.

"When I find a wife, I'm sure she'll be grateful."

The words echoed in the silence around my head. One of the women dropped the dishes she'd been gathering, while the men stood with mouths hanging open, heads swinging from Moira to me and back again.

"Okay everyone, let's get back at it." Mr. Miller's voice broke through the blood pounding in my ears. He came over and put his arm around my shoulder. "It's all right, son," he said quietly. "I'm sure lots of them have stories too."

"I'm a dollybird," Moira said, rescuing me. She stood straight, ready to take them on, the baby pushing out against her work dress, sleeves rolled up, sweat shining on her brow. She wasn't no different from the rest of them. But they stared at her a moment and then one by one lowered their gazes and ate their food in silence. The crew was quiet after that, thanking the women for lunch and heading back to the sod. I followed at a distance, hearing the whispers drifting in the air.

"Well, I never."

"And in her condition."

"Bad enough to be a dollybird, but a pregnant one?"

Shame burnt my ears hot. I wanted to explain about Taffy, about Moira being the only one willing to help, to tell them she was good to Casey and smart and capable. More capable than me if I was honest. But I couldn't take their dirty glares and wagging tongues. I couldn't look at Moira, caught Carla's eye a moment and looked away quick. She must think me a bugger for not sayin' anything.

The men worked faster now, wanting to beat the gathering clouds. And all the while they were looking at me from under their hat brims, at Moira, shaking their heads at one another, raising their eyebrows. The voices of Arichat wandered through my head.

"*Obviously no morals in either of 'em.*"

"*Knocked up. She should be hiding out in a convent somewhere.*"

"*Why doesn't he just marry her then? That would make everything okay, wouldn't it?*"

People are the same everywhere.

Every step I took was like walking in mud. The walls were almost done and the men brought sod for the roof, arguing a little about which had the most grass roots that would make it strong. One of them said they should just put up a dirt roof, as though dirt was good enough for the likes of me and Moira. I recognized the man, knew Moira had helped his son with a rash that about drove the boy crazy with itching. The bastard. I wanted to shout that I had lied to no one, that I hadn't invited them here, that Moira would be as grateful for that house as any wife or mother.

Mr. Miller stepped in. Stroking his chin, starting and stopping, fixing each of them with first his good eye and then the bad, he said very carefully, "No. I think we will build a sod roof." And when they snorted and mumbled, he added, "You know dirt. One day of rain and it's pouring inside the house for two. There's going to be a baby in there."

The men grumbled, but started back to work. I tried to smile a little at Mr. Miller. He nodded slightly in return and turned to help the men lift the logs needed to support the roof.

CHAPTER 23

MOIRA

Dearest Aileen,
  We have a house, an honest to goodness house...

There was no party. The sodding done and the house complete, the women entered it quietly and congregated around the table and chairs brought in from the tent. Light filtered through two windows, splashing a patch onto the dirt floor. Casey wouldn't go near the dim corners, stayed close to me instead, gazing tiredly at the strangers who sent tolerant smiles his way. I sat at the table and received their mumbled congratulations, the gifts they offered one at a time as they came forward from the group that stood back just a little. Any intimacy now seemed impossible. But it was for the better. If these women had been allowed to believe Dillan and I were married, and found out the truth only later, the hurt would have been all the greater.

I sat straight and accepted blue embroidered curtains from Mrs. Rehman; a set of tin pots from Mrs. Miller, who squeezed my arm hard before sitting down with Casey on her lap; a green hand-stitched baby blanket from Hazel Baker; tiny baby gowns from Rebecca Long, a woman Silas called the chronic widow. After these things had been passed around and admired, Mrs. Koch's husband came in carrying a worn, but still functional, crib.

"All my babies, all eight of them, slept in this crib." Mrs. Koch looked around at the other women. Worry etched her eyes. "See these marks on the wood? I couldn't get little George to stop chewing, his teeth bothered him so." The women peered at gouges in the railing, glancing up to ensure I appreciated the significance of such an heirloom being offered. "And here," Mrs. Koch caressed a spindle, "is where Emily rubbed the bar between her fingers every night for comfort." Her eyes teared and the other women made small comforting sounds and patted her shoulders.

It was bewildering. If the woman didn't want me to have the crib...

"Little Emily was taken by a mysterious disease when she was only a two years old," Carla said quietly.

"I'm so sorry. I can't possibly take this. It's beautiful, but..."

Carla shook her head in warning. "Take it," she mouthed. "Just take it."

"Thank you so much." I gave Mrs. Koch a small hug.

The women nodded their heads in approval and began to gather their things and their children, hollering at the men that it was time to go. Their husbands were enjoying a drink outside, disappointed the clouds had dissipated for today. Everyone needed a rain to encourage the sprouting green crops.

"The wheat's come up real nice. But it's been dry too long." I'd heard Dillan speaking to the men earlier like he knew what he was talking about, but they didn't pay him any attention, acting like everything he said was now suspect after finding out the truth about me.

"Not much of a party, I guess." Carla sat down beside me and fingered a baby sweater on the table. She suddenly covered my hand with her own. "It'll be okay. You just gave them a shock. Me too. But they'll be all right once the baby comes. Maybe if you marry Dillan?" She stared at the sweater.

"That is not going to happen," I said firmly.

She smiled a little, seemed almost relieved.

"Carla." It was a command. A large woman towered over us. She pulled Carla up and out of her chair. "We should leave now." Her voice carried a trace of accent I couldn't place.

"You must be Carla's mother then?" I extended my hand. "I'm so happy to..."

"We should leave now," the woman repeated. She gave me

a pointed look and turned to push Carla ahead of her out the door.

I caught Carla pantomiming strangulation, rolling her eyes and sticking out her tongue just as she went through the door. I laughed and shivered all at once, wondering if everyone in this small world now felt it their right to judge me. The wind had picked up and was coming through the windows.

"Better put some greased paper in them, or at least hang some canvas sacks if you have any." Mrs. Miller was at my elbow. "It'll stop the wind a little and keep the flies down. You'll need something more than those curtains. Nice idea, but not very practical. When it gets cold, put that extra sod in or it'll be so drafty the little ones will get sick."

It was so much more than anyone else had offered. "Thank you."

Mrs. Miller gave me a quick hug and a peck on the cheek. "It won't be easy, out here all alone." I followed her to the tiny front porch and we watched a few stragglers leaving for home. "You'll need to keep your wits about you. Silas says you're smart, the both of you, that you won't be too proud to ask for help when you need it." She raised her eyebrows. "Never mind the rest. They'll come round. In the meantime, we're only fifteen minutes north by horse should you need anything, or help when the baby comes."

Mr. Miller pulled up in front of the house, his horses prancing, eager to head home.

"Goodbye now." Mrs. Miller climbed in.

Dillan and Casey appeared from the back of the house to see them off. Like a family in a portrait, we stood smiling and waving, as though basking in the idea of our new home and the many comforts it would bring. It was ridiculous. I lumbered off to the tent. It was empty, as everything had been moved to the house, and I thudded heavily onto the floor, wondering if I'd ever get up, cradling my head in my hands. Then Dillan was there, confusion on his face, the stupid red dog with him. Apparently the dog was a gift too.

"I thought you'd be happy."

"I am." But it was his home, not mine. I had no home. "The house will be wonderful."

"I made a fool of both of us." He hunched into himself and sat down across the tent.

"We're not fools. They are."

"Then why are we sitting in an empty tent moaning?"

"Well you're sad because your wife died. They can't blame you for that."

He looked at his hands, lying calloused and dark in his lap. When he raised his face it was ashen, his brows drawn together, mouth clenched, cheeks sucked in with pain.

"What? I'm sorry. Did I say...?"

"It was my fault she died. I've never told anyone."

Time slowed, matching the beat of my heart in my ears. I waited, not wanting his revelation, fearing he'd expect something in return. The confessional at St. Joseph's popped into my head. The parted curtains had revealed a small, dark interior, Mother kneeling in front of the window cut out halfway up one wall. A screen over the window hid the priest from any guilt-ridden soul searching for heavenly absolution from an earthly mediator. I'd always pictured the devil on the other side, laughing at Mother, patronizing her with promises of forgiveness while knowing she would leave his company only to slap my small hands for the least infraction, miserable as always, her clean slate giving her new space for misery. I couldn't be Dillan's confessor.

"Don't. Just don't." Rising quickly, I started out of the tent, then stopped, wanting to explain and couldn't. "We'd better get back to Casey."

As his shoulders slumped, I wondered if the shadowy figure that had listened to my mother possessed more empathy than I.

CHAPTER 24

DILLAN

SOMETHING PULLED at the cotton that stopped up my head with sleep, tearing me out of my dream: Mule hanging in a tree as if from the gallows, a rope round his neck and hood over his head.

"Dillan, Dillan, wake up."

The tree branch was thick and high off the ground. I watched myself try to climb up to cut him down; but the tree grew as I climbed, and the branch was always just out of reach.

"It's time, Dillan."

"Huh. What?"

"The baby. It's time."

"But Mule is dead."

I opened my eyes to see Moira looking at me. "Dillan. Listen to me." She said it slowly like she was talking to an imbecile, her voice calm but pained. "It started yesterday, small contractions, but I didn't know how long to wait. I thought it might be nothing, but my water broke and now..."

A shaft of moonlight beamed through the cracks around the window curtains, and I saw her beside the bed. Suddenly she doubled over, moaned and grabbed her belly with one hand, the bedpost with the other.

"Oh my Christ." I grabbed my pants from the floor and pulled them on.

"What do I do?" I asked, and she was seized by another pain. I'd never felt such terror, not even when Taffy died. I'd been too stupid to know what was possible. Looking for something I recognized, I started toward the door. "I'll go to town and get the doctor." But a picture of Doctor Gibson reaching into Taffy flashed through my head. "No, Mrs. Miller is closer. I'll go there."

"Stop. No time. You have to help," Moira said through clenched teeth.

I shook my head no, while she nodded yes.

"I'll tell you what to do." She was already turning away, groaning. "Help me to the bed."

I wanted to run, but forced myself to her side and took her by the elbow. She leaned into me, hunched and breathing deep, one hand under her belly propping it up. When the pain passed, she straightened a little and shuffled across the kitchen. Finally we were beside her bed, where the sheets were twisted round themselves. Helping her down to the mattress, I felt the dampness of her sweat. She must have been awake and alone for a long time.

"I don't know what to do, Moira." My voice cracked out a whisper.

"It's okay, Dillan." She tried to smile. "I have to do most of it anyway."

She was trying to be brave and funny, and I was being an idiot, needing her to make me feel better.

"Just light a lantern and the stove and put some water on. We'll need hot water before long."

She stopped real quick, her mouth open like a scream, another pain wrenching her face. The moonlight played round her wild hair, making her a little frightening to look at. I was happy when she turned away and slowly rolled over so her back was to the room and her knees drawn up to her stomach. I listened for her breathing, loud through her nose at times, soft and light through her mouth at others.

I shook awake, forcing myself to get busy. I built a teepee of kindling in the stove, stoked it into a small fire with wood chips and dried cow dung, then filled the large copper kettle and set it on top. It only took a few minutes. I wished there was more to do. Shuffling closer I could hear Moira quietly moaning on her bed; across the room Casey whimpered.

"Are you all right?"

"I think…," she paused for breath, "…that it will come soon."

My chest was collapsing in so tight I could hardly breathe. When Taffy had moaned in the livery, I'd only prayed, trusting in God. But he didn't give a fug then either. Shit, I needed more time to figure out what to do.

"Moira. I don't know. I'd better go get someone."

"No," she almost shouted. "Don't leave me alone."

She grabbed my hand so hard it felt like our finger bones were mashing together. Her eyes were full of pain and fear and something else too. I wanted to snatch my hand away.

"Oh my back," she groaned. "Prop me up with pillows, please Dillan."

It was hard to look at her and hard not to. I set the lantern by the bed and she squirmed like she was trying to get away from her own body, her face dripping with sweat, nightgown up around her thighs. She acted like I wasn't there, like she didn't care if I saw her nakedness. It made me want to try harder not to. Her face was squished up into itself and she was breathing heavy. I tried to help, propping her up with our few thin pillows, twisting a blanket into a roll to shove behind her. She pushed her back into it.

"The baby must be upside down." Every word came out in a pant. "The back of its head must be pushing on my back."

"What does that mean?"

"It means it hurts like hell," she yelled.

I'd only asked a question.

"If it won't come when I start to push, you'll have to reach in and turn its head."

"What? I can't do that. I don't know how." It was an impossible thing.

She screeched and Casey sat straight up, calling out. I went over to him. "Go to sleep. Whatever happens you stay in your bed. You hear me?"

He nodded, found his thumb, eyes drooping as he lay down again. I went back to Moira. She grabbed my face hard between her hands.

"Look. If you don't do this, the baby won't come." She let

go, pain washing into her face. When it left again, her dazed eyes found mine, and she spoke slowly, as though I was a two-year-old and this was her only chance to make me understand. "If the baby won't come, it'll die. And so will I."

I stared at her.

"Dillan," she shouted so I jumped back. "Do you understand?"

"Yes, yes," I stuttered, trying to ignore the fear lodged in my throat, the pictures in my head of Casey howling for his dead mother. My breath came shallow and fast, keeping time with Moira's. "All right then. What do you want me to do now?"

"Rub my back." She whimpered the words, as though my agreement to help had released her from needing to cope. "Please. It hurts so much. Right at the base of my spine. There, right there. Rub it harder."

I was afraid to push too hard, afraid to hurt her.

"Harder."

She was frantic, up on all fours now, back arched like a cat rising to my fist digging into the spot she'd guided it to. I'd expected her to lie still and bring her baby into the world calm and organized like she was. All this twisting and screaming and carrying on; it was unnatural. Sweat beaded her forehead and ran down the wide bridge of her nose, dripping onto her upper lip. That instant she tucked her lip in, sucking it dry. The next she let out an animal grunt, her body twisting toward my hand again. I rubbed for hours, changing hands each time one went numb. We didn't speak. She was away someplace where I was an outsider; yet if I took a break from kneading her back, she'd look at me quick and sharp.

"Sitting," she gasped suddenly. "I should be sort of sitting now. Help me."

I arranged pillows and blankets behind her and tried to cover her. She kicked the sheet aside, legs thrashing and hands grasping the sides of the bed. The fits were more intense now, closer together.

She looked at me quickly, eyes narrowed, clear and alert. "It's coming now." She took a deep breath. Her face shot

through with red and purple veins, eyes bulging, heels digging
for traction. When the push ended she sagged into the pillows.
In an instant another seized her, this one ending in a scream.
Casey's eyes were wide when I looked at him.

"Quiet, okay."

He nodded, his face gone white, knuckles pushed into his
mouth.

Moira rested a moment.

"I don't think it's coming." She breathed hard. "Something's wrong, Dillan." The edge of fear in her voice sent me
reeling again.

"What do I do?"

"You need to look." And at my shock, "well what does it
matter now, Dillan? Look."

I slid slowly further down the bed, fingering the flowered
cotton edge of her nightgown. She yanked it up and pushed
me toward the end of the bed, tears in her eyes.

"Please, Dillan," she whispered. "You have to."

All the people in my life whirled about us – Taffy, my father, Casey – fingers pointed, their eyes cruel, mocking my
impotence, my sorry life. But Moira wanted me to do this. I
didn't know how to take control, had no talent for power. But
she was giving it to me. I looked at her and she gave me a small
smile. Taking her hand, I smiled back and nodded.

She was beyond tired, lolling back and drifting off between
spasms. I would have to be quick or she might not be able to
finish the job. Fighting off embarrassment, I looked between
her legs at the mound of wiry black hair, the swollen opening,
gaping and wet with fluid. The mountain of her belly was the
only sign of a baby even though she'd been at this for hours.
Slowly touching her, gently as I could, I pushed my rough fingers in. I didn't know what I was supposed to feel.

"Reach as far as you can." Her teeth were clenched.

"I don't want to hurt you."

"Just do it."

Pushing harder, her body tightened around my hand, and I
had to wait for the pain to pass before I reached again. Until

finally there it was, a tiny mound of fuzz soft against my fingertips. Gently as I could, I felt the dip of its eyes, the small rise of its nose, the tiny mouth that would give it a voice to say its own name. It was face up, the back of its head wedged against Moira's spine.

"I can feel it, Moira." I hadn't expected the tears or the catch in my throat.

"Turn it just a little to the left." She was gasping, the pain making her voice fill up the room with each word.

The top of the small head fit easily into my fingertips. I turned it as gently as I knew how, but Moira screamed. It was the cry of the wounded rabbit I'd once found in Da's trap in the woods near our house. Knowing there'd be no supper, I'd released it anyway, holding its small, furry body close an instant. But I couldn't give Moira such relief. Instead I left my hand inside her while the baby's movement brought on another fit of pain, and then I turned it again, just a little. Then waited and turned, waited and turned. Moira was getting weaker; she didn't seem to know when to push. All the while Casey was whimpering and edging himself off his bed and closer to me.

"I can't do it any more." Moira sagged between the spasms, nodding off, coming to again. I watched her, squeezing her calf now and then to try to send encouragement. And suddenly the baby's head was moving freely. I wanted to shout, but when I looked up Moira's eyes were rolling back, her head lolling to one side.

"You have to push, Moira. I think it will come now, but you have to push."

"I can't. Leave me alone."

"Moira, just a little bit more. You can't give up."

"I can't do it." She wept as another wave hit her. "Just let me die."

"What?" My voice roared out of me and her eyes opened wide. "All this and now you want to die? I won't let you die. You can die later. Right now this baby needs to be born."

I was glad for the hate in her eyes. She was back with me. I steadied her then, lifting her so she had more support for her back, and her feet could push against the bedposts. I felt old, like this moment had been coming for years – a lifetime of bad choices and worse decisions bringing me here to prove myself. I took a deep breath.

"Now push, Moira. Hard. Just a few times. I'm sure it'll come."

She gathered herself into a clenched ball and pushed, her scream shattering the night. Three more times, and the baby dove into my waiting hands. Slimy and red and wrinkled, it sat cupped there, stunned by the light. I could only stare like a jackass, relieved and amazed. And then I knew just what to do. I wiped her small face with a cloth and squeezed her tiny nostrils together and down to get rid of the nasty stuff in there. Then I held her upside down and smacked her bottom. She cried out, angry, just like Moira.

Moira was looking at me like I was someone she didn't recognize. I smiled. "You can thank Doctor Gibson." I settled the baby on her slack belly, found scissors among her things and snipped the cord like I'd seen Gibson do for Casey. Moira gathered the now-howling baby girl into her arms, and I covered them both with a light blanket.

I brought Casey over. He reached out a shy finger to touch the baby's head and then shrunk into my arms. I took him back to his bed asking him to wait a minute, and went to Moira.

"Thank you," she said, looking at the baby, then smiling up at me.

We were awkward again, like when an intimate thing happens between people and suddenly the lantern is lit.

"You can clean up later. Right now you should get to know each other."

Pictures of Casey and Taffy rushed into my head and I fled outside, ran to the corner of the house and threw up, legs damn near buckling. After a long while I pulled myself to the well, scrubbed my hands and face and slicked back my hair. The gift I'd been working on was hidden off behind the house under an old tarp. It had taken weeks to finish. Carefully I crept into the house and set it at the foot of Moira's bed. The baby was sleeping in her arms, her mouth slightly open, eyes squeezed shut. I reached down to brush the hair from Moira's face.

"Thank God," I whispered.

She stirred and opened her eyes. "God had nothing to do with it," she said, and drifted off again.

Maybe she was right; maybe none of it had anything to do with God. Maybe we're just proving ourselves to each other. I felt brave thinking it, but lonely too, realizing some-one you'd called friend for so long a time was not who you thought he was.

I grabbed the heel of bread from the table, picked up Casey and set out to the Miller farm, the red dog trailing behind.

CHAPTER 25

MOIRA

ALARM RANG THROUGH my head when the baby shifted and stretched. I'd actually forgotten she was in my arms, had left her unattended as it were, and subject to harm. Her tiny, pursed lips sucked at the air, her fingers grasping, seeking comforts, perhaps the solace of my womb. Maybe the world was traumatizing in its brilliance, its overpowering smells, its cold air touching her virgin skin. She was minute and fragile and new, but wise with instinct, rooting now, signalling her need. I had forgotten what my breasts were for and fumbled with those foreign appendages, afraid her nose and mouth would disappear into their fullness and she would suffocate. She suckled weakly for a moment and promptly fell asleep as though knowledge of my presence was enough. For now.

Seconds later I was nodding away with her again, acutely aware of how sore and naked I was, unable to address either of our needs. I was draped with a blanket, the blood and sweat of labour drying on everything. A mother. That's what I'd become, what Dillan had helped me become, what was expected of a pregnant woman whether she was ready or not. Little choice. None really. Except now. Silas believed the birth would shake sense into my life, make my choices clear, the answers obvious. I looked at the baby. She was tiny and needy, but did she have to be mine in order to belong in the world? I was about to give in to exhaustion and sleep when I caught sight of the rocking chair, a beautifully crafted piece, the finished sheen of cherry wood.

It seemed only moments later I was awakened by Mrs. Miller bustling at the stove, warming water, readying soap and towels. She whisked the baby from my arms and bathed her, then diapered her, dressed her and cocooned her in a blanket. Mrs. Miller's competence was a relief. For all the babies I'd helped deliver, I had no idea how to care for one. Finally the tiny thing was settled in Mrs. Koch's crib. A startling combination of fear and hope shot through me. The bad luck of the crib's forbear might reach my child. Maybe I would be released from the responsibility and choices to come. But of course nothing would happen.

"She's beautiful, Moira." Mrs. Miller turned to me and smiled. "And now it's your turn."

"It's all right. Really. I'm fine." I pushed myself up, pulling the covers to my chin. "I'll just clean up and get dressed."

She laughed. "No, my dear, you'll do no such thing." She quickly grabbed the sheet and swept it off, grinning when I shrieked and pulled at my bunched nightgown. "There's a little warm water in the tub, enough for now. We'll get you in and heat some more so you can have a nice soak. Are you very sore?"

"No. Yes. I'll be fine."

"Moira, believe me. At this point you need to take any help you can get. That baby will be nursing at all hours. You won't get much sleep, and you'll wear yourself out keeping up with everything else, including Casey and Dillan." She pointed at the tub. "Get in."

The warmth of the water slid over parts of my body that had never known such pain. I was only vaguely aware of Mrs. Miller stripping the soiled bedclothes and replacing them with clean sheets and blankets she'd brought from home. She added more hot water and gently washed my hair, back and legs, rinsing away the sticky evidence of birth. Reclaimed at last, my body felt itself again, my slack stomach a welcome, if wrinkled, sight. I was a freed hostage, released from the baby and the fear of its birth.

The baby cried in the crib and I leapt to my feet, splashing water on the floor. A pain, almost as intense as a contraction, gripped me. I doubled over, my euphoria premature.

"It's okay, Moira. It's an afterpain. Try to breathe." Mrs. Miller's hand on my arm was strong, steadying. "You get dried off and dressed. I'll rock her for a bit 'til you're ready."

Father claimed afterpains were nonsense, a woman's attempt to get back the attention transferred to the baby on its arrival. I'd have something to tell him.

"Thank you." The rough towel rubbed over the pores of my shivering skin. I dressed in a clean nightgown and gingerly sat in the rocking chair. Its arm fitted snugly in my hand, each spindle perfectly carved. I swallowed hard around the lump in my throat. Mrs. Miller caught this moment and nodded.

"Why are you doing this?" I asked.

"Why?" She didn't appear surprised by the question. "I'm here because I know how alone a person in your position can be."

"Did you have no one to help you when your first baby came?"

"They could have helped. But they chose not to." The edge in her voice carried a hint of sadness with it.

Exhaustion overcame curiosity about what she might mean.

"Here let's get her fed." She settled the baby in my arms. Her tiny tummy met my own. "It's a little tricky the first few times. You have to tuck her right into you."

Positioning her, learning to have her latch on rather than nibble and bite, burping, diapering. By the time we laid her in the crib again, I could barely stand. "I think you must have been a very good mother."

"I did all right."

"But why would no one help you?" I crawled into bed, melting into crisp sheets and blankets that smelled of pure summer days.

"Let's just say I'm more like you than you know."

My eyes fluttered open, but closed again of their own accord.

"I'll be leaving now and coming back in a few hours. If you need anything sooner, have Dillan come for me."

"Thank you." I didn't hear the door close.

✥ ✥ ✥

CHAPTER 26

ONLY THE MILLERS came to see us in the month after the baby was born. I was happy when Carla finally showed up, riding bareback on a small pinto pony.

"I'm so sorry I couldn't come sooner," she said, and jumped down lightly where I stood surveying my neglected garden, looking past me then at Dillan standing in the doorway. A blush spread to her throat. Dillan came toward us, Casey in his arms, light-footed, almost dancing, and kicking up a little dust. I took Carla by the arm and led her over to him.

"Dillan, you remember Carla?"

"Yes, um...hello," he managed before Casey shrieked.

"HELLO. I CASEY."

"Well hello Casey." Carla was almost as loud.

We laughed, awkward adults saved by the silliness of a child, and trooped into the house, where I fixed cold tea.

"Your place looks wonderful." Carla swallowed her drink in one long chugging gulp, then blushed at Dillan. "This heat."

"It's taken a little while to get everything arranged," I said, conscious of how pleased I was she'd noticed, how domestic it was of me to care.

"And there's the infamous crib." Carla nodded to the corner where it stood next to my bed, all made up with the sheets and blankets the women had given me, a tiny handmade mobile hanging above it. "And such a beautiful girl," Carla crooned, bending over to stroke the baby's downy head.

"I think she's crazy to use the thing," Dillan said loudly.

"Dillan! He thinks me daft for accepting the bed of a dead infant."

"Well, you had to accept it." Carla looked at Dillan. "But I didn't think you'd use it, what with the ghosts and all."

"I've told her, but she won't listen to me." Dillan was a little too pleased to have found an ally.

"Don't tell me you're as superstitious as he is." Shaking my head, I got up to bring more tea and turned back to discover the two of them smiling shyly at one another. Carla reached up to smooth her hair. Dillan brushed dust off his work pants.

"It's just a crib and it's in perfectly good shape," I continued, though they barely nodded at me, so engrossed were they in their simple actions. "Besides, I'll only need it for a short time until the baby is weaned and I can find her a good home."

There was silence as the words sunk in. Then Carla drew a quick breath and stared at me, horror in her eyes. "You're not going to...I mean, how can you think of...?"

My pulse quickened, ears turning hot. "I can't raise a baby out here all alone."

"But if you took her home with you, back East." Her voice trailed off. I caught Dillan sending her a warning look. "Well, surely your family would help you?"

"I'm going home to be a doctor. I can't do both. It'll be better. For everyone."

Carla's eyes filled with tears of pity. For me. How dare she.

"You don't know what I'd be giving up." I hated that my voice broke. "What I already have."

"It's just that I look at you, this house, the baby." Carla stood up and flung her arms out. "You have everything," she whispered. "How could you throw it away?"

"Believe it or not, Carla..." What I wanted to say was angry and mean, but I couldn't stop. Carla was naive, her world narrow, her situation desperate. "This is hardly everything."

"Leave her alone." Dillan sat Casey in a chair and went to stand beside Carla. "Maybe some of us believe a child is important."

"Is that what you think? That I'm selfish?" My hands clenched. "I'm the exact opposite, and you're a fool." Eyes fixed on Carla, I gathered the baby in my arms. "I want to make sure this child has a good home, the life it deserves."

"But who can do that better than its mother?" Her eyes were wide with an innocence I wanted to slap away. It was a simple question, but I couldn't answer it.

"This is none of your business. Either of you. You don't know anything about me."

Quickly laying the baby in her crib, I fled outside, my legs stiff when I wished for swiftness, out of breath with anger. I yelled at the dog to stay home and walked past the corral where Mule stood slumbering in the sun, past the small garden. It was spindly and ugly, ungrateful for my efforts to pull the immortal weeds and haul endless buckets of water.

I looked back an instant. Dillan and Carla stood next to her horse, their heads together in discussion. I stormed into the field, knowing full well I left a trail of mangled stalks through Dillan's precious Red Fife wheat.

Finally I sat down in the neighbour's pasture near a few scrawny cows, the anger that had spurred me now a dull throb in every muscle. The horizon was flushed pink with the setting sun, and distant thunderclouds were coloured soft by the light. I heard the geese calling. They were scattered across the field, dining there on Dillan's hard work; and as I listened, their noise grew, filling the air like voices at a ceilidh, all cackling and giggling and grunting and posturing. Gossiping. Everyone thought I was wrong, my plan stupid or worse, selfish. Maybe I was the one who was naive to think it could all be decided so easily, and with such certainty. A life was in the balance and I was the scale. I was impatient with the uncertain woman I'd become, my old self weighed on one hand, the newborn girl on the other.

"She's expecting," people would say of a pregnant woman. Until now I hadn't known what that meant. It was the expectations I hadn't been prepared for. Expectations came from everyone, parents, friends, acquaintances. They saw a pregnant woman and instantly made assumptions. She was married, she was desperately happy to be having a child, she would love it unconditionally and she would never, ever, think of giving it away.

Who better to raise my child? If Carla knew my mother she'd have proof that some women lack the basic instincts for mothering, the unconditional kind of love required. Maybe

I'd inherited my mother's inability. Maybe I just didn't have it in me. Or maybe Dillan was right, and I was being selfish. I'd seen how children robbed women of their own lives. I'd delivered babies into homes already stuffed with them, the mothers overwhelmed and left with little room for choices.

Sitting there on the edge of the field, I wrapped my arms around my belly and felt the slack skin where the baby had made its home, remembered slow ripples across taut skin, the swift jab of a tiny foot. Rocking back and forth, my thoughts mingled with the sounds of the party in the wheat field. I had my answer for Carla.

CHAPTER 27

DILLAN

THE WIND SWARMED round the house, sucking at the greased paper hung across one window, pushing the canvas sack out the other. I stood in the door and watched it come, shoulders hunched with listening. It had been building for hours, the thin grey horizon gathering itself into a long barrel that rolled toward us. The cloud was almost white where it moved and spun high above us, black on the bottom part surging ahead.

I went out into the yard for a better look. The great white thresher, Silas had warned, telling me the stock would fend for themselves in such a storm, leaving out any mention of what it might do to the crops. The Red Fife was almost ready for harvesting, and now there might be nothing to show for it.

Moira was standing in the doorway, the baby in her arms, Casey clutching her thigh. She searched the sky, then looked at me like I had the answers. "What's it doing?" she called.

Casey followed close. He'd been twitching all day, like the boiling sky and sharp air were scaring him too. The wind grew then, lashing out and drawing back, gusting harder every time. The hot, dry air crackled, needing some kind of release from the late-July spell of heat and dust.

"I think we're in for it." The wind died a little just as I spoke, tempting me to hope, but then seemed to take a deep breath and pushed it out hard and fast from the southeast, the change in direction making it seem more of a threat. The dust and grit stung my face. Casey covered his and cried, sending Moira inside with him.

I kept my head down against the wind. It was hard to see for the dust blowing. Mule and Nelly were in the small corral

I'd built from small trees. I'd finally been able to buy the big Percheron from Silas. She lowered her head, waiting for the scratch I always gave her. Instead I slapped her on the neck. She jumped back, wheeled around and trotted out the gate toward the dried-up slough. Mule looked confused. He never left the corral except when I took him out. He waited, looking at me like Moira had, like I could somehow change what was happening. It was a relief when he finally followed Nelly.

We had a half-dozen small pigs. Local families had given them to Moira as payment for bits of doctoring. They came running, looking for slop. The animals had learned to get along in their small space, and the open gate and my waving arms surprised them. Any other time, I'd have chased them with sticks, thrown rocks to head them back to the pen. They rushed around in circles, tried to head back to the corral, bolting away at the last second when I stomped at them from inside the gate. Finally they shuffled off with their heads down, ending up under the tree by the house. It was all I could do for them.

The red dog was running circles around me. He was a useless thing, shittin' in the yard and chasing the chickens. I kicked at him now and he ran away round the side of the house.

The field was just beyond. My gut felt heavy seeing the heads of wheat bent almost to the ground by the wind. The brittle stalks couldn't survive. Blinking dust, I headed to the house. It wasn't much of a fortress, just stood there looking puny in the wind. We'd survive or we would not. The storm didn't give a fug either way.

The long barrel of cloud swirled right above my head. I started to pray, the words whipped out of my mouth and flung at the sky. "Please God, let us be all right, and if you could somehow keep the crops standing?" I didn't want to ask for too much. I hadn't prayed since Taffy. Dust blew into the house with me, and I heaved the door shut. The thick sod insulated us from the noise, but Casey's eyes were still huge, his body rigid. He ran over and threw his arms around my knees.

"I think we should put that extra sod in the windows

for now. I thought we wouldn't need it until winter." Moira laughed nervously.

Soon the house felt like a tomb, all light blocked by the chunks of dirt and grass stuffed in the windows. I lit a lantern and we sat on the two chairs, facing one another, Casey between us on the floor, each of us alone in our listening.

"Do you think the wheat will be able to stand this?" asked Moira.

"I don't know."

"It would be a shame if it was flattened." She was like a crowbar trying to open me up to the fear hiding just under my skin.

"Uh-huh."

"What'll we do if we lose the crop?"

"It's just a storm. Stop harping." The muscles in my jaw hurt.

"I need material to start some new clothes for Casey. He's grown so much. And you'll need some decent things to wear into town this winter." The words came rushing out of her, and she jumped a little as another blast of wind rattled the door. "The produce from the garden won't last long. It was a pretty dismal first attempt." Her hand played round her lips.

"Why don't you just shut the hell up?" The words leapt out of my mouth, and she sat back quickly. "It's just a storm. And what the hell do you care what I wear? You're not my wife."

Casey started to cry. He wasn't used to anger or the big voice with it.

"I'm only trying to be realistic." Her voice was pinched.

"But all your worrying won't help. You can go on talking but it won't change what God delivers. I know that for sure." I heard Mother's defeated voice in the words, felt washed out by their truth.

Moira stared at me for a long minute. "What a complete truck of horse manure," she finally said. "You tell me how God is responsible. It is just a storm, like you said. Not revenge, not a curse, not anything your voodoo Catholic brain can come up with."

The house groaned. She sounded like my teachers in Arichat, their voices saying it was useless trying to get anything through my thick skull. Casey had got down on the floor and was playing. He was getting used to the sounds of the storm, us raising our voices to hear over it.

"Maybe it's a punishment," I said.

"For what? For being alive?"

"For taking Taffy away." My face felt like it was crumpling in on itself. "For letting her die."

The tension in my shoulders started my head pounding.

"What is it, Dillan?" Moira's voice came from far away.

"I took Taffy to Halifax where we had nothing and no one. She tried so hard, did everything she could to prepare." My chest hurt so I could hardly breathe. "And she still died."

"But if there was nothing the doctor could do...?"

The answer to her question was one I hadn't ever wanted to say out loud. But the storm, the possibilities of what could happen, I wanted her to know. Moira leaned over the baby in her arms to hear me.

"I didn't call the doctor. She didn't die because of Casey. She had the typhoid."

Moira didn't move.

"She got it because we lived in filth." I could barely hear my own words. "She got sicker and sicker because I didn't think a doctor could help."

The wind rose and shook the house. I had taken away any chance Taffy had. Casey could have died too. I looked at him sitting on the floor, playing with a cup and spoon, startling at the bang of the door in the wind. "Oh God." I clutched at the pain in my skull and felt her hand on my knee, real gentle.

"Silas told me about the typhoid," she said. "But Dillan, things happen. When you love each other" – her voice seemed to come from a great distance – "you don't think anything bad can possibly happen because you've got all that love to bank on." She stopped talking and stared at the floor. "Or at least you think you do."

"We did."

"Oh I'm sure you did." She studied me, and then straightened. "But tell me, why didn't Taffy tell you to get a doctor?" Her voice was harder now. "And earlier, why did she stay in Halifax if it was so terrible?"

I tensed. "She was a good wife."

"Oh yes, a good wife." She was being sarcastic, and I flinched, wishing I hadn't. "I think you mistake devotion for love. She stayed with you because she wouldn't do what her good common sense told her to do, wouldn't just put her foot down." Moira's voice rose above the sound of the wind. "She was taught to be obedient until death do us part. And it did."

I felt like she'd kicked me in the head. I stood and backed away from the fire burning in her eyes. Moira hadn't been there when Taffy stood up to her father, stood up for me. "You would damn yourself to a life of poverty for this man?" her father had asked. "Wherever he goes..." I heard Taffy's answer like she'd said it just yesterday. Saw her father shake his fist. "Be damned then. The both of you."

Moira was wrong. "She stayed with me because she wanted to," I said, knowing it was a poor defense of my dead wife. The house seemed to be humming now, the wind testing the sod's strength.

"She went with you because she was weak. Let a man decide her fate. It wasn't your fault," Moira said, glancing up at the ceiling as rain began pounding against the roof. "It was her own choice. When you realize that fact, you'll let go of this useless guilt you wrap your whole life in."

"She was weak? If you were half the woman Taffy was, you wouldn't have ended up here. Knocked up and alone, practically selling yourself. At least Taffy had her dignity."

"Dignity?" said Moira. "While dying in her own filth? I've seen typhoid, Dillan. I know how ugly it is." She glared at me, poking at me worse than any man ever had. "There is no dignity in dying because she didn't have the courage to make decisions for herself."

"What the hell do you know of courage?"

"I'm here aren't I? That took courage."

159

"And what does that prove?"

"That Taffy's not."

"You bitch."

I raised my fist at her. The fear in her eyes quickly turned to defiance, as though this was what she'd expected, that my anger proved her right. Fear was in Mother's face when Da came home drunk and angry. It was in Taffy's face when she'd stood up to her father. There was movement on the floor, Casey still there between us. He was watching me close, his eyes turning to my raised fist, a kind of awe coming over him as though he sensed what was about to happen. My anger dissolved; I'd allowed my son to see the violence of a trapped man. Shame filled me up.

And then the storm hit.

The door flew open. Rain drove in at an impossible angle and quickly puddled on the floor. Casey screamed and Moira grabbed him up in her free arm while I rushed to push at the door.

"Oh my good Christ." The rain shot like slivers into my face and instantly soaked through my clothes. Lightning flashed so bright I could almost see the bones in my hands held out in front of me. Another bolt shot across the sky, white veins of power sparking off in every direction. A crack of thunder exploded around us and the house shook. It was like my feet had grown roots. I couldn't move, couldn't take my eyes off the blackness outside. Another flash lit the land like an instant of sun and I saw it again. Not more than a half mile away, a black funnel hung from the boiling mass of cloud. The wind was so strong I had to brace myself against the door frame to stand upright. Another crack sounded, as though the sky and earth were in a fight to outdo one another. Casey screamed. I turned to see the fear in Moira's eyes. She had seen the funnel too.

"Shut the damn door," she yelled. The dishes rattled in the cupboard. "Oh God, my china." With Casey and the baby in her arms, she rushed to rescue the china, as though that mattered now.

"Leave it, Moira," I hollered. "Get them under the bed."

In the battle to close the door, I lost my grip and it banged against my shoulder and across my forehead. I fell backward, but grabbed the door in time to steady myself by pushing against it. I felt something warm trickle down my cheek. Anger gave me the strength to heave the door shut. At the last instant I caught sight of the monster, only a quarter mile away now, but a little to the north. "It might miss us," I yelled, but when I turned there was only blackness.

The lamp had blown out. The roar of the wind was like the sound of a train, drowning out all other sound so I wondered if I was even breathing. I stood an instant in a darkness that had swallowed my world, life cut down to what I was at that moment, a man at the mercy of God. Another flash of light came through the cracks in the sod, and I saw feet sticking out from under Moira's bed. Casey's feet. The storm could take me, but I would not let it take Casey.

"I'm here, boy," I shouted into the darkness.

I felt my way over to the bed, then reached underneath and touched firm flesh. Another flash of lightning, and I saw Moira's face only inches from mine. Casey was clutching at her neck, the baby buried in her breast. She inched back toward the wall to make room, and I quickly rolled under as another strong gust of wind blew the sod out of the windows.

"My teacups," Moira moaned as the dishes rattled in the cupboard again. "I can't lose them." I felt her body shaking.

"It'll be okay." I said it like I knew what I was talking about. "I think it's heading north."

"I've never heard anything like it," she said, her voice a choked whisper.

I reached across the small ones and put my hand on her shoulder, feeling awkward. What the hell did I know of comforting? Her muscles tensed and she shifted a little closer to me, Casey's small bum pressing into the curve of my stomach. The wind slammed against the house again. Rain beat on the roof so hard I could hear it leaking into the room. I was almost getting used to the fury of the storm, and my fear. We lay there listening for the thunder after each flash of lightning.

Gradually Casey's breathing became even, and before long he was snoring lightly.

"I think he's asleep." Moira sounded relieved.

There was another long silence, the baby gurgling, and then I could feel Moira tensing to speak. "I'm sorry about Taffy," she said quietly. "About what I said."

I didn't know what to say to her apology. I'd never been offered one.

"You loved her. You did what you thought was best."

"It wasn't though. The best."

Casey turned toward me, grabbing at me with his tiny hands. I couldn't say anything for the tears in my eyes, my throat working against the lump growing there. The wind seemed less bent on killing us now. There was a faint glow coming in the windows, and I knew it was almost dawn. I started to drift between wake and sleep.

"I knew you wouldn't hit me," she said. "You're a decent person, Dillan."

"You think so?"

"Yes, I believe you are."

CHAPTER 28

MOIRA

A VOICE FROM OUTSIDE pushed through the fog of sleep and I woke, struggling for breath against Dillan's arm heavy across my neck. Casey started to wail. Dillan swore as he woke and quickly rolled out from under the bed, pulling Casey behind him, then reached back to take the baby from me. I squirmed out, my dress twisted above my thighs, and I pushed up on all fours. Silas was across the room trying not to look, holding up the door, which hung crookedly from the top hinge. He righted it and then came in to take the baby from Dillan.

I straightened my dress and smoothed my hair, stupidly hoping to avoid the inevitable: the mess, the dirt floor transformed to mud by the rain, sod blown out of the windows, the soaked crib. The house smelled of dank earth and musty bedding.

"Needs a bit of cleaning up, is all," Dillan said.

I barely heard him, my eyes fixed on the blue-and-white china fragments littering the cupboard top. I went over to it, something disintegrating inside as I gathered one small piece after another in my hands.

"Maybe we can fix them...," he said.

I glared at him. "You wouldn't let me save them."

"You needed to save the kids more than this junk."

I was suddenly hot with anger and shook my fist in Dillan's face. I could have saved both.

"It's okay, Moira," Silas said sharply. "You're okay now."

He led me over to a chair and put the baby into my arms. In silence the two men picked up the remaining shards and piled them into the tin wash basin, still intact after the storm. Only the strong and ugly survive in this place, I thought.

I watched Casey squish mud through his fingers.

"It's a mess," said Silas. "But at least you're all alive."

"The animals?" Dillan's eyes were suddenly frantic.

"The big draft is in a field over by my place. But I haven't seen Mule. And you've lost two of the pigs," he said.

Dillan raced outside calling for Mule and Nelly.

Silas eyed me then, as though measuring my ability to handle more bad news. "Moira, I need you to come with me." His voice was suddenly urgent. "Mrs. Schmidt's broken her arm. She fell down the cellar steps, rushing to get out of the storm. Carla came by this morning. Says her mother's in a lot of pain."

I couldn't imagine being more exhausted, but the news brought me to my feet. Carla would be frightened. And I had to help. She was a simple person, but good, the only woman besides Mrs. Miller and Annie to make an effort at friendship. Silas went outside with Casey while I quickly nursed the baby and wound my hair up into a bun. Remarkably, the bucket by the door had not spilled, and I splashed a little water over my face. Grabbing my black bag in one hand, I scooped the baby up with the other and headed outside. The two men stood talking by the wagon, Dillan's face bright with relief.

"The wheat doesn't look too bad from here," he said.

"Yes, considering." Silas nodded and hoisted Casey up, pushing him into Dillan's arms. "We're going to help Mrs. Schmidt."

"But what about the mess here?" Dillan whined. "Who's going to help me?"

His voice in the night had been so reassuring, his arm strong across my shoulder – where did that man get to in the light of day? Maybe only the thought of death gave him courage. The thought made me shiver.

"We shouldn't be long," said Silas. "Clean up what you can, and we'll help when we get back."

Dillan scowled and stalked off into the house with Casey.

"He's not very happy about this," I said.

"He'll get over it. That man needs to understand he can handle some things on his own." Silas stopped for a moment to survey the scene. "Just some boards need fixing on the corral, sod to repair the roof. It'll be good for him."

He grinned and helped me into the wagon. Within minutes he was pointing out small buildings in the distance that were the Schmidt farm. I'd never noticed them before, but somehow the sun burning off the previous night's rain made the flat expanse shimmer and images rise up out of the ground, closer, bigger.

"It's a mirage," I said. "Seems like I could reach out and touch it."

"Every once in a while, when the air and light are just right, it'll do that."

Simple. Air and light in the right combination rescuing the landscape from its sameness, giving it a new look, new possibilities. Maybe the transformative light would find me, offer up a bigger life than what I'd expected from the prairie, make me more than the forsaken daughter, the not-quite doctor, the dollybird. It was a comforting thought, lulling me along with the creaking of wheels and harness, the plodding of the horses' hooves.

To the right of the trail, several planks lay askew on the ground, looking like broken bones. I meant to ask Silas if they'd been deposited there by the twister, but he seemed distant.

"Is your place okay?" I asked.

"I've got some roof repairs to do, windows that need replacing."

For the first time, I wondered about where he lived and imagined a large farmhouse, Silas alone in all those rooms with the ghost of his wife in the kitchen, that of his child peeking through dust-caked second-storey windows.

"The worst thing," he continued, "is I lost most of the trees I planted when I first bought the place. They were finally getting a good size to provide some shelter. Some beauty." He shook his head. "They take so long and then, bam, a storm can take them out like they're no more than matchsticks."

"It was really frightening," I said, surprised to hear myself say so. "On the island we have bad weather. Winter storms with lots of snow. Takes days to dig out. And in the summer, wind and rains that scare the life out of you. But we have neighbours to help if we need it. I don't know how people expect to survive out here."

"Luck and common sense. Maybe a little prayer," Silas said.

"Hmmph."

"I imagine you offered a prayer or two through last night."

I hadn't actually. Dillan had muttered his own wishes to God, but hearing them made me angry. He seemed to reach for prayer only when he'd already lost courage, and I'd needed Dillan to be brave in that storm, more than I'd needed God's help.

"I'm not one to preach. But I think there's something out there." Silas nodded toward the horizon. "Something can help us figure all this out. How to be deserving of being alive. And in the worst times, like last night, how to endure our circumstances."

"People die from their circumstances all the time, prayer or not."

He laughed, a big booming laugh, and pushed his glasses up to rub his eyes. "Oh come on now, Moira. It's not all that serious. Just a bit of talk."

It was not simply talk. His blue eyes shone with the wisdom of a man who had lived much. We came over a small rise, and beyond was a farmyard with a small wooden house resting like a lean-to against a large barn. The barn doors were open, and as we drove up I could see the line of horses' rumps protruding from their stalls. One of the loft doors had been torn off by the wind and lay in splintered pieces on the ground fifty feet away. What must have been a small chicken coop was flattened, the surviving chickens darting about the yard, pecking at the dirt, their wings flapping in a flurry of distress.

Carla came running from the house, scattering the hens, her long braids flying. She ran alongside the wagon and pulled on my arm before my feet hit the ground.

"Thank goodness you're here, Moira." She took the baby from me and hurried toward the house. "Mother is hurting really bad."

The faces of several young children peered out from behind the barn door. They vanished quickly when I smiled, so I wondered if they'd been real.

"We were all so frightened. The children wouldn't stop screaming. It was awful," Carla said, and started to cry. I put my arm around her shoulder. "There was a big bang and I thought the house was going to fall down. It was only the loft doors, but we didn't know that and went to the cellar. That's when Mother tripped." She hugged the baby tighter.

Silas came up beside her and steered her toward the barn. "You take care of the baby and keep the kids busy. Moira will have a look at your ma. I'm sure she'll get her fixed right up." He darted a glance at the house.

The bright morning light blinded me to the darkness inside. I stood in the doorway, pupils adjusting, and heard the woman's low moans and then an impatient male voice hushing her. He came into view out of the murkiness, a large, thick man with thinning grey hair and bushy eyebrows that knit together to form a peak. His appearance was comically threatening as he looked me up and down, his gaze wary, measuring. Maybe he'd been at the sodding, shared the contempt his wife had shown to me when she'd dragged Carla away as though I might corrupt her. After a moment he nodded.

"This way." He motioned to a corner of the room where the moaning had started again. I could only make out a bulky form sitting in a chair. He pulled sod out of the windows as we entered, the light spilling into a room surprisingly tidy, given the chaos of the storm the night before. Beds were tucked into every available corner, all made up, the floor swept, dishes neatly stacked on shelves in an oak cabinet.

A long bench ran the length of one wall, providing seating on one side of a huge table that was surrounded by chairs on the other three sides. The black wood stove in the middle of the room was unlit, yet warmth emanated from the room. This was Carla's mother's home, a home she cared to make welcoming. Now that I was helping her, perhaps she'd accept me as Carla's friend.

She sat in an armchair, a light wool blanket thrown over her, grimacing with pain. I took a step toward her, and she threw the blanket off with one hand and tried to stand.

"No." I had spoken too loudly. "I mean, you're fine where you are. I can examine your arm there."

"I don't need anything." Beneath Mrs. Schmidt's gruff voice, the flutter of tears.

"But maybe I can help."

"I don't need anything," she said again, a little softer now.

"You let her look, Mama," Mr. Schmidt barked, as though he simply wanted the whole episode over with, then left us to go outside. Mrs. Schmidt shrank from me. I'd seen it before, patients afraid my father might inflict worse pain than what they were already experiencing.

"I'll try not to hurt you. I just want to see if there's anything I can do for your arm." When I reached out to reassure her, she seemed to relax a little, and gazed past my outstretched fingers into my face.

Mrs. Schmidt was not as old as I'd thought, maybe thirty-five, and considerably younger than her husband. When I reached for her arm, she squirmed, then took a deep breath and gingerly lifted it with her other. Wincing again, she kept her eyes on my face. The upper wrist plate was jammed over the bottom, and the bone in her forearm possibly broken. I went outside and called Silas and Carla. Mr. Schmidt was no-where to be seen.

"She'll be all right, Carla. But she must be in a great deal of pain. I can give her a cocaine mix for that." Carla moved to hug me. I hurried on. "But right now I need to realign her wrist bones. Can you explain that to her while I get my things? I think it'll be better coming from you. Tell her it will likely be painful, but if we don't do it, her wrist will never set properly."

Silas and I returned to the house just as Carla finished ex-plaining. Her mother nodded and looked resigned. I instruct-ed Silas where to stand, how to pull, and stood across from him with my hand around Mrs. Schmidt's forearm. Silas and

I looked at each other for an instant, gathering courage, then took a deep breath and pulled hard. The crunch of bone on bone was drowned out by shrieking. Mrs. Schmidt passed out just as her husband came crashing in.

"What the hell did you do?" he hollered and, seeing his wife slumped in the chair, he went still, his voice become a whisper. "Oh my God, you killed her?"

Silas almost laughed. "No, Gerhard. She's fainted." He patted Mr. Schmidt's back. "It's probably for the better. This way she won't feel as much pain."

I busied myself setting the splints on her arm, then wrapping them around and around with lengths from an old sheet Carla had cut for me. The arm was huge from the elbow down, but our contraption would keep it immobilized. Carla bathed her mother's face with a warm cloth and, when Mrs. Schmidt came to, we carefully helped her into bed, clothes and all.

"She'll need to rest now," I said pointedly to Mr. Schmidt. He'd been agitated and muttering to himself. I didn't like the man. "She's had quite a trauma. I've given her something for the pain, and she'll sleep for a while."

"Sleep?"

"Yes, she needs to sleep." I pronounced each word carefully, loudly. "And she'll need help if her wrist is going to heal. She can't be doing any work."

"Well." Carla's father puffed himself up to object, but Carla came over from the doorway where she'd been watching with some of the small children.

"I'll help her." She glared at her father. "You won't need to worry. I'll make sure everything gets done around here."

"But you're going to school," I couldn't stop myself from saying. "How will you...?"

"I think the Schmidts will work this out for themselves." Silas cut me off and handed over my scissors, motioning for me to put them in the bag, keeping me busy, keeping me out of the way. "Your work here is done, Moira," he said quietly.

He took the baby from the child who now held her and pulled me along out the door. When we were outside, I yanked my arm free and planted my feet.

"Carla can't do everything – all those children, and her mother. She's just a girl."

"Leave it alone, Moira." His impatience stung.

"It'll be weeks before her mother's arm is healed. She can't miss school."

"She has no choice right now," he said.

Carla called out just as we reached the wagon. She ran to us and flung her arms around me. "My mother says she feels better already."

I felt a familiar flush of pleasure at her gratitude, at my ability to help.

"I'm sorry for what I said to you, Moira," she said suddenly. "What you do with your life is none of my business."

I'd been so angry at Carla, and had imagined chastising her like she was a small child with a small child's limited experience of the world. I had wanted to tell her I was not like the women of this godforsaken place. I would have control over the direction of my life.

But her honesty was breathtaking. "I'm sorry too, Carla." She grinned wide and I hugged her quickly, felt the small knobs of her spine, the smooth contours of her ribs.

The trip home was quiet. I ached all over, my body suffused with exhaustion and tension from the storm, the night spent on the floor, the encounter with Carla's father. Every time the wagon hit a bump my lower back went into a spasm and my legs throbbed right down to my ankles. I'd barely had time to recover from the trauma of giving birth, for heaven's sake.

Silas remained silent, seemed disapproving.

"Well what?" I said.

"You have to accept that some people are different. The way they do things is different."

"I understand people."

"Your people, yes." He held up his hand to my objection. "But not these people, not parents who can't send their kids to school because they need them to work. It's not always the choice they want to make. They have to."

"But tell me why it's the women who always suffer most. I've seen poor women, Silas. Trapped women. I've treated their infected and stinking wombs, the venereal diseases they never asked for, their skin so chaffed it oozes. And they'll never escape, can't even imagine themselves doing more than working in the house, raising chickens and having babies." He thought he knew so much. "I've seen them, Silas. That's why I want more for Carla. For her to have choices."

"It's not that simple."

But how I wished it could be. Simple like the morning's mirage with its balance of light and air, all of us given whatever perfect combination might lift us beyond our circumstances. My doctoring had already given me choices, allowed me to be more than what people expected of a woman in this place. Maybe the light had already found me. Maybe it could find Carla too.

✥ ✥ ✥

CHAPTER 29

DILLAN

I WAS MAD MOIRA had gone off again, leaving me with the mess. But then, if I was honest, being mad made me feel worse about everything. She'd listened during the storm, when I was telling her things I hadn't told anyone. It was embarrassing, her knowing so much, but it was good too, like saying it out loud made it not as bad – Taffy and me and Taffy's dying.

I let Casey play in the mud in the middle of the kitchen while I picked everything up and took the mattresses and blankets outside to dry in the sun. Finally I carried him out to the well and ran water over his muddy arms and legs while he hollered like I was killing him. He giggled fits when I threw him up onto my shoulders, using fistfuls of my hair for handles. He bounced and whooped as we jogged to the other end of the field, checking for damage. There were plenty of bent stalks, but few had broken completely. A surprise and a relief. I ran my hand over the carpet of green.

"It's tough, that Red Fife. Just like they told me."

Casey bent his head around to look at me from the side. "Tough." He nodded.

We found Nelly nearby in a patch of scrub brush, asleep with her nose to the wind. A piece of twine from my pocket was enough for a halter, and I threw Casey on her back and led her home. Mrs. Miller was on the porch waiting for us.

"Where's Moira?" There were deep furrows in her forehead, and she looked half worried, half mad. "Is everyone okay here?"

"We're fine. Moira's gone with Silas to help Carla's mother. Hurt herself in the storm."

"Oh for goodness sake, Dillan." Now she was mad. "With the baby? What were you thinking, letting her go?"

"Hey, they never asked my opinion, and she wouldn't listen to me anyway." I hoisted Casey down. "Say, could you watch him for a while? I'd like to go find Mule."

Out back of the house, I found two weanling pigs huddled together against the wall, their slick pink bodies one on top of the other, dead. They might have died of fright, or been suffocated by one another, or been slammed against the house. I ran my hand over the firm back that was just starting to prickle with wiry hair and pulled the piglet off its brother. It was a shame. I found the others wandering nearby, rooting at the grass and dirt.

I went looking for Mule, walking about half a mile to a slough ringed by thorny buckbrush and wild rose bushes. Getting closer, I saw the coyote before it saw me and quickly loped away. There was another movement in the bush, and then Mule's nasal bray. I ran into it, the sharp thorns raking my arms and tearing at my shirt sleeves.

At first Mule looked kinda contented standing in the shade. But the horror rose up at me as I got closer, and Mule's bulging eyes came into focus, his throat working hard. His tongue was huge with swelling and stuck out the side of his mouth, hanging there like a thing already dead. His halter was tangled in the branches and his thrashing about had wound the knot at his throat into a tightening noose. The coyote had been there. Small chunks of meat were gone from Mule's haunch and rear end. I was close to sick.

Mule stood still now, his eyes fading and rolling back in his head. Moving closer to him only scared him, and he thrashed his hind legs, trying to find footing in the mud he'd already churned into a slick mess. His carrying on made him weaker still, and he fell back and to the side. And the noose tightened.

"Oh shit." I ran to his side, but he flailed again, his front hooves just missing my head, so I had to get back. "Stop, Mule. I gotta help you."

His strength sputtered out. He stopped struggling and

waited for whatever was coming. A high-pitched wheeze squeezed out from his pinched windpipe. The cheek strap was pulled tight across his one eye, crushing it. The strap at his neck had gouged through hair and skin; white flesh pulsed under it. I rushed in and worked at the leather halter with my knife.

"Shit, shit, shit. Come on goddammit." It was like the knife wasn't attached to my hand. No matter what I did, I couldn't make it cut faster. One by one the strands broke while Mule's gasps became small puffs, and finally there was only the sound of the blade scratching through rope. The last strands split, the rope snapped back and Mule's heavy body fell, knocking me on my ass in the mud, his head in my lap. I searched his eyes; they were glazed and gone black.

"Jesus Christ, Mule. Not you too." I heard a wail that grew louder, not knowing the sound was coming from my own mouth. I sat there stunned a minute. And then I wanted to yell. At Moira for taking off again. At myself for not getting here earlier. For Mule being dead.

I rubbed Mule's stringy mane, hard at first and then more slowly 'cause it made me feel better doing it, my breathing slowing down too, so's I could think. Sometimes bad things happen, Moira had said. They just happen. Like Taffy dying. Like now. I didn't make it storm, didn't lead Mule to this bush or sic the coyote on him. And I might have taken my time coming out here anyway, fixing something in the house, or nailing a loose board on the corral, or cleaning up the dead pigs. I'd spent a lot of my life looking to blame myself for all the bad things, strangling myself with guilt. I was like Mule pulling on his halter, doing the very thing that made it worse, that killed him. But there was no need to blame anyone. And maybe I could stop killing myself.

CHAPTER 30

MOIRA

"HAVE YOU NAMED her then?"

Dillan was pouring water into a basin to wash up. He'd just come in from the field, face black with dirt, his dusty coveralls now in a heap by the door. His red-rimmed eyes blinked constantly, swollen nose dripping.

"Not yet." It was none of his concern. "I'll name her when I'm ready."

"But she's three months old for God's sake. You can't just keep calling her baby."

When I didn't answer, he shrugged as though I was daft, lathered soap to wash, rinsed and grabbed a towel off the chair next to the table.

"Hey that's my dishtowel." He was absolutely infuriating. "Maybe you should help with the washing, and then you'd stop making so much of it."

He laughed. "Moira, I can't help getting dirty. The binders kick up so much dust I can hardly see. It's bound to stick to me."

Dust was embedded in the creases of his eyes, awns stuck in his hair. He was quiet, studying me. I was ugly, hair barely contained in a bun, clothes the same as I'd worn the previous day, no powder to hide dark rings under my eyes every morning. The baby had croup.

"Baby up all night again?" he asked.

"Not that you'd notice."

"Who could sleep through that racket? But there's nothing I can do for her."

"I know." The kettle of soup was heavy, and it landed on the table with a thud. I could never have imagined this kind of exhaustion. I was in some kind of purgatory, wandering from one chore to another, constantly reminding myself to stay awake.

"The wet nurse used to dip her finger in whiskey and let Casey suck on it." Dillan sat down beside the boy, who banged a spoon on the table. "It put you to sleep every time, didn't it?" Casey giggled when Dillan tickled him.

"Whiskey for a baby. I would never."

Dillan dished up some soup, sharing a slice of bread with his son. "You told me once," he said through a mouthful, "what you planned to name her. I recall it was a good Scottish name."

It would have been justice to smack the sarcasm out of his voice. When I watched her obsessively, marvelled at the purity of her sleeping face, worried at the pitch of her insistent cry, I knew what I wanted to call her all right. But I couldn't bring myself to make it official, the weight of the choices preventing it, the weight of her small life in the balance. I let him eat his lunch in silence.

"I'm taking some harness over to the Millers' to get fixed. Nelly's gonna walk right out of the field on me if I don't." He laced up his boots. "I have to get the rest of the crop cut. Threshing crew will be here soon."

He stood up tall, proud to use the words in relation to himself. Farmers' words. I wondered if the language of motherhood would ever find my tongue.

"I'll take Casey with me so you can get some rest." He held out his hand to the boy.

I nodded from where I stood at the sink. The door slammed, and I released my breath in a ragged sigh. How easily he made me question everything. The baby's cry sent a quiver through my tender breasts. Early on it had been torture every time the baby latched on; sometimes it still was if I didn't get to feeding her soon enough. No one had warned me, not the good doctor Berkowski. Not even my father.

Sitting in the rocker, breasts relieved, I watched the baby, stroked her downy head and crooned small ditties remembered from childhood. I was becoming sentimental, every spare minute spent watching the child, listening to her, wondering that she had come from me. A dusting of sadness came over me. Evan didn't even know his baby had been born, or that she was a girl, that she was perfect. It wasn't fair. But it wasn't fair to leave her without a name either, to keep her waiting as though she weren't important enough to have one.

If I was honest it wasn't only her life in the balance; I'd delayed her naming for my sake as well. The dreams I had for my future had never included a baby. They were of myself, alone with my black bag, riding off like Father to help people, to cure them, even to save them from themselves as he'd tried to do. I would be respected, maybe revered for my wisdom and knowledge, and I would not be shackled by the demands placed on other women. If I was really honest, the picture hadn't included Evan either. For as much as we'd shown love to each other, his love wasn't something I'd thought I would need.

But the baby was mine. That was one true thing. I looked down at her, clasping my finger in her small hand, kneading my breast with the other, her small mouth pursed and rooting for my nipple. Suddenly she looked directly at me, gazing intently until the clouds dissipated from her small grey eyes and the pupils became clear and quizzical, seeing me, all of me. We looked at one another a long moment before her eyes relaxed into recognition of a bond that belonged with the smell and touch already imprinted into her trust. It was her trust that swallowed me up, crowded out the sadness and pain of the past few months, pushed away the deadness. And in that moment I knew she would always be mine, that somehow whatever my future held, she would be part of it.

"Shannon Louise," I whispered. "Your name is Shannon Louise."

"It's going to be hard doing it all," said Mrs. Miller when I showed up in her kitchen an hour later. "Doctoring. Raising her by yourself."

"I know, but I've decided to take her home as soon as I can." I'd walked to the Millers' farm, inhaling the pungent air of late summer, the smell of ripened crops and crisp grasses reinforcing my confidence in what was possible. I took a knife from the counter to slice bread for the lunch Mrs. Miller was preparing for her husband and Dillan. "My sister and father will help."

"Well, whatever happens, you'll manage because you have to. That's what I did. With George." She nodded out the window to where the two men worked on the harness just outside the barn doors.

"You had the community," I said, still prickling from the treatment I'd received.

"No dear, we didn't." She hesitated, smoothing loose hair back into the bun at the nape of her neck. "You see, I was a dollybird too."

"Oh." I felt a kind of relief. She knew me better than I thought.

She frowned. "I wasn't in your situation. Pregnant and all. But I had been working in the rooming house in town. The one you lived in." She paused. "With Annie."

I tried to keep the shock out of my face.

"Now I help the girls out when I can. Make sure they're eating properly, that they stay healthy as much as possible."

"I had no idea."

I recalled then the occasional surprise of freshly baked cinnamon buns and pies. Thought too of Annie. She'd only seen the baby once when I'd taken her to the doctor in town. Since then, I hadn't seen Annie for weeks.

"I was destitute. I didn't have a choice."

"But you're here." I gestured vaguely around her perfectly arranged kitchen.

"Yes, someone took pity on me, saw I wasn't made for that kind of life. In fact -" she sized me up-"I had already tried to kill myself. Cut my wrists. But I'm not very good at it I guess."

"Mrs. Miller!"

"There wasn't a reason to live." She smiled out the open

window and across the yard at the barn where the two men worried over the harness, their heads close. "Then George came along."

As though her thoughts had travelled across the yard, he looked toward the house.

"So he married you then? His dollybird?"

"No, we were never married. We live like a married couple, yes." She continued to set the table, carefully placing a knife and spoon alongside each setting. "That's what people couldn't abide. You see, George was already married to a woman down south in North Dakota. She was supposed to come up here after I got the place livable. But it never happened."

I looked out at the men. "You mean you just let her wait?"

"No. George sent her a letter, but she was so angry she wouldn't get an annulment. A Catholic, you know. Visions of hell I suppose."

"But think of her." I pictured a young woman waiting expectantly, her life carefully packed into a trunk, growing ever sadder as time passed and her hope wore thin.

"I'm sure it was terrible for her," said Mrs. Miller, wiping vigorously at the cupboard. "But she had family. She had choices that I didn't have. I'm quite sure I'd have been dead long ago if George hadn't come along."

"So you've lived this way, all this time?" I cringed the moment the words came out, the judgment in my voice making me a hypocrite.

"Some people call it sin." Mrs. Miller gestured around the room. "But is this life more sinful than living in a brothel?" Her eyes were probing. "I can tell you, I understand now I was never a bad person, only desperate. And it's the people who wouldn't help me, who've judged me all these years, who should bear any guilt. My conscience is clear."

I realized I was thinking like my mother, forming intractable opinions of everyone but myself, thinking my life and the choices I had to make were so much harder than anyone else's. Suddenly mine seemed almost easy. I picked up the baby and held her close.

"Mrs. Miller, I'm sorry."

"It's all right, dear. I thought you should know." She put her arm around my shoulders and squeezed hard.

"I've named her then," I said. "It's Shannon Louise."

She told me it was perfect.

PART 3

Moments of Grace

CHAPTER 31

DILLAN

I'D BEEN ABOUT to wake Casey from his nap and head out to the field when Carla showed up to see Moira and the baby, but they were gone with Silas to look after another patient. Didn't really have time for visiting, what with how busy I was cutting the crop, but I was glad to see Carla. It was awkward being alone with her. Felt like I had twelve tongues and none of them working, and finally I told her to wait and I'd make some tea. When I was done, bits of leaves floated in the pot and I gave it a quick stir. The tin cups rattled when I set them on the wobbly table in front of her, and I felt bad I had nothing better to serve it in. It was the only time I understood Moira's attachment to her fancy china.

"She finally named her," I said at last. "Shannon Louise."

"It's a strong name, don't you think?"

"She had the name already picked when I first met her. Don't know why it took her so long to say it."

"A name's an important thing," Carla said, staring into her cup.

She glanced up real shy, and my neck grew hot. I looked over at Casey snoring in his bed, his face still flushed with tears from our struggle over nap time. I guess the world was far too interesting to give up his exploring time. Carla poured tea for both of us, pretending not to notice the floating bits, then added a little cream. I liked how her small hands wrapped themselves around the cup, her fingers wound round it to hold it close to her chest, a small appreciation in that.

"Being a doctor makes things harder for Moira," she said. "She thinks she has more to prove than most. Most women anyway. People won't say it, but they think she's all right. You too."

"I don't know."

She cocked her head.

"It seems I haven't handled things very well. Farming. People," I said, and wished I hadn't, embarrassed at the whine creeping into my voice.

"Your crops look pretty good, considering the storm." She shrugged, her lips pinched tight like she was measuring me up. "And your animals are doing well."

"Mule died."

"I heard. But there was nothing you could do about that." She stirred her tea. "Just bad luck, I'd say."

Her grin was like a warm blanket, her words so sure. She'd set it all straight with two words – bad luck. I laughed at myself.

"And you helped Moira with the baby. The whole countryside's talking about that." Her small face grew big and alive. "Most of the men around here would have run the other way. They're saying you saved her life. The baby's too."

I was embarrassed she was looking at me like I was something special. "My wife, Taffy, you would have liked her," I said to change the subject.

"Yes? I heard she died giving birth. Sorry." She glanced at Casey. "I think she'd be glad you were able to help Moira."

I didn't set her straight, wanted her to believe my good deed was enough, a kind of redemption. Maybe it was. We both started at the sound of a wagon driving up. She leaned in close, and I could smell something sweet in her hair.

"I think you're a good person even if others want to talk." Her lips were warm and light on my cheek.

The wagon had stopped. A loud voice rang out. "Carla, what are you doing here?"

"Oh Lord, it's my father."

Her fear got into me. I told myself this was my home, and we'd done nothing wrong. I opened the door and stepped outside, Carla behind me. Her father stood by the wagon, hands on hips, feet planted like trunks an axe couldn't budge.

She went over to him.

"Tell Moira I was here then," Carla said loudly. "It's too bad I missed her. I wanted to see the baby again, especially now she has a name. Shannon Louise. Isn't it beautiful, Daddy?"

He didn't say a thing, just stood there with his hooded eyes fixed on me.

"Oh, and tell Moira I'll come by to help her with the preserves, and we can get that pork salted. She'll need help, what with the baby and all," Carla said, her words coming fast and forced.

Mr. Schmidt tied Carla's horse to the back of the wagon and heaved his large frame up. I chanced a wink at Carla and she grinned.

"The crew," Mr. Schmidt called out. "They're on their way here." He clucked to the horses. "You got everything cut and stooked yet?"

"What? Today?" I wasn't ready.

"The foreman says they'll start your wheat in a couple days." He was watching me, probably hoping I'd show some sign of panic. I went to work like an idiot then, finished cutting the crop, stooked it into sheaves so they'd be ready for the crew, my heart pounding with the thought of my first harvest.

The huge thresher rolled into the Red Fife two days later as promised. I jumped off Nelly, who was suddenly nervous. Or maybe it was me making her twitchy, excited about the massive machine, the wagons, the fifteen men busy hitching horses, preparing for the day. The crew boss was hollering instructions, and the others were shouting back and forth. The work was familiar, but new too, and the excitement of it churned in my gut. I was a little crazy, worrying that the men on the wagons were pitching the stooks carelessly and leaving the odd one twisted on the ground as though that grain didn't matter. It mattered to me. And when I ran about picking them up and throwing them into the thresher, the men gave each other a look, like I was a lunatic. Screw them.

Steam poured from the machine into the clear blue day and mingled with the dust and chaff so there was a sun-drenched haze over the field. My eyes itched and I was sneezing all the time, but I ignored it. My harvest was on.

The crew was paid by the bushel. A weighing device on the thresher tripped to make every half-bushel bag. I watched for a while, jumping up to check the scale myself, though the men didn't look too happy at my being there. But I'd heard of tampering, the scale set too low, farmers being cheated. Underweight bags caused trouble at the elevators too, buyers believing it was the farmer'd done the cheating.

The hours wore on, the bags stacking up on the wagon. When it was loaded, I drove it to the yard and neatly stacked the firm canvas sacks in the small shed I'd built off the corral. I counted them out loud, and Casey recorded each with a nail mark on the wall. I couldn't get the smile off my face. It was my crop, started as nothing but dirt. I'd seen it through to the end, the results of all the sweat and fear now safely stored. I'd be able to provide. I almost laughed out loud.

"There it is Casey." I threw him onto the top bag and spread my arms. "It's ours. All of it."

"Yeah well." Gabe stood in the door of the shed. "You got lucky."

"What are you doing here?" I wanted to take a hammer to the quiver in my voice.

"Had to get a job." He held one side of his nose and snorted a stream of snot from the other to the ground. I stepped between him and Casey sitting on the bags. "Seein's I lost everything in the storm. Need something to live on."

I'd heard about Gabe's crops being ruined and had been quietly glad, recalling the suffering in the girl's face and the beating he'd given me. I was thankful for God's good judgment in choosing whom to smite. "Bad luck I guess."

"Looks like you'll do all right," he said, and laughed a mean little snort. "But good luck runs out too." He swaggered away.

Mrs. Miller hollering "lunch" was met with a general roar

from the crew at the prospect of roasted chicken, fresh bread, preserves and pies. Moira tried to be pleasant, laughing at jokes I knew she didn't think were funny, gracious when the men complimented the food. They were respectful. I wondered how they'd treat her if they knew our real situation. Afterward everyone stretched out for a short rest, some talking quiet, some sound asleep on the ground. Gabe was eyeing Moira up and down like an animal sizing up prey. He gave her tits a good long stare – full with milk they were – and smirked. I tried to catch his eye, to warn him off, but the crew boss showed up at my elbow.

"Thought you should know. We'll work late as we can to-night and start about ten tomorrow." Joe rubbed dust out of tired, red eyes.

I hadn't trusted him at first, his accent being heavy and gut-teral like Gabe's. But I'd watched him run all day, feeling bad I couldn't keep up. He was a good boss. A good man.

"The dew should burn off by then if the sun's out strong," he said. "We'll get breakfast in town seein' as the missus has the new baby and all." He nodded at Moira collecting plates and coffee cups.

I didn't set him straight. There were at least some things I'd learned. "She'll be thankful for that small mercy, then."

Joe laughed and stomped over to the crew resting in the field. "Let's get back at it boys," he hollered. "Soon as we finish here, we gotta move south."

Row by row the thresher ate the stooks, the field left look-ing like a rough-shaven jaw. The end of the day brought a mix of exhaustion and happiness like I'd never known. By sunset the next day, the crop would be in.

The crew showed up a half-hour late the next morning, some holding their heads and sodding on about how much whiskey they'd drunk. Others moaning and walking as though their private parts were all but worn off with the heroic effort it took to keep the local whores happy. Moira shook her head, disgusted, while I only hoped their carrying on wouldn't affect the day's work.

"Shut up, you idiots," Joe hollered. "You're late and we've got plenty to do."

The men grumbled, but quickly got to work, climbing on the equipment to grease bearings and set the machines, harnessing horses. Those with the least experience and the biggest hangovers lined up, leaning on their pitchforks, ready to feed the giant thresher. By midmorning I could see we'd be done before dusk. My heart was thumping with the thought of it, though I was about ready to drop.

Moira served lunch without Mrs. Miller, who'd gone home to prepare for their harvest. She'd laid out the meal on a large rock, and the men stood or sat in small circles eating. With the belching of the steam engine stopped, it was peaceful in the field. The whir and grind of it had egged us all on like someone standing behind you ready to kick your ass if you even thought about slacking off. I sat with my back against a wagon, picking my teeth with a sliver of wood, my belly full and eyes heavy.

Gabe headed up to the rock to help himself to seconds. Moira must have felt his breath on her neck, he was that close. My vision was blurred with the heat and dust and midday stupor, but I saw Gabe's arm brush across her chest. It took a second to clear my head, but I knew what I saw. Moira flinched and jumped back. Before she could get far enough away, he grabbed her ass. She shrieked, turned real quick and slapped his face. I couldn't believe she'd go after him and was proud of her, considering my own fear. He raised his arm to fend her off and laughed. The other men looked at me to do something.

"What are you doing?" an older man called out, and moved slowly toward Gabe.

"Don't worry, boys. She don't mind," Gabe said, sneering.

"How dare you," Moira said, then looked at me. Finally I found my feet and took a quick step.

"You." Gabe pointed his stubby finger at me. "What does it matter to you? She's just a damn dollybird you found at Penny's whorehouse."

Moira gasped and Gabe made a point of looking her up

and down. "Although a mighty attractive dollybird, wouldn't you say?" He reached out and flicked at a strand of her hair. "I was with Annie last night. She says hello."

Moira looked at me with wide eyes, asking me to help. The men seemed as shocked as I was to think she'd come from that place. She'd been living in my home, raising my child, but I didn't know her, hadn't even thought to ask, just trusting her like an idiot. Some of the men were watching Moira with growing interest, like she was on sale at Obi's hardware. Others stared at their boots. When I finally looked at Moira she was staring at me, waiting for me to stand up for her. When I didn't say a thing I saw how angry she was, the red flush creeping up her neck.

"I am a dollybird." Her voice was loud and defiant. "And now I am a mother."

Gabe snorted.

"And I have never sold myself to anyone," she said to me, then turned back to Gabe. "Don't you ever touch me again."

My ears felt hot with shame. There was hurt and disappointment in her eyes. And I knew what I'd done.

"No difference between a whore and a dollybird." Gabe stared at me. A challenge. "Maybe you're screwing her, now the bastard baby's out of the way. Maybe you'll share her with the rest of us."

"That's enough, Gabe," someone muttered and walked away.

Joe came round from the back of the house. "What's going on here?" His voice was low with suspicion.

It broke the spell they'd been fixed under, and one by one the men shuffled past Moira with their heads down. House building, well digging, the tornado; she'd been through it all with me and Casey. She'd said I was a decent human being. My gut did a little leap thinking of how I'd helped bring Shannon into the world. Right then I hated myself more than I ever had. Even more, I hated Gabe for making me a coward. My tongue seemed to thaw then, rage building like a fire in my gut so it felt like flames were searing the back of my throat.

"Get him off my property." My voice came out a bark.

The other men looked back at me, sharp. One or two nodded. With big strides, I went after Gabe. I wanted to feel the
crunch of his nose under my fist, hear the scream of pain when
I kicked his groin, let Moira see I knew the truth about her:
she'd been struggling just as hard as me. But Joe grabbed my
arms too fast, held them from behind, saying, "Whoa, Dillan.
He's not worth it." Joe couldn't know how wrong he was.
He nodded to two men nearby, and before I could shake Joe
off, they had hustled Gabe away. And then I stood in front of
Moira with nothing to offer, not even Gabe's crushed nose.

"I am more sorry than I've ever been in my life." I said
it loud.

She nodded, breathing noisily as though she might finally
let herself cry.

CHAPTER 32

MOIRA

THE HARVEST DANCE was in full swing. Silas and I stood watching, a sleeping Shannon in my arms. A grey-haired fiddler scratched out a country tune, while his son strummed a guitar and sang slightly off-key. Young men with scrubbed, shiny faces cautiously crossed the hall to approach even younger women, who stood waiting, shy but hopeful. I'd never been a wallflower, my dance card always full. I swallowed hard at the memory. At how much had changed.

Silas had heard about the episode with Gabe. "It's such a small place. How could Dillan not know I lived at Penny's brothel?" I asked him.

"Excuse me for saying so, but sometimes Dillan has his head up his ass and can't see what's happening right in front of him."

I laughed and Shannon stirred in my arms, smiling, rooting for her thumb. I had missed Silas through the long harvest. His straightforward way.

"Look at how he is with Carla," Silas continued as Dillan and Carla stumbled by, hands touching, eyes radiant. "She couldn't make things any more clear. Some things are just so obvious."

It didn't seem all that obvious to me. There was Casey to consider, and Shannon. I needed to live with him until I figured out how to get home. I hadn't considered it could be Dillan who might help Carla, who might rescue her and give her the choices she deserved.

"Listen here, Moira. Even though Dillan didn't know about Penny's, he should have stepped in." His face drew tight. He turned suddenly and looked into my eyes, then whisked

Shannon away and into the arms of Mrs. Miller, who was standing nearby. "Let's dance, Moira Burns."

My protest went unheeded.

"Go on girl." Mrs. Miller gave me a small push, nodding toward Silas as he stood waiting, tapping his foot to the rhythm of the waltz that had just begun. His hand was on my back, guiding me to the middle of the dance floor and into his arms, my right hand clasped lightly in his, his other encircling my waist. One, two, three. One, two, three. We waltzed in sweeping circles, the fiddler's music filling the room with a plaintive keening, and I succumbed to Silas's guiding hands. He was gazing down through his thick glasses, a slightly dreamy smile at the corners of his mouth. I grinned back at him and slowly let my arm rest against his.

The song ended, the fiddler becoming businesslike again as he announced they'd resume playing after a short break, suggesting we enjoy the refreshments laid out near the coatroom. Silas walked me back to Mrs. Miller. Shannon was winding up to cry. I kept my eyes down, but no one was paying the least attention to us. Except for Dillan. He sent me a small wave from across the hall while Carla, standing at his side, beamed up at him. Silas was right; it was obvious. I smiled back. Then Shannon began to wail.

"I should be taking her home." It was a disappointing thought.

Silas nodded and I went to gather our things before making my way over to Dillan. "Are you ready to go then?" I asked, and he looked dismayed. Casey leaned against his knee, tired from a full night of dance and strangers.

"I'll take them home," Silas said from behind me. He helped me with my jacket and picked up Casey, arranging us like a family about to head out.

Relief spread across Dillan's face, and I saw the barely contained joy in Carla's eyes as she pulled him onto the dance floor again. As we headed out the door, I caught sight of Gabe leaning against the wall in the corner, his hat pulled down low. He watched Carla and Dillan spin past him, shaking his head and muttering to himself, his eyes following their every move. I shuddered and rushed out quickly, unsure of what Silas might do if he saw Gabe there.

The air outside was fresh and autumn crisp. Casey promptly fell asleep on the wagon seat between us while I fed Shannon, a blanket thrown over her head and my shoulder. She, too, was quickly dreaming.

"I hope you don't mind, but I'd like to go by my place first." Silas sounded casual, but his voice betrayed there was something on his mind. We were alone but for small babes who would keep all secrets for now. I trusted him and his good-natured way, but I'd begun to doubt my instincts.

"That's fine," I said finally. "How is it I haven't seen your home? You're one of the first people I met when I arrived in Saskatchewan."

"There's not much to see, I'm afraid. I don't spend much time there," he said.

"A person's home says a lot about them, don't you think?" I spoke quickly, suddenly conscious of my current homelessness, wondering if home still existed for me in my parents' house. I hadn't received a single response to my letters and had stopped asking Dillan about the mail, my disappointment harder to hide each time he shook his head. Instead I hoped to be surprised one day by some correspondence from my family, some sign that I was indeed still one of them.

We were pulling up to an old two-story frame house where beautiful big elms loomed over the verandah, their branches reaching into the shadows, dwarfing the house. At least these giants had survived the storm. He took Casey down from the wagon and helped me with Shannon.

"I haven't kept it up," he said as we mounted steps to the double front door.

"I'm sure it's wonderful."

It was less than wonderful. When Silas opened the door, I was startled by an orange tabby cat shooting out between my feet. The air coming from the house smelled musty. I hesitated to go in, able to see only the outline of furniture until Silas hurriedly laid Casey down on a cot in one corner of the room and lit a lamp. An oak table sat in the middle of the kitchen with four chairs around it, one of them resting precariously on three good legs against the table. Everything was covered with a thick coat of dust except a small area on the kitchen counter, a chair and a clean circle on the table in front of it where Silas obviously had his meals.

We walked in silence to the sitting room. A davenport and two armchairs were covered in white sheets turned grey with dust. Through an open arched doorway, we emerged into a small adjoining room with varnished floors and what had once been a luxurious area rug. An upright piano stood in one corner. I ran the fingers of my free hand lightly over the keys, their worn sheen. They'd been played a great deal.

"Do you play?" he asked quietly.

"Some."

He was watching, searching for my reactions maybe, or simply letting the house reveal itself. I wished I'd kept quiet earlier.

"It's a lovely house. Just needs a little cleaning." I wiped a finger through the dust on the banister of a staircase and peered up into the gloom to see the closed door at the top.

He laughed – a small, relieved sound that broke the tension. Shannon stirred, yawning a smile in her sleep. We watched her for a moment before Silas took my arm and guided me to another corner of the room. He pulled a sheet from a large oak cabinet framed by ornately carved mouldings. Inside it was a full set of four beautiful rose-patterned china teacups and saucers, a teapot and an assortment of dinnerware. Silas opened the door and gestured for me to look inside. Picking up the pieces one by one, I admired the red-and-white detail, their fine pattern a reminder that, somewhere in the world, such beautiful things were still admired.

"I have a proposition for you. No, that's the wrong word," he said when I stepped away from him. "Look. You are in a predicament. And if something happens between Dillan and Carla, where will you be?"

I didn't want this conversation. "Surely she'll finish school before she's allowed to leave home."

"I think you know that's not how it works." He was growing impatient. "It would be good for Dillan. And for Casey. He needs a real mother."

I stiffened. "And not a dollybird."

"Oh God, Moira." Silas looked stricken. "That's not what I meant. Come, let me show you something."

Grabbing a lantern, he took me by the elbow and guided me up the stairs. When he reached the top he stepped in front of me and the door swung in, opening to a large room. The light threw shadows on the gabled walls as he hung the lantern from a hook in the ceiling. The hardwood floors had been recently polished. Against one wall was a wide bed with a small dresser next to it, a bassinet on the other side. The bed was covered with a worn comforter, the lovely blue of my grandmother's shattered china. A desk and chair were arranged on the opposite wall with a few books stacked beside them. I walked around the room lightly touching things, running my hand over the bedspread, the top of the dresser. I turned to find Silas watching me.

"It's for you," he said, and took Shannon from me and laid her in the bassinet. All the blood rushed to my head as he approached and put his hand on my arm. "You can live here, in this room. For now."

There were times in the past few months when I would have given anything to have this room. To feel at home. To feel safe. A strange sense of calm overtook me. He thought I was like the china in the cabinet, too fragile for everyday use, needing to be kept out of harm's way as though I might shatter at the first sign of trouble-blue teacups in a storm. But I was not so fragile. I had choices. I pulled away.

"Silas, it's wonderful, absolutely wonderful, but..." I wanted desperately not to hurt him. "I've decided to go home, to Newfoundland."

"Moira." His hands reached out and then fell to his sides.

"I have to go back and set things straight with my father."

"But he's abandoned you," he said, his voice cracking.

"Father reacted the way any father would."

It all came rushing at me. I wanted to give Father a second chance. And perhaps he'd give me one as well, mentoring me, teaching me the rest of what I needed to know to be a good doctor, perhaps even to be a good parent.

"If I don't go back I can't become a doctor. Not the kind I want to be. They can help with Shannon so I have time to learn. And they are still my family."

Silas shook his head in disbelief, and anger burned in his dark eyes. "I'll take you home now."

The ride was stiff and silent. As we pulled up I saw the sod hut as Silas must see it, cramped and musty despite our best efforts to spruce it up. Small wonder he'd thought I'd jump at his offer. He came in and helped Casey into his pajamas and tucked him into bed, gave the slightest of nods and was out the door. I wanted to go after him, to make amends, but what could I say to make things different?

CHAPTER 33

✣ ✣ ✣

DILLAN

I WALKED HOME from the dance, my heart still thumping with the excitement of dancing with Carla and holding her small hand. Didn't matter I'd tripped over myself and stepped on her feet a few times. She'd just laughed and held on tighter. Her father had watched the whole time, looking about ready to nail my ass to the wall, but that didn't matter either. Out in the night air now, with all the good feeling inside me, I could have walked for hours.

I heard a wagon coming toward me. It was Silas. He'd dropped Moira off at home and was heading back to his place.

"I'll take you partway. Then you can head across country home," he said without looking at me. He cursed the horses to git up. Don't know why he offered me a lift when he seemed in such a hurry, trotting the horses, shaking the hell out of us both. We were silent for a mile or so.

"I saw you dancing with Moira." My voice sounded loud in the night.

Silas jerked upright, his lips set in a hard line. "Stay out of it," he warned.

"Why don't you tell her?"

He hauled on the reins to stop the wagon, and I almost pitched over the horse's rump. "Get out, you son of a bitch," he said.

I jumped down and fell as my feet hit the ground. He was spitting mad when I looked up at him. But I couldn't help myself. "Just tell her, Silas."

"Son of a bitch." He said it again, but the mad was suddenly leaving his face. He whipped the reins hard and the wagon lurched away.

I lay there looking at the stars with the brittle fall grass poking my ass, wondering what had happened to put the fear in his eyes. I got up and started walking west, calculating Carla's farm to be only about a half mile away.

I stood there considering the door of the Schmidts' house, thinking of what to say to Carla's father. But when his large shadow passed the window, I turned and went to the side of the house where I knew she and the children shared a room, feeling scared and stupid at the same time. I rapped on the window and a small girl appeared. She smiled and then her blonde curls disappeared. Seconds later, Carla was there. When she saw me she pushed the window up.

"Can you come out?" I asked. More than anything, I wanted to talk. "Come to the old tree by the dugout."

"Ssshhh." She turned to hush the snickering behind her. "I'll try. But if I'm not there in ten minutes, I'm not coming. Father keeps a close eye."

As I rushed away I had the shivering thought that if her father had his sights on me, I'd be a hopelessly easy target on the open prairie. The trunk of the old elm didn't offer much more protection. A few mosquitoes buzzed round my head. I heard muttering first, then footsteps in the grass.

"Dillan?" Carla called softly.

"I'm here." The breath rushed out of me. "By the tree."

She tumbled into the shelter of its boughs and sat on the ground beside me, her breath heavy at first – she must have run the whole way – and then her breathing slowed and grew shallow with her lungs filling up.

"This is ridiculous, you know," I whispered. "I'm a grown man. A father. What can he do?" I spoke louder, tempting fate I suppose.

"He can make my life miserable. That's what he can do," she said, and I saw the gleam in her scared eyes.

There was a long pause. A far-off cow bellowed, announcing her heat to any bull that might be interested or unfenced. Carla buried her head in her arms, and I moved in close beside her, putting my arm around her, not knowing what to say.

"It's okay," I whispered.

"Dillan, he wants me to marry Gabe. I heard them talking, making a deal. Gabe will partner up farming with my father when he marries me." Her voice broke. "Father says it's best for all of us. He needs the help, and he figures I likely won't find any better prospect."

The words hung between us. I knew what she wanted me to say, her body gone taut with hope. Bloody Christ. I couldn't let her father give her to Gabe. But I couldn't say the words she wanted to hear either, just sat there wondering how in hell I could help her without promising too much. We sat a long time not saying a thing. It was like the air between us was loaded with dynamite, and the wrong words would set off a million sparks.

"I'm afraid." There, I'd said it.

"Of what?"

"Of trying again. I wasn't very good to Taffy. I didn't listen. Didn't think enough about her."

She interrupted. "You're so hard on yourself, Dillan. You gave her what she needed."

I waited, hoping Carla had some wisdom I didn't possess, some divine gift of understanding. It seemed to me we were all sitting on the edge of the world, all of us, staring down at what might make us happy, but not seeing it for all the bits of trouble floating between us and what we wanted.

"You loved her."

We sat there, the hair on my arms moving against the scratchy wool of the wrap she wore. Our hands didn't touch, but her fingers were so close it was like the blood pumped a current through the ground until my fingers ached. Something fluttered in my stomach, ached in my groin. And suddenly I was doubled over with guilt. I couldn't recall Taffy's face. Not exactly. Only shadows, bits of her, blue flirty eyes, the vague shape of her nose muddled in with lines in her forehead, the lobes of her ears. I couldn't get her straight in my head. It was like a brick was resting on my chest, and I started breathing hard. The sky had clouded so the night was like pitch, dark enough to make a man disappear altogether. But Carla's fingers brushed my hand, brought me back from the livery and the fear and the pain.

"Taffy," I said. It was a moan coming up from some godforsaken hole in my gut. Carla leaned toward me, took my hand in her own and squeezed. I held on tight, like she was saving me from drowning right there in a sea of grass.

"She's gone, Dillan," Carla whispered.

And for the first time it seemed real. I searched the black night like something might appear in the stars, telling me what to do. But I only saw my life with all its mistakes and pain. I'd filled the hole where Taffy had been with hating myself. But Casey was surviving without her. A picture of the boy jumped at me, him waving like a fool with a huge smile on his tiny face. He was happy. I imagined the light touch of Taffy's hand on my cheek, remembered her as she'd been in life, not sick or dying or afraid. "Be happy," she'd say when I was crazy about what was going to happen, about failing both of us. She seemed to be saying it now. "Be happy."

I smoothed Carla's hair, took her chin in my hand and lifted her face to my own, my lips against her eyelids, her cheek, her nose, my chest opening up with the feeling that life was possible again. Finally I kissed her long and deep.

We snuck back to her window, whispering promises about being together, about making a home someday. We'd convince her father he didn't need Gabe, that they'd all be better off with me. Walking home, my head spun with the excitement and fear of it. It was so late it was early, the horizon lightening with the sun somewhere close to rising. I wondered if Moira was worried. Wondered too if what had broke between her and Silas could be fixed.

✣ ✣ ✣

CHAPTER 34

I HEARD THE SCREAM before I saw the house, the sound like a terrified animal. It stopped me quick and then I started to run, barely daring to breathe.

"No!" The word pierced the murky dawn and echoed. I couldn't run fast enough. It was like I was dreaming something terrible was happening and I just couldn't get there. Where was the dog? Pain in the ass since we got him. Where was he now? And then I almost ran over him a few hundred yards from the house, his throat slit, eyes bulging and teeth bared. It was obvious he had tried, for once, and now he was dead. I ran past, trying not to look, legs pumping harder.

Another scream. Moira? Casey? Oh God. Whoever was in there with them still had the knife that killed the dog. Closer now, the window only a few feet away, I began to hear voices.

"Please, no." It was Moira.

"Another fucking word and I'll shove my fist down your throat."

My stomach damn near vaulted up my insides. Gabe. I crept slowly to the window, keeping my head low.

"You're not human," Moira said, trying to sound brave.

"You're a whore. And I told you to shut the hell up."

If he saw me, who knew what he'd do? Slowly, I lifted my head until I could just peer over the windowsill. Casey sat on his bed, eyes big and scared. Gabe had Moira around the throat with one arm, the knife pointed at her chest with the other, while he pushed her toward the bed. They disappeared and I heard the loud creak of the bed's frame. Oh God. I was afraid he'd kill her if I just ran in. The tears were rolling down Casey's face, and he worked his thumb to keep from crying out.

"Don't do this," Moira said, loud and harsh.

"He took everything that son of a bitch. My land. And now my woman. Dancin' with her all night, the prick." Gabe was breathing hard. "She's mine. Her father promised her to me."

There was a ripping sound and Casey whimpered.

"Roll over, I want you from behind. That's what a whore likes."

Oh God, Oh God. There was a shriek of pain and Moira went flying past the window, blood all over her nightgown.

"I won't let you do it, you bastard," Moira panted. "You can kill me, but I won't let you do that." She tried to wrap the torn and bloody nightgown round herself.

He waved the knife in the air, grabbed Casey and threw him over his shoulder. Casey howled and I went crashing through the door. Moira was huddled by the crib, her face filled with fear, but something else too, something saying she'd win or die. Gabe threw Casey on the bed and spun around to face me. Slowly he raised the knife, pointed it at me and smiled. His eyes were fired with a kind of hate I'd never seen. Crazy eyes.

"Get out of my house."

He lunged and I jumped out of the way. His shoulder caught mine and we both crashed into the table, the knife clattering to the floor. I pushed off the table and pain rocketed through my head as he punched my nose.

"Ha." He was enjoying this, sick with loving to hurt people.

I threw myself at him again, swinging hard, and connected with his chin. His head shot back, teeth snapping together, stunned an instant. And then he was on me, spitting blood, his arm across my throat so I couldn't breathe, and I was thumping on him, thrashing my legs, trying to break his hold. I thought I might be done, but suddenly his arm went slack and he slumped, his bulk heavy on top of me. It took everything I had to roll him off. Moira stood above us, her bloody nightgown wide open and pale tits hanging out, Gabe's knife in her hand.

"It's over," she said, looking at the pool of blood growing round Gabe, her voice weirdly calm. She dropped the knife onto the table and went to the crib, where Shannon was whimpering.

I stood real slow, picked Casey up from the bed and hugged him tight. He clung to my neck, his soft little hands pulling so hard it was like he wanted to become part of my body. Then he drew back and touched my nose where the blood was drying, and looked into my eyes.

"Daddy?"

"It's okay, Casey."

His tears let go and he sobbed, me rocking him like he was a baby again, just holding him 'cause I'd come so close to not bein' able to. He kept glancing at Gabe, who'd started moaning. I turned so Casey couldn't see him. I don't know how many minutes we stood rocking, but finally his breathing slowed, and when I looked down he was drifting off on my shoulder. I laid him on his bed and turned back to Moira. She was standing over Gabe, just looking down at him. She'd tied her nightgown to cover herself up, but I could see her shoulder was bleeding bad. Then she bent and put her fingers to his throat.

"He's still alive," she said. "Get my bag."

I couldn't believe she would want to save him. She took the bag from me, and I rolled him on his side, like she asked, seeing the hole the knife had made between his ribs. She said to bring water and towels, calm-like, as though she was in a trance. She pressed the towels tight against his wound, soaking up the blood, grunting through her own pain the whole time. When the leaking finally slowed, she cleaned round the wound while I ripped sheets into lengths, and then helped wind them tight round his body, holding everything together. When we were done she stood up and looked across the room. "A pillow," she said. I brought it, wanting to tell her he didn't deserve any comforts as she put it under his head.

Finally she sat down, leaning into the chair, exhausted, her face gone white and slack. The door flew open. Silas stood there, framed for a second by sunlight, loped his long legs across the room, giving a glance first to Casey, then Shannon in her crib. He stepped over Gabe, looked at us both and then picked Moira up gentle, like she was a broken sparrow. She put her good arm around his neck, her head on his shoulder and went limp with fainting.

I brought Shannon to the wagon, laying her on the blankets beside Moira, and covered them both with another. Silas said he'd take Moira to the doctor in Ibsen and then back to his place. I could only nod, watching Moira drifting in and out of sleep, thinking how Silas didn't know the half of what had happened. Moira had fixed Gabe even though he'd hurt her, and would have done worse if I hadn't showed up. I didn't understand. But I knew one thing; she was a bigger person than me, better than any of us.

Gabe was moaning when I went back to the house. He hadn't moved, but I tied his hands to the table leg anyway, just in case. I filled a canteen with water, put some bread and cheese in a sack, picked up Casey and headed outside to tack up Nelly for the long ride into Moose Jaw to see the Mounted Police. To tell them what Gabe had done and where to find him, to finally make him pay, for everything. As I was about to leave, I went back to the house, walked over to Gabe, and pulled the pillow out from under his head.

CHAPTER 35

MOIRA

GABE HAD CUT deep into the muscle of my shoulder, and I needed help with the most basic of things. After taking me to Doctor Berkowski, Silas had brought me to his place and arranged for Mrs. Miller's help. She was wonderful, dressing the wound, cooking and cleaning, caring for Shannon when Silas wasn't home to do it. But mostly he was home, and for two weeks had nursed me in the large room at the top of the stairs.

Dr. Berkowski came for a follow-up visit, to put everyone's mind at rest, though I knew he'd taken great care with the sutures, the positioning and length of each stitch perfect. Even with the severity of the wound, the scar would be minimal. While the muscle was still weak, I was healing well. He paused an instant as he packed his things away.

"I have to say you did an excellent job treating that hoodlum, especially in light of your own injury," he said. "More than he deserved from the sounds of it."

"I did what needed to be done," I said, trying not to blush.

"Hmmm." It seemed he wanted to say more, but instead he looked me in the eye and formally shook my hand as he left.

I remembered the smell of that early morning two weeks earlier, my loathing and fear making me a madwoman. But while standing over Gabe's wounded body, I'd thought of my father, his patients, the lowly patients he treated without question, his firm belief in a doctor's obligation to preserve life. All life. And I thought of the oath I'd memorized as a young girl, especially the part that said, "To hold him who has taught me this art as equal to my parent." I had to treat Gabe. Not out of any sympathy, or heroism. But because I was my father's daughter. I was a doctor.

With Berkowski's blessing, I decided it was time to move back to the sod hut. Silas was hurt, but I was beginning to feel trapped by his good intentions. The next day Dillan came to get me, and I met him at the wagon. He held his hat in his hands, his shoulders stooped a little, a question in his eye. I hoped he was glad I was going home with him, at least for the time being. As we rode, a cool breeze swirled skiffs of snow on the ground, arched the dead grasses above it, waving like flags of truce surrendering to winter.

"It's beautiful." My throat clicked. "Every season."

He looked at me suddenly. "You could have stayed with Silas, you know."

"Would you have liked me to?" It was petty.

"Well it's hard for him, living alone in that great big place." He was watching for my reaction. "Must get lonely."

"What are you suggesting I do?"

"I'm not suggesting anything." He shook his head.

We'd arrived home and stopped in front of the house. Dillan helped me down, careful of my arm. Casey ran ahead as we trooped inside. I lay Shannon in her crib and turned to Dillan, grabbing his arm.

"What's really going on here?" I asked.

"Jesus, Moira. I don't know what to do. Carla." He blushed. "I like her, you know. But Casey is very fond of you. I am too," he quickly added. "It's just so hard. So complicated."

"It's okay." I couldn't help but smile at his distress. "I've been wondering how I'll fit into the arrangement if you and Carla get together. Obviously I won't. Can you imagine two women around this place?" I shot Casey my best mock-horror look and tickled his neck. "But don't worry. I've decided to go home. As soon as possible." The shock in Dillan's face made me laugh. "You go ahead and do whatever you need to do without your infernal guilty conscience haunting you."

"To St. John's? But your mother, Shannon." His hands flew into the air.

"I don't have a future here." I bent to hug Casey, who tugged at my skirts. Tears sprang to my eyes. "You little rascal. I will miss you."

"Miss Moira too," he said seriously, and gave me a long look before running to see why Shannon was fussing. "She hungry," he announced.

"Yes, I believe she is."

Dillan brought her to me, his face clouded with questions I didn't have the energy to answer. I sat down in the rocking chair to let her nurse, running my fingers over its carefully carved wood, imagining Dillan's large hands gently moulding the lathes into perfect arches. He stood by the sink, helping Casey to wash his hands.

"I'll have to leave my chair when I go," I said as the realization hit me.

He glanced up sharply, sighed. "I suppose."

"I want to take it. It's so lovely. But, the train you know." I felt pregnant again, my huge body wading through very deep water, pushing against the current. "It would be very expensive to have it shipped."

"I suppose," he repeated. He was quiet for a moment. "But Moira, what about all of this?" He spread his hands to encompass our small world. "What about Silas?"

I didn't answer, instead climbed into the bed he'd put in front of the west window so that, when the weather was fine, I could push the canvas sack aside and watch the sunsets as I recovered.

⁘ ⁘ ⁘

In the days that followed, a lump would rise in my throat every time I looked at Casey or thought about the dying garden I'd cleaned up and readied for someone else to plant in the spring. I'd always begrudged Nelly and the pigs the time I spent feeding them. They'd only been a nuisance. Now I wished I could help with the chores, linger out in the corral and listen to the birds, smell the farm smells. And Dillan had spoken as though

I might stay for Silas. I was fond of Silas; he'd been so kind. But did they all think his kindness was enough? Damn Dillan and his questions.

"Hello in the house," Silas's voice carried through crisp fall air, and I pushed myself up on my good arm, wincing at the pain.

"Hello." It was a woman's voice, small and tentative.

Dillan answered from somewhere outside. "Nice to meet you too. Moira is just inside. Here, let me help you across that."

I could see over the window ledge to make out an improbable hat, a city hat, not one of the prairie bonnets farm women wore. Its wide brim shielded the face of its wearer, and as I watched, the woman picked her way across the yard in polished boots. She glanced up again and I gasped. Aileen. My heart began to thump, so loud I was sure they would hear it. I got up and took deep breaths to steady myself and stop the fluttering in my stomach.

"Moira," Silas called as he entered. "I've brought someone."

"Aileen." My voice squeaked past the lump in my throat.

"Moira," she cried, and rushed into my outstretched arms, careful to avoid my battered shoulder.

We hugged for a long time, laughing through a few happy tears, hugging again.

"But how...?"

"Dillan found the address in your things," Silas interjected. "I thought it best your family knew you'd had an accident. Aileen has come to see how you are."

"And are you all right then?" she asked, standing back a little as though to survey.

"Yes, yes, I'm doing fine. It's just such a shock to see you so unexpectedly." I gave Silas a raised eyebrow.

"I'll go unhitch and water the horses," he said.

"I'll help." Dillan had been standing aside, watching our reunion.

Aileen glanced between Silas and Dillan and then at me, confused. The two men donned their hats and left. I hugged her again.

"You're so thin," I said. Her frame was bony under layers of dress and petticoat and corset, while I could feel how strong I'd become since I'd last seen her.

She stiffened and looked at the floor. "Oh, you know me. I've always eaten like a bird." She looked me up and down. "You look wonderful, so much colour in your cheeks. You must spend a lot of time outdoors."

It might have been a slight. Only labourers acquire the sun's colour. "Thank you. Yes I do spend a great deal of time outside. It's so lovely here in the summer."

Aileen glanced around the sod house, her small eyes adjusting to its dim light.

"It's not much," I heard myself say. "But we lived in a tent at first, as you know. I was so grateful when the neighbours came to build the house."

She looked about skeptically, as though imagining neighbours who sported two heads and a very unclear vision as to what defined a house.

"This is much better than some places I've seen here on the prairie." I wanted to bite off my tongue for making excuses. Casey saved me, running in to greet Aileen, throwing himself at her, wrapping his arms around her legs.

"Oh my." She swayed under his assault. "He's certainly a friendly little thing." She reached down to pat his head.

It was a surprise to realize that, while I'd been raising Casey and learning to be a mother to both him and Shannon, my sister knew nothing about children. I scooped him up and nuzzled his neck, showing off the ease of our relationship, how he depended on me and trusted I could give him what he needed. I put him down and went to the crib, where Shannon grumbled to herself in tiny, fitful gurgles, her delicate chubby feet waving in the air in front of her. She tried to grab for them and missed, tried again.

"And this," I picked her up and brought her into the light, "is Shannon." I wished she'd been dressed in more than a plain white nightdress, wished Aileen could have met her dressed in the frilly pink dress and booties Mrs. Miller had given her. Her hair had filled in so its shiny blonde curls fell around her face like a halo, like the dolls we'd been given for Christmas with solemn warnings not to soil them.

"Oh," Aileen gasped. She stayed where she was. "She's beautiful."

I brought the baby to her and placed her in my sister's un-practiced arms, adjusting Aileen's hands and Shannon's head so Aileen could see her clearly.

"Oh Moira," she gasped again, her eyes shining with tears. She looked from the baby to me and back again as though she didn't quite believe I could have managed anything so perfect. "Moira," she said again.

We looked at each other and at the baby for a long time, the silence filled with all that had happened in the time we'd spent apart. Dillan and Silas came in, stomping their boots.

"We'll talk later," I whispered to her.

"Come." Casey ran to Silas, pulling Aileen along. "Come," he insisted. Aileen glanced back and I laughed and waved her out the door. "Chickenths."

The lisp accompanied Casey's every word now. He point-ed to the birds as they ran in a fluster away from them. As I watched, Aileen picked her way past tufts of weed, reaching down to brush dust from her boots. "Pigth." Casey pointed to the mud they wallowed in. I watched him pull my sister around the corner of the house, his monologue keeping time with their progress.

Rushing behind the curtain of my room, I pulled on my one good dress, yellow with tiny red roses around the hem, grabbed a brush and viciously pulled it through my hair, count-ing the strokes as Aileen and I had done every day of our lives, wondering why it seemed important to do it now. Pulling the unruly mess back into a tight bun, I caught myself in my one tiny mirror, grimacing from the pain of lifting my arm to hold the pins. I tucked in loose tendrils and applied a little powder and lipstick. Turning, I stretched on my toes to see how the dress fell over slightly larger breasts, craned to see myself from behind, wondering if Aileen noticed my expanded hips.

"She's only your sister," Dillan said from the other side of the room.

I emerged from behind the curtain. "I haven't done anything special."

He shrugged. "I don't know why you think you need to impress her." He sat down on the one good upholstered chair we'd managed to buy. I cringed, hoping the back of his pants were free of the dirt and grease he usually brought in on them.

"I don't. It's only that..." The words wouldn't come because I didn't want them to be true. "She expected things of me, her little sister. I wasn't supposed to end up in a sod shack on the bald prairie."

Dillan's eyes clouded.

"I mean, it's fine. I know. But she won't understand what we've done here. Not any of it — how hard we've worked, how nearly impossible it can be to make a garden grow, or the crops, just to keep things alive, including ourselves. She has no idea of the impossible things we've done."

I turned to the window and took a deep breath. Aileen and Silas were making their way back to the house. I shouldn't have said that. Not to Dillan. He didn't need my sister's judgment to point out our meagre existence. I turned back to apologize. He was grinning and shaking his head.

"For a smart woman, you can be an idiot."

It was my turn to be hurt.

"You haven't learned a fug from all this..." He waved his hand around the room, gestured outside, toward the crib where Shannon gurgled. "Surviving? You think you should worry about some dame with fancy shoes thinking it's not enough?" He threw his hands in the air.

We laughed then, full belly laughs that felt good and true.

"Thank you, Dillan," I said.

"You're very welcome," he said, and smiled.

Just then Aileen came back in and Dillan got up and went to do chores with Silas while we fixed supper. Aileen was awkward, searching for things that were right in front of her, unaccustomed to functioning in such a primitive domestic situation. The peas and potatoes were from my own garden. The salt pork I'd managed to preserve with Carla's help. At supper Aileen barely touched anything on her plate, and when I glanced at it yet again, she blushed.

"It's fine, Moira. Really it is." The silence from the men was resounding. "I'm just tired from the trip is all."

"Of course." I shrugged to hide my disappointment and started to gather the plates. "Well, that must be the first time." I pointed to Casey's plate, hated that I was trying to make a point where none needed to be made. "Look, Dillan, he's finished everything on his plate."

Dillan nodded and, to my surprise, got up to help. "Silas has offered me a bed for the night." He stood beside me at the big metal basin used for washing both clothes and dishes. He spoke quietly. "I'll go so you two can be alone."

"It's really not necessary. Aileen and I will have plenty of time when I'm home." Glancing at Silas, I could see him nod his head and smile faintly at something Aileen was saying. He was gazing out the window toward the setting sun, his posture aloof.

"I'll come back early and do the chores," Dillan mused.

"It's up to you, but it's not necessary."

He put a few things together, picked up Casey and, before we knew it, Aileen and I were alone. Shannon muttered to herself in her crib while we cleaned up. The effort to make small talk was exhausting and disappointing. Aileen radiated a growing sense of gloom. I'd pictured a meeting with my sister filled with breathless talk, the two of us stumbling over one another, anxious to share. After so much time there should have been so much to tell. But looking around our hovel, I didn't know where to start.

"Did you enjoy my letters then?" I asked finally. "Maybe they gave you a sense of the adventures I've had."

"Mother never gave them to me." She sounded apologetic, as though it was she who'd made the choice.

"What?" I'd revealed myself in those letters, imagined Aileen at the other end of the pen, hearing my thoughts, sympathizing, listening. "She had no right to do that."

Aileen looked away, clearly uncomfortable. I busied myself feeding Shannon, readying her for bed. With the baby finally tucked in her crib, I beckoned Aileen to sit across the table from me, determined to overcome whatever was holding us apart.

"So. Now you need to fill me in. What have you been doing with yourself?" It was the question I'd asked every time I came home from another trip with Father. The answer had always been the same.

"Well," Aileen started, and I heard myself sigh. "Mother has been quite ill."

My world had been turned on its head, but at home, for Aileen, nothing had changed. "Then you didn't get to take those literature classes?"

"No." She looked down, her face reddening. "But I'm singing in the church choir now."

It was hardly imaginable. She had no voice, no talent for anything requiring public display. "Mother put you up to it?"

"Well, yes, they were short of voices. But I really do enjoy it."

"Hmmm."

She frowned. "I do."

"I'm happy you've found something you like. At least it gets you out of the house." I winked at her. "And maybe there are some nice boys who sing as well?"

Blushing, Aileen waved her hand as though this were silliness beyond compare. There was a short silence while I tried to corral all the scattered ideas and questions galloping through my head. Taking a deep breath, I finally blurted, "And what about Father then? Is he very busy?"

"Oh yes, very. Runs off every morning and isn't back 'til dark." Aileen's voice crackled with sarcasm. "Saving the world you know."

It was Mother's voice. Anxiety collected in my throat. "No, Aileen, how is he? Really. I miss him so much. And not a word from him in all this time. From anyone."

"I know," said Aileen. She seemed only mildly apologetic, mostly impatient, fidgeting with her hands.

"At first I was disappointed. But then I thought Father must be busy. Or Mother was demanding all his time again. I knew what you were doing. I guess not much changes." She looked up sharply at that, but I forged on. "And my letters. I can't believe she'd keep them from you."

I searched Aileen's face for any sign the tired excuses were true, that a father could be too busy to write to his own daughter, that a sister could give up trying, that they wouldn't have fought for even a small connection.

"She's crazy, you know." I nodded vigorously when Aileen started to protest. "It's true. I can see it now. Being away from her. I've thought about it a lot, how she manipulates. I mean really, Aileen, it isn't normal. She just says and does whatever terrible things she likes and then pretends nothing has happened. And we're supposed to act like her behaviour is normal, even forgive her."

Aileen stared across the table at me. I could see the truth was sinking in, revealing itself to her as I spoke, my words like a light into her dark world. I waited, but still Aileen didn't move. Of course she hadn't the benefit of time and distance to reach the same conclusions.

"I'm not afraid of her any more. Things will be different. I won't put up with it. And you and Father won't have to either."

Slowly Aileen raised her head, eyes filled with a mixture of pain and pity and something else too — a hint of anger. Her chest expanded with a huge drawing in of breath and I waited, mesmerized by the apparent effort it took for her to speak. Eyes averted, she spoke very slowly as though she was capable of saying this one time and no more.

"Father doesn't want you to come home." She lowered her head and her entire body slumped as though it had been kept upright all this time, not by bones and flesh, but by the responsibility of carrying those few words.

I didn't know if I'd heard right. Perhaps she was lying. Aileen hated me as much as Mother did. They had concocted some sort of scheme together, these two sick women. The blood rushed to my head.

"He sent me to tell you." Still Aileen didn't look up. "Not in so many words, but that's why I'm here. Your accident gave him an excuse to send me."

"You're lying." I stood, breath coming shallow and fast, looking at my sister's bowed head and hating her and her stunted, shallow life. "He would never say that."

"Why wouldn't he, Moira?" Slowly, finally, Aileen raised her eyes to meet mine. They were black with contempt, her face suffused with anger. "Because you're perfect? Because you're his favourite?" She stood, her face so close to mine I smelled the stale familiarity of her breath. "You have no idea what you've done."

Turning abruptly, she walked quickly to her bag on the floor by the bed and retrieved an envelope from the side pocket. Eyes blazing, she thrust the letter into my hands, turned and walked out the door, leaving it to swing shut behind her. Father's sloppy cursive rolled across the front of the envelope. When I looked up, Aileen was silhouetted against the pink glow of the horizon. I wanted to call out, to make amends for whatever I'd done to cause her grief and anger. Instead, I opened the letter and sat down next to the lantern at the kitchen table.

Moira,

The lack of any endearment tied a knot in my stomach.

Such a difficult letter to write, though I am sure you will agree with my conclusions once you have read it through.

You have always been a very practical girl, someone who deals with matters in a reasoned and responsible manner. And so, though it pains me, I will get to the heart of the thing quickly and assume your usual wherewithal to deal with the obvious, and manage as you always have.

I was very impressed with your ability to learn quickly and was so much looking forward to seeing you thrive as one of the few female physicians in this country. As difficult as your indiscretion was in becoming pregnant, it was not insurmountable. However, your commitment to keeping the child and bringing her home is another matter.

If you were to bring a baby back to St. John's, you would have no opportunity to enter a residency or to find employment as a physician. No one will allow an unwed mother to be a serious candidate for either. And, my dear, Evan is not coming back. His father has repeatedly told me so. The boy is staying in Scotland and has given little thought to you or his offspring since he left. If you were anticipating any help from him, there will be none. His father is a bastard – they both are – but I can't say I blame them for what they've done. His career might have been ruined.

Mother says you are practicing in the small community where you live. Perhaps the people there have already grown accustomed to your situation and are comfortable with what you have to offer. I could send some resources, books and medicines and the like, and maybe over time you could build a reputation and some clientele. It will never happen here. The standards are too high and, frankly, they would never accept you.

And your mother is very ill.

You have no idea how she suffers. Her illness has progressed to where she is bedridden most days and medicated to keep away the vile humours that torment her. Still she rants, mostly about you, I'm afraid. So much so, I know the presence of you and your child in our home could only worsen her condition.

And so I find myself at this crossroads with the impossible task of navigating between two people I love. My wife is far off down one road, a small shadow of the woman I married, our relationship a strange mix of contented familiarity and sometimes unbridled difficulty. Down the other stretch is you, my dear daughter, who stands closer, our history short and so less fraught with pain, your future malleable, full of potential despite this one mistake.

We will manage somehow, Moira, if you do come home. I only think you should know how difficult it will be. And if you should stay in Saskatchewan, as I suggest, I have confidence in your ability not only to survive, but to flourish. Do you remember, dear, when you were small and asked us why we chose your name, what it meant? Your mother admired the lilt of its sound, but I never liked its Scottish meaning – sorrow and bitterness. Since then I have discovered a Latin interpretation – Moira: Goddess of Fate and Destiny.

You must have faith now, as I do, that the Latin meaning of your

name will find you and guide you. Confidence and hope, my dear.
Hang on to them. And to the knowledge of my love.
  Always,
  Your father

My head sank to my arms, to the table, the room growing dark as night fell. Outside, the brittle fall grasses rubbed
together in a shushing sound as though they knew I wanted
to shout loud enough to reach Father's ears. Instead I sat in
silence, more exhausted and alone than I'd ever been.

CHAPTER 36

AILEEN HAD COME back and stood now in the doorway, but I ignored her, rushing instead to fuss at great length over Shannon, who was awake and clamouring to be fed. Aileen washed at the tin bowl, removed her clothes and laid them carefully on the bed. Out of the corner of my eye I caught a quick glimpse of her nakedness before she pulled a nightgown down over her head. She was a jumble of angles, thin arms and legs that would be flaccid if they had an ounce of fat on them, hips protruding like the pin bones on a starving cow. Her skeletal ribs were encased in skin translucent as fine parchment. The extent of my sister's frailty was heartbreaking.

"You're barely keeping yourself alive," I blurted out.

"Oh." She quickly pulled down the nightgown and tied the cotton strings at the throat. "I'm fine."

Aileen stood by the bed, fingers working at a sore on the side of her mouth, staring at the floor in front of my feet. Her weakness raised something terrible in me.

"Did you ever, in all your twenty-three years, do anything for yourself?"

Her lip quivered and my voice rose.

"Don't you want to get married? Have you never thought of a man, what it might be like to touch someone, have him touch you back?"

"Moira, really." Aileen held back tears, feigning shock.

"At least I've had that much." I glanced down at Shannon and lifted her toward Aileen. "And I have this," I said triumphantly. "If she is all I ever have, at least I can say I have lived. But you...," I stabbed a finger toward her "Are not living. Your soul is dying, bit by small bit in that house, just like Father's."

Aileen shrunk away from me, helpless in the face of my anger.

"It's your own colossal lack of courage that allows a woman

who can barely get out of bed to hold sway over you. Both of you. You and Father."

Aileen began to weep, sniffling at first, then crying hard. My rage melted into sadness as I watched, puddled into thoughts of what I'd done to survive the past few months in the certainty that I would go home and start again. And I wept, finally, overcome by huge, gulping breaths of sorrow. Because none of it meant anything.

We cried together for a time, Aileen sitting on the bed while I sat with Shannon in the rocker. I got up, finally, put Shannon in her crib and went to sit beside my sister. Slowly, I put my arm around her, lightly at first, then hard, aching with how much I'd hurt that frail soul, squeezing her fine bones, kissing her soft, fine hair, willing forgiveness from her.

"I'm not angry with you. I'm sorry."

"I know." Aileen sniffled and leaned into me a little.

"He shouldn't have sent you to be his messenger. It wasn't fair."

"He couldn't come. His patients, and Mother. He takes on too much."

"Oh Lord, don't you go worrying after Father too. Let him worry about himself."

"I wish you were home. You could always make him laugh." Her shoulders slumped. "He doesn't laugh any more."

We didn't speak for a while. Shannon stirred, whimpered a little and slid back into sleep. Outside the pigs grunted in their pen.

"It's okay, Aileen. We'll all be okay."

"You will, anyway. Look at you, Moira," she said. "You've got friends, a beautiful child. You can practice at least some medicine. You have a future. I wonder why you'd even want to come home."

I gazed at her then, sister become philosopher. We were silent again, glancing at one another, letting go the occasional heavy sigh. I looked around the sod hut, toward Shannon in her crib. In loving her, I'd determined her future was with me in St. John's, but Father's letter and Aileen's frailty reminded me of the pall cast over our house by Mother's illness, the darkened windows and hushed voices, the absence of joy. I pictured Shannon in that place and shivered. It was not a home. Aileen gave me a puzzled look.

She was right; I'd done more than survive. Shannon and I had people in Ibsen who cared about us. Father said I could not doctor with him in St. John's only because Shannon was too great an embarrassment for his colleagues. And suddenly I was embarrassed for them, their stuffy arrogance, their assumption that because they were men of education and power they were to be respected. The people of the prairie had no such notions; you proved yourself or you didn't. And I had already proven myself. I was needed here and could gain their respect with my skills. I felt sorry for my father then, for everything he faced. But I couldn't rescue him from my mother. He'd made his choices. Now I'd have to make mine.

"I don't even know where I'll live," I said. But the thought wasn't frightening any more, and the relief of it made me laugh. Aileen looked at me like she thought I was a new kind of crazy.

"We're sad. And we're damn pathetic now," I said, smiling. "But we will be just fine."

"Do you think so?" Aileen wiped tears from her eyes and looked into mine.

I fingered the embroidered bedspread, recalling the primitive conditions in which I'd started prairie life, remembering what had already been proven.

"Yes, I do."

At the train station, Aileen's cheek glistened under my kiss, her frail body almost crumbling into bits with the force of my arms around it. She couldn't speak, but looked from myself to Shannon and back again. She turned to take in the station, gazed toward the center of Ibsen, as though she'd become accustomed to it and might miss the people she'd only barely met. She shivered in the late fall breeze.

"You can still change your mind," I offered. "Stay here with me."

"We've been over it, Moira. I can't." She brushed at the tears. "But I will take that class, go out once in a while with friends." She shrugged self-consciously.

"I know you will."

Aileen's guard had dropped a little the past few days. A smile played around her face; there were small glimmers of the person she might have been in a different life. I desperately hoped she'd find one place of solace back home, one other person who could help her to see how unique she might become. She looked down at Shannon resting in her arms. One by one, she kissed her baby fingers, tiny feet and, finally, her smooth, soft cheek. Her eyes filled with tears as she handed Shannon back.

"You two take good care of each other," she whispered.

Before I could reply, the conductor hollered his all aboard and Aileen was gone, up the steps and swallowed by the steel hulk of the train. I strained to see her shadow move down the aisle through the dark windows and felt a calloused hand touch my arm. Dillan stood at my side. He'd brought us to the station earlier, leaving us to our goodbyes.

"Are you all right?" he asked, looking after the train.

"I suppose I have to be."

The engine bellowed a last time, huffing thick black smoke, and its massive wheels rolled forward, the beginning of its noisy passage east. Taking one of Shannon's small hands in my own, I waved it at the receding caboose, and then laid her in her carriage. We were alone on the platform now, everyone else turned back from their farewells and wishes for a safe trip, back to the regularity of their lives. The wood echoed hollow under our shoes as I steered the carriage toward Dillan's wagon waiting at the bottom of the stairs.

"You can stay with us, you know. As long as you need," he said. "Carla's father is coming around, but it's going to take some convincing."

I smiled at him. It was enough for now.

"I need a few things at the hardware store," he said. "It won't take long."

"I'll wait here."

He jumped down to get Casey from the wagon and headed off down the street, comfortable, finally, in his own skin. A man. His offer meant more than he could imagine; it wasn't made to a dollybird. It was made to a friend.

I sat down on the hard floor, my legs dangling over the edge of the platform, and gazed at the train's smoke, a charcoal smudge drifting across the blue sky. That was how I'd arrived, in an unremarkable puff from the east, my fate sealed without my having yet imagined it.

"Hey there." And there was Annie, walking heel to toe on the steel track, balancing with her arms outstretched. "I heard your sister was visiting." She ran up the steps to the platform and went to the carriage to stroke Shannon's head. "She's grown. And so beautiful."

She looked toward the train in the distance. "She's gone now?"

"Yes."

"And?" Annie came to sit beside me, her legs swinging in time with my own.

"She's gone...and I'm staying." The finality of the statement caught me by surprise. "I can't go home, Annie," I whispered. "Too much has changed. I've changed."

"That's not so bad, is it?" She reached over to put her hand on my shoulder, glancing up as Shannon cooed from her carriage. "Most people around here think you are remarkable. Your doctoring. They have to pretend they're not impressed by you. But of course they are. You've taken your fate and made something of it."

"It's hard to believe there would be so much talk of my small triumphs."

Or perhaps it wasn't. The whole place was built on just such moments of grace, small mercies making up for endless difficulty and disappointment. Maybe Father was right; maybe my path was meant to be more than the maladies my mother's name choice had offered, to be something else, something exotic and flowing. Goddess of Fate and Destiny. I laughed, deep and real. Shannon gurgled and thrust small fists into the air.

"I guess I have learned something from all this. I'd rather be a goddess." I smiled at Annie's confused face. "Never mind."

We watched the train grow smaller until it was a spot on the horizon, and then it was gone, swallowed into the miles of empty blue sky. That big sky. With all its possibilities.

ACKNOWLEDGEMENTS

A HEARTFELT THANK YOU TO:

My editor, Sandra Birdsell. Your superb skill and insight have made this a better story.

Mentors Sarah Sheard, Byrna Barclay and Connie Gault. And to my writing friends, Leeann Minogue, Anne McDonald, Shelley Banks, Annette Bower and Linda Biasotto: your commitment to having us all succeed is humbling.

The Saskatchewan Writers' Guild for retreat time at St. Peter's Abbey, an oasis of quiet in a distracting world, and for participation in the Mentorship and Facilitated Retreat programs.

Geoffrey, Barbara and Nik at Coteau Books, for believing in the story and guiding me through the publishing process.

My parents, Gerald and Ann Groenen, for their support always, and especially Mom, who lives for good reading and has indeed lived long enough to hold my book in her hands!

My kids, Sara, Anita, Logan and Maddy, who have become amazing people and are a constant source of inspiration.

And finally, David, I couldn't have done it without your faith in my writing, and your love.

An important resource on diseases, medicine and attitudes of the period was Donald Jack's *Rogues, Rebels and Geniuses: The Story of Canadian Medicine* (Toronto: Doubleday, 1981)